Wow!

BY MICHAEL BAMBERGER

The Green Road Home

To the Linksland

Bart & Fay (a play)

Wonderland

This Golfing Life

The Man Who Heard Voices

BY ALAN SHIPNUCK

Bud, Sweat, & Tees

The Battle for Augusta National

Swinging from My Heels (with Christina Kim)

the Swinger

A NOVEL

MICHAEL BAMBERGER
AND ALAN SHIPNUCK

SIMON & SCHUSTER
New York London Toronto Sydney

Sports Illustrated
BOOKS

Simon & Schuster
1230 Avenue of the Americas
New York, NY 10020

This book is a work of fiction. Names, characters, places, and incidents either are the product of the authors' imagination or, if real, are used fictitiously.

First Simon & Schuster hardcover edition July 2011

Designed by Ruth Lee-Mui

Manufactured in the United States of America

3 5 7 9 10 8 6 4

Library of Congress Cataloging-in-Publication Data

Bamberger, Michael, 1960–
The swinger : a novel / Michael Bamberger, Alan Shipnuck.
p. cm.
1. Golfers—Fiction. 2. Golf stories. I. Shipnuck, Alan, 1973– II. Title.
PS3602.A63455S95 2011
813'.6—dc22 2011020045

ISBN 978-1-4516-5755-5
ISBN 978-1-4516-5757-9 (ebook)

For James P. Herre

The tree was dead. Still, the children climbed it.

—*Chinese proverb*

You should know one thing from the start: I have tried to make this whole write-up as accurate as possible. Looking for a single quote, I just spent twenty minutes trying to find one particular notebook, marked PEBBLE/FATHER'S DAY on the cover in blue ink, with Johnny Miller's cell number written sideways in pencil on the last page. Turns out it was stuck to another notebook, one marked AMANDA/OFF COURSE with a red felt tip. Their spiral metal bindings had become enmeshed in a crowded storage box. How fitting.

Tree Tremont's guy hired me. Someday, he said, Tree would write a book and he'd need a record of the details. Did Tree really go into a GNC and buy $945 worth of dietary supplements in one fifteen-minute shopping spree? He did. Did Tree really say to his nemesis, Will Martinsen, on Masters Sunday, "You'd make way more putts if you went to a cross-handed grip?" He did. Did Tree really drink a bottle of Macallan and half of another by himself on one Scotland-to-Florida flight, hours after winning the British Open? He did.

I found the quote I was looking for in the Pebble Beach notebook on a page crammed with my semi-legible late-night handwriting:

> *2:10 a.m. Wake up to high heels descending circular wooden steps, Tree a step behind them, barefoot. He's been up now for 20+ hours. Started weight lifting poolside at 6 a.m., grunting like a porn star. At breakfast he talked to Belinda/kids for 30 minutes on speaker: new countertops, soccer strategy, down-the-street gossip. I open the bedroom window. Burning cedar in heavy Pacific air. Tree walks High Heels to her car. The gate opens. As she leaves (Toyota Prius?), a Lincoln Town Car arrives. Ships passing in the night. From backseat, out comes a tall shimmering redhead. "Hi, I'm Tree," he says. She says, "I know."*

A driver had brought the girl to our rented castle, on a hill above Pebble Beach, U.S. Open week. Not somebody in Tree's tight little circle, just a random middle-of-the-night driver. It seemed so reckless. How was Tree going to get the redhead home? The circle would expand. Did he really think Belinda would never find out about any of it? What about the position he was putting the rest of us in?

I have to say one thing in Tree's defense. There he was, the most famous athlete in the world, introducing himself to the next girl in the parade by name. *Hi, I'm Tree.* There was something so charming and unassuming about it. I think that's how he got good, by taking nothing for granted.

Of course, getting good and staying good are not at all the same thing.

the Swinger

1

I took my bills to work, stuffed into the big pocket of my Target backpack with the crappy refurbished Toshiba laptop that the paper gave me five years ago. For the longest time, I'd still find eyelashes in the keyboard from the guy who had the computer, and the golf beat, before me.

"Joshuamon, what brings you to the paragraph factory?" Pete, the sports editor, asked me.

It was late December. The new golf season was still weeks away. The high school football season was over. I wasn't on the copy desk rotation. My paycheck—$1,362.50 biweekly, after all the deductions—was on automatic deposit. There was no reason for me to come in, no good reason.

"My kid needs mold samples for a science project," I said to Pete.

The truth was that I had to make some calls that I couldn't do on my cell phone from my usual office, the crowded Starbucks on First Street in downtown St. Petersburg. I had to call the mortgage company about refinancing, I had to call Visa and American Express to figure out some kind of payment plan, I had to call my ex-wife and ask for more time on our son's tuition at his summer lacrosse camp, and I had to make sure my girlfriend, Lily, didn't get wind of any of this. I needed multiple phone lines and a soupçon of privacy. Ten in the morning on a Saturday in winter, there shouldn't be anybody in the sports department of *The St. Petersburg Review-American*. But there was Pete, wearing his short-sleeved plaid shirt and plaid pants without a hint of irony.

I worked my way into a corner. I swept a week's worth of old papers into a big blue recycling bin. There was something comforting about being at the paper. We were dying a little death every day, but there was still an undercurrent of macho arrogance in the place, like *We might not be relevant now, but you should have seen us back in the day.*

I got out my Visa card and squinted at the 800 number. I had tried on some 1.0 reading glasses at CVS, but I'd left them on the rack, not ready to make another concession to middle age. Pete came ambling over. "I heard something that might interest you," he said.

I knew the various preambles of Peter Henry Hough down cold, and this was one of his favorites. Pete loved everything about the reporting game, and the editor-as-tipster was near the top. Pete loved news. If you had news, he wanted it. In the paper, on RevAm.com, on our blogs, in our Tweets, he didn't care, as long as we had it first and had it right. A few days earlier he had taken great delight in a little item I had posted about a local high school baseball coach who got ticketed and breathalyzed for doing 62 in a 25. The coach called and read Pete the riot act. That made Pete's day.

"I heard Tree's been stepping out," he said.

Pete, drawling Southerner, milked this most unlikely of sentences, dripping Spanish moss on the whole thing.

Tree. What everybody called Herbert X. Tremont, Jr., the damnedest golfer who ever lived. Tree's father was a black Creole from rural Louisiana who spent twenty years in the army; he had a master's in political science from Howard and a jazz collection that rivaled Kareem Abdul-Jabbar's. Tree's white mother was from Chicago, where she had been a schoolteacher. The parents, who had married fairly late and were now separated, hadn't worked in years. Tree was their job. He was an only child, homeschooled by his mother and coached exclusively and secretly by his father until Tree entered, at age nineteen, the first tournament of his life, a U.S. Open where he finished ninth. Since then he had become not just the most dominant golfer of all time but also the richest, most powerful, and most popular athlete in the world. He was modest and handsome, with perfect Hollywood teeth and the family to go with them: the beautiful wife, the adorable twins. Everybody wanted a piece of the action, and before long, Tree Tremont became the first celebrity ever to have endorsement deals with Coke *and* Pepsi. His Crest deal alone was worth $5 million a year. Tree could have lived anywhere in the world. He lived in Florida because the Sunshine State has no state income tax. He lived in St. Pete because he fell in love with a boat.

Only one sportswriter knew what the *X* stood for. Me. And I was sworn to secrecy.

"Stepping out," I said, incredulous.

"That's what my peeps are telling me." Pete's slang was always outdated by a few years, not that he knew it.

"You've seen his wife, right?" I asked.

Of course Pete had seen his wife. Snaps of Belinda DeCarlo Tremont, a former Italian bikini model, sunbathing topless had become an Internet sensation ever since plaything.com paid a fired housekeeper a reported $250,000 for them. When I saw the pictures, I couldn't stop looking at the beads of moisture deep in Belinda's cleavage. I didn't know if the droplets were sweat or Mediterranean seawater, and I didn't care. Lily caught me looking at the pictures one day. She pushed up her A-cup breasts and said in a fine mock-Italian accent, "Good golf buys hot tits." I loved that girl.

"Hey, it's like I always say, dudes want a piece of strange," Pete said. He had seen it all and done it all. "I hear Tree's been going upstairs at Gents, dealing Benjamins like he's working a Vegas blackjack table."

I made a mental note: *Steal line for screenplay.* If I could just sell my screenplay—the one I'd been trying to write for years—I could make everybody happy.

"Let's say it's true, Pete," I said. I took a good look at my boss, standing in his brown Wal-Mart shoes on the linoleum floor of our dumpy sports department, wearing his extraordinary plaid-on-plaid ensemble, casually offering a tidbit that could bring down an empire. A tidbit that could fell the Tree Corp. "Let's say we could get the girls on the record."

"You'd have to," Pete said. "You'd need to have it dead to rights."

"Fine, you got it dead to rights."

"You'd need pictures," Pete said. "You'd need art."

"Okay, you have art," I said. "You have some girls on the record. You give Tree the chance to deny it. What are you gonna do with it?"

"We run it."

"With our publisher?" The patrician, silver-haired Charles B. "Salty" Morton IV. Ringer for the pompous blowhard in *Caddyshack*, Judge Smails. He owned the paper free and clear, having inherited it from Salty III, who got it from Salty Junior, who got it from the first C. B. Morton, who predated Morton Salt and the family nickname. Salty IV was more interested in his golf than in his newspaper, and he was on the fast track to becoming a player in the hierarchies of both the United States Golf Association and the Augusta National Golf Club, home of the Masters. "You really think Salty's going to let us run that story?" I asked.

Pete ran his thick fingers through his fine hair, leaving an oily film on his nails. "I don't know," he said. "But you'd like to give him the chance, right?"

He grabbed a reporter's notebook off my desk. He wrote a name and a phone number under a scribbled quote from the high school football coach in Tampa who had let his kids score seventy points against a team that managed one lousy field goal. *Did it kill 'em? Don't see no dead bodies over there.*

I looked at the name. Emerson. I looked at the number. Area code 917. A New York cell phone.

"You didn't get it from me," Pete said. He actually sounded giddy. Which was weird. Because Pete didn't do giddy.

2

Lily and I ate dinner at my house that evening, eggplant Parmesan on a cold December night. She had her own apartment and I had my house, a 1950s-development rancher three miles from the nearest Gulf beach. I shared the house with Josh Jr., getting close to fifteen, several nights a week, or whenever he felt like coming around. Sometimes the three of us would have dinner together. Lily and Josh had an easy rapport, talking about teachers and swimming and movies. She was my first real girlfriend since my divorce from Meg, and she was nearly ten years younger than I. We were very different people, but we shared some significant interests: cooking at home, movies, newspaper reading, ocean swimming. She looked great coming out of the water. We'd read movie reviews out loud to each other, or she'd read about Belize in the travel section of *The New York Times* and say, "Can't you get an assignment *there*?" She believed, as I did, that being a reporter, done the right way, was a noble thing.

Cleaning up, I put the eggplant peels in a compost pile that I kept for Lily. When I leaned in for a goodbye kiss, she turned her head away, like they do in the movies.

"It's a goose chase," I said.

It didn't sound good, going to Gents late on a Saturday night for a story.

Lily said, "That better be all you're chasing."

St. Pete is loaded with beach dives and hotel bars and suburban taverns and cycler hangouts, but Gents is the town's only swanky nightclub, a nexus of silicone and Italian tailoring and, in the parking lot, German engineering. The club attracts all manner of flush men: professional athletes, businessmen, trust-fund college kids, fugitive husbands on golf junkets. Sparkly women from as far away as Tampa flock to it. I had been there only once, when an off-duty NBA star tried to throw an uppity fan through a plate-glass window, à la Charles Barkley. But the window was shatterproof, and the fan went splat and broke his nose and sued the baller. "Next time," the doorman had said to me that night, "if there is a next time, come correct. No tennis shoes. And no fuckin' pleated Dockers, neither."

For my second visit, I tried to dress the part. I got through the front door and entered a dark, womb-like tunnel. The music was so loud, the bass was thumping in my chest. The walls were upholstered in red leather. Large chandeliers hung from the black ceiling. The place smelled of spilled champagne and perfume. I went to one of the many bars.

"Coors Light, please."

"Fourteen."

I slid a ten-dollar bill across the counter. "Just the one."

The bartender, heavily pierced, looked at me with pity. "Fourteen dollars, sir."

I fished out a five, leaned against the bar, and tried to look like I knew what I was doing. At the center of the room was a dance floor, a blob of sweating, flailing limbs. The men wore designer jeans and bejeweled shirts, many sporting inflated biceps and shaved chests. On the edges of the room were roped-off red sofas and tables with signs that read BOTTLE SERVICE ONLY. Here the patrons were slightly older and more debonair, and the women were particularly spectacular, with their sculpted thighs, pierced navels, and gravity-defying breasts. I felt woozy and old.

In one especially dark corner, there was shrieking and whooping. A patron was spraying his posse with champagne as if they had just won the World Series. Security stepped right in.

I could not imagine Tree Tremont hanging at Gents. He despised it when fans slapped his back. You almost never saw him shake anyone's hand. He refused high fives. He avoided crowds. He avoided anything public. He was a germophobe. He made you think of a straitlaced basketball savant off an Iowa farm, circa 1958. Most people didn't even think of him as black.

He really was one of a kind: polite assassin on the field, model citizen off it. The whole of America—urban, suburban, and otherwise—couldn't get enough of him. Nor could France or India or China. He wasn't even thirty yet, and *Fortune* had pegged his net worth at $1.2 billion and his annual income at $150 million, only one tenth of which he made on the golf course. It was his image that made him Wall Street–rich. It was people like me who helped create and maintain that image. Tree chasing tail at the Sporting Gent? I couldn't see it.

I walked by a 330-pound NFL lineman I knew slightly. The two girls with him might have checked in at 230 combined.

"Zandy Clarke," I said. "What are you doing here?"

Zandy Clarke leaned down to my level and said, "Snatch by the batch, my man. By the *batch*."

I laughed.

"Serious," he said. "A *sportswriter* could get laid here."

"Hey, Zandy, you ever see—"

I never finished my question. The offensive lineman, with a girl on each arm, had other things to occupy him.

I moved on, middle-aged sportswriter on an expedition. I reached a stairway that was guarded by a large man dressed like Johnny Cash. A waitress sashayed by. Her getup was like that of all the other waitresses: five-inch stilettos, tiny black skirt, black shirt unbuttoned halfway to the navel, lacy red bra.

"What's upstairs?" I asked.

"You know what they say: If you have to ask, you can't afford it."

Her smile made you want to reach for your wallet. She walked over to a nearby table and leaned in to take an order. Her shirt rode up, revealing a tattoo on her lower back: two rows of intertwined circles, in blue, black, red, yellow, and green. I recognized the ink and then placed its owner: Cari Coleman, who got the tat and a bunch of long lectures when she was a senior at Calvary Christian and held three age-group world records. Back then she was all set to become a star Olympic swimmer. The paper ran a close-up photo of the tattoo to accompany a feature I had written about her. Angry church ladies wrote in to complain, saying *The Rev-Am* was getting too risqué. Somewhere on her MapQuested trip to an Olympic podium, Cari Coleman missed an exit.

She stepped back from the table. I tried again.

"Aren't you Cari?" I asked. The music was so loud, I was practically yelling. She smelled like vanilla. "I'm Josh Dutra. From *The Review-American*? I covered you at Calvary?"

"I remember you," she said. "You were the one with no camera, no tape recorder, nothing but that little notebook. You had a thing for Coach."

St. Pete is a hard place to keep a secret. "Not as bad as that lady cameraman from Channel 63 did," I said.

Cari smiled.

"I'm trying to find Tree Tremont," I said. "You ever see him here?"

"We're not allowed to talk about that kind of thing," Cari said. "I'm sorry. I better go, Mr. Dutra."

That's what she had called me in high school. She started to turn away.

"Cari, I'm not going to quote you. I won't use your name, nothing like that."

She tilted her head, gave me a serious look, and said, "You gotta keep me completely out of this."

Cari understood the ridiculous power of a third-rate website like RevAm.com. She was making a trade. She didn't want to be mentioned in a story about Tree, a where-are-they-now column, or anything else. Her life as a public figure was over. She was a cocktail waitress in a short skirt at a nightclub called Gents.

I nodded sympathetically. Young promise will follow you around for the rest of your life. We both knew things about the other.

"He's been in here," she said. "He comes by himself, meets up with these two nerdy Asian guys with glasses. They hang out upstairs."

"With women?" I asked.

"Yes, with women," she said. I thought I saw her roll her eyes. "They're spending a thousand dollars for a bottle of Patrón you can get at a liquor store for forty bucks. Of course there are women. Two girls for every guy. *That's* what you pay for upstairs—that and a lot of privacy."

I started to ask another question.

"I gotta go," Cari said. She still looked like a swimmer, long and lean, with broad shoulders. I noticed that she'd had her ears pinned back. They used to protrude. I wondered what that had cost her. "I can't lose this job. Take care, Mr. Dutra."

She walked away. The dance-floor crowd swallowed her up.

My head was spinning from the noise, the flashing lights, the story I was chasing. I pushed my way outside and plopped into my ten-year-old pale blue Camry, 160,000 miles on it but all paid off.

I looked at my phone. One missed call from Lily. Any other time, I would have called her right back. Instead, for the third time that day, I dialed the 917 number Pete had given me. For the third time, it went to a generic voice mail. I resorted to texting. I had learned it was the only way to reach my son and most everybody else under the age of forty. I clumsily thumbed a greeting: *Emerson, this is Josh Dutra of The Review-American. I would love to talk to you about Tree Tremont. Please reach me at this number. Thanks!*

I couldn't stand the fake cheerfulness of the electronic

exclamation mark, but there I was, another abuser. I was calling Lily when my cell phone vibrated, alerting me to an incoming text:

Meet me in 15 at gad

Me, texting:

How will I know it's you?

Nothing.

I made the drive to the Great American Diner to talk with a total stranger about one of the most famous men in the world, a man who represented not just family values but something far more valuable: *country-club* family values. Could it possibly be all facade? I was actually starting to wonder. I felt my shoulders shimmy in a cold chill.

3

I knew within a minute of my arrival at the Great American Diner that Emerson was not there. There was a truck driver at the counter. A couple in a booth. Some high school kids in a corner table. I took a booth that faced the door. Early on, most of my interviews with Tree's father had been at the diner. I thumbed through a menu I knew by heart, passing by the familiar pictures of the various specials. Grandmother's Famous Meat Loaf. The Honest Indian Turkey Platter. My mind drifted. I thought about my history with Tree.

I met him about three months before his first U.S. Open. Actually, I met his father first. Big Herb. I was covering a Yankees–Red Sox spring-training game at Legends Field in Tampa. Scads of New York writers were there, plus ESPN, FOX Sports, NBC Sports—all the big bats. Another steroid scandal had erupted.

A tall, elegant, long-fingered black man in a Kansas City Monarchs hat approached me in the quiet press box five hours before first pitch. "Young man, do you know the sportswriter Mitch Albom?" he asked. This was during the *Tuesdays with Morrie* craze.

"Sir, I don't think Mitch Albom is here," I said. He had moved way beyond *sportswriter.*

There was a movement then to get old, forgotten Negro Leaguers in the Hall of Fame, and I figured this man in the Monarchs hat was connected to it. He looked hurt.

"Can I help you?" I asked.

The man said, "My son's gonna be the greatest golfer of all time. I was gonna let Mitch Albom do an article on him."

In the '80s and into the '90s, when there was space galore in *The Rev-Am,* I used to write stories that Pete called Profiles in Kookiness. The man in the Monarchs hat, I thought, would have fit right in.

"Herbert X. Tremont, Senior," the man said. He shook my hand vigorously. "Father of Tree Tremont. Nice to know you. Keep an eye on Tree. He's gonna change the world."

Big Herb spent the next hour telling me about Tree. None of it sounded credible, but it was irresistible. A few days later, I found myself on a sod farm on the outskirts of Brooksville, Florida, watching Tree knock rising 4-iron shots through a Hula-Hoop held high by his father. Any errant shot could have knocked Herb out, but he had total faith in his son. The day Tree qualified for his first U.S. Open, my 3,500-word piece on him was ready to go. The story was picked up everywhere. After his ninth-place finish in the first tournament of his *life,* I was interviewed by *CBS Evening News* and *Good Morning America,* by a dozen radio stations and NPR, by Golf Channel and ESPN. For a while there, I was the Tree Tremont expert. It landed me a side job, a writing contract with *Golf Digest.* For a couple of years I had access to Tree that nobody else had. I got the word on his engagement to Belinda before anybody else.

But by the day of the wedding, on an island off Key West, I was in the media boat like everybody else. When the baby pictures of the twins came—a boy and a girl—they went straight to *People.* By then I couldn't get one-on-ones with Tree anymore. He was the Tree Corp.

That day at the sod farm, Tree was funny and smart and likable. Little Josh was a toddler then, Meg was pregnant, and I was feeling my way through the father-and-husband business. I admired Tree and Herb's father-son bond. They almost seemed like contemporaries.

"You know what has two thumbs, speaks French, and loves blow jobs?" Tree asked me one day at the sod farm.

I said I did not.

Tree dropped his club, pointed his thumbs at his chest, and said, "Moi!"

I kind of doubted that Tree actually knew anything firsthand about oral sex—his life was so cordoned off.

Big Herb just about fell to the grass. When his back was straight again, he said, "Now, I know you ain't gonna put that in the paper, Josh." And I didn't.

That was the tradeoff for the access. They could be themselves around me, trusting that I knew what to print and what to leave out. I didn't know if Pete would have approved, but it felt right to me. My father had taught me golf, and though I never got even close to good, there was something about Herb and Tree that felt familiar to me. I was on the inside of a once-in-a-lifetime story, and I liked it.

Big Herb and Tree's mother, Helene, were still together when I first started coming around. Helene had a kindly manner and an old-fashioned correctness and the kind of skin that burned after ten minutes in the Florida afternoon sun. She popped in at the sod farm every time I was there, pouring pink lemonades for us from a giant thermos.

Mrs. Tremont asked me a series of courtly questions about where I had grown up and how I had become a sportswriter. Her "hobby," she said, was poetry; every so often she sent one of her poems to the editor of her church's newsletter. But she didn't have much time for that. "Not with this guy and *this* guy," she said, pointing to her husband and son. They were working in the dirt, discussing how you add bounce to a sand wedge by opening up the face. "*They* believe in six squares a day. We have *two* refrigerators *and* a freezer. Have you ever heard of such a thing?"

When Mrs. Tremont wasn't there, Big Herb worked blue. One day at the sod farm, he said to Tree, "I want you to move that left thumb to the right just a cunt hair and hold it down hard." Tree did exactly as told and started hitting beautiful low draw shots. I could only dream about hitting shots like that.

"For the British Open, into the wind, right?" Tree said.

"You got it, Bo."

That name came from Bill "Bojangles" Robinson, Shirley Temple's black tap-dancing partner. Herb said to me, "My son might sound white to you. Lord knows his mother is whiter than Billy Graham. But Tree knows a lot of brothers danced a lot of soft shoe for white folks so he'd have the chance to make more money in a week than most people will make in their lives."

I didn't use any of that, either. There was more than enough good stuff, and I figured I'd be writing about Tree for years to come.

I came out of my drift and looked at my watch. It had been nearly an hour since Emerson had sent me his text.

A breathtaking woman entered the diner alone, wearing a short skirt and high heels. As she came closer, I could see she was expertly made up.

She came right to my booth. "You're Josh."

I must have looked shocked.

"Your picture's on the website." She sat down. "I'm Emerson. Before I say one word, I want to know where you got my name and number."

She had immediately put me in a tough spot.

"Unfortunately, that's not something I can tell you."

She got up.

"Wait, please."

She stood at the table.

"I got it at work."

Emerson sat. "Look," she said. "Some very nasty shit is about to go down, and some powerful people and powerful companies are not going to be happy about it."

One of the old-gal waitresses came by, took Emerson's coffee order, and said to me, "Be sure to say hi to Lily for me."

Emerson's eyes were bloodshot. Her hand shook as she raised her water glass. "I'm telling my story to *Eye of the World*. My girlfriend's father knows the editor there. I talked to them one day, and the next there was a contract and a check at my front door. I didn't even give them anything *close* to my best stuff. What I did, technically, is sell them a picture of Amanda and Tree and me together upstairs at Gents. It's a very revealing picture."

My mind was racing. I opened my notebook and said, "So they paid you for the picture. If you don't mind me asking, what'd you get?"

She read an incoming message on her cell phone and said, "This has to be completely off the record."

I closed my notebook.

"You know what that means?" she said.

"It means I can't use what you tell me unless I can confirm the information with another source and leave you out of it," I said.

"I was told that's background basis," she said.

Emerson was correct, and I knew it. I wondered where she had learned the difference.

"I'm saying you can't use *any* of this," she said. "Not a word. Do you know the power these people have?" Her chin fell in her chest. She was a surgically enhanced party girl, but there was something vulnerable about her, too. "Twenty thousand," she said. Her voice was low.

Not a lot of money, really, when you consider what Tree might have paid for the picture. Maybe she felt the same way.

"Can we start over?" I asked. "How can I help you?"

She looked around the quiet diner, then at me, and she was off.

"I started dating Tree two years ago. Our anniversary is coming up. You know, he was really nice. A freak between the sheets but a gentleman on the street, you know? He'd say, 'The thing about Belinda, she can't give me what I need, but she's the mother of my children. I can't walk.' Very, you know, honorable.

"What you got to realize is that he can't give me up. He's like an addict. He texts me like twenty, thirty times a day. He'll text me from the car with his wife right next to him. He'll say, 'When can I see you? I gotta see you.'

"I actually feel sorry for him. All that money. Good-looking guy. Great body. But he's led such an army life, you know? Up at five and all that. With me, he always wanted to experiment, get a buzz on, try things. And I introduced him to my best friend, Amanda. He wanted three-ways, and that was cool, 'cause Amanda and me, we're fine with that. He liked to watch us. So that went on for like the past year. We'd be with him at his golf tournaments. But never on Sundays. Belinda doesn't miss Sundays. You know that special black shirt he wears every time he's in the hunt on a Sunday? He told me he didn't give a shit about it but that Belinda was all into that Catholic superstitious shit and she makes him wear it, that black shirt with the red armbands. He said his sponsors like to see the twins and Belinda on the eighteenth green whenever he wins, that it's worth an extra twenty million a year. It's so funny. He wins and his wife gives him a little peck on each cheek, like they're meeting at the airport or something. It's so pathetic. And the kids are on his legs like dogs pissing on a hydrant.

"My dad's like, 'Look at them kids. What kind of fucking sport is that? You don't see kids running around after a football game, do you?' I told that to Tree. He laughed his ass off. He goes, 'Your father's right.'

"So it was all good. But then, about ten days ago, 'Manda goes, 'Don't be mad at me, but I gotta tell you something.' She's like, 'Tree told me not to say anything to you, but I didn't think that would be, you know, ethical.' So I know this is gonna be good. She says, 'Tree wants to take me to Maui for the first tournament of the year. He's gonna stick around afterward to look at a hotel project, and he wants my design ideas.'

"Design my ass. You should see her condo. She's got like artwork made out of Fruit Loops, the stupidest shit you've ever seen. Design. That's just Tree looking for cover. So now I'm out? That skank over me? Fuck that, and fuck Tree, too.

"I know *Eye of the World*'s gonna be in Hawaii. I want the story out. But then I start freaking out, because you know people will say, 'Yeah, what do you expect, it's the *Eye*.' Last week they had that mother delivering a Martian baby. They got all that crazy shit. So if it comes out in the *Eye* and nobody believes it, then the joke's on me. So I was telling Pete all this, and he said for the story to be credible, it had to be told by a real sportswriter, by somebody who knows Tree. That's why I'm sitting here with you."

"Pete?" I asked.

Emerson look confused. I hadn't given up Pete when Emerson first arrived, but now it was obvious how I came to have Emerson's cell number.

"Your boss. From the paper?" she said.

"Pete Hough," I said.

"Yeah. Sweetheart. Hangs out upstairs at Gents. I'm a hostess there. We call him Payday Pete. He comes once every two weeks on Friday nights."

Pete, in his plaid-on-plaid, upstairs at Gents, writing numbers on matchbooks. Unbelievable.

Emerson took a Marriott pen from my breast pocket, removed the cap with her teeth, and wrote down flight information on my Great American Diner/Great American Generals place mat. According to Emerson, Amanda was flying to Maui on the first Wednesday in January, on United out of Miami through LAX.

Emerson dropped the pen back in my pocket. "I'm going to the ladies'," she said. "Lose my number."

I watched her get up and march straight out the front door. I wanted to call Lily. I looked at my watch. It was one in the morning. It felt much later. I made a slow drive home, dazed.

4

Pete said he wanted the story, and he sure as hell didn't want the *Eye* beating us on it, so a few days into the new year, I found myself flying a gruesome combination of flights engineered by Pete and Travelocity.com for maximum cheapness: Tampa to Dallas, Dallas to San Francisco, San Francisco to Honolulu, Honolulu to Maui. Four legs, middle seats all the way. But with one breath of the fragrant, humid Hawaii air, the flights were a bad memory.

I used to make regular trips to Maui for the Kapalua Championship, to write state-of-Tree stories, but in recent years the trips had been canceled because of the paper's vicious cost-cutting. I was glad to be back.

A PGA Tour event is comprised of four rounds that are played over four days, starting early on Thursday mornings and finishing late on Sunday afternoons. When Tree was in contention, a hundred million people around the world watched. When he wasn't playing, the number was less than half that. PGA Tour officials—and just about everybody else with a financial stake in the game—prayed for him to play well.

Tree opened with a first-round 63, tying his own course record, the best round of the day by three shots. What a way to start the year. Virtually every person at the tournament was following Tree, thousands of people, traipsing the canyons of Kapalua's Plantation Course. As soon as I saw Tree toiling in his vineyards, I stopped caring about Amanda and Emerson, whether Pete was a regular at Gents, *Eye of the World*—all of it. I was watching the greatest athlete in the world at the height of his powers. It was mesmerizing for the casual sports fan. For the serious golf aficionado, which I still was, it was intoxicating. Tree used his mind and his body to make a golf ball do things that others could not.

Even from two hundred yards away, Tree Tremont was an unmistakable figure. He was built like a martini glass, with powerful shoulders and a chest tapering to a thirty-inch waist, all of it accentuated by his tight European-cut clothing that Belinda hand-picked for him, as Tree liked to remind reporters. (He was giving himself plausible deniability.) By comparison, the other players looked like they had just stepped off a shuffleboard court. Tree's stride radiated athleticism, confidence, superiority. There was something virile about his presence, certainly for women but for men, too. Twenty weeks a year, whether you saw him live or on your flat-screen TV, people watched Tree Tremont throw grass in the air, and it excited them in ways they couldn't even articulate.

In theory, I was paid to be a neutral observer, but you couldn't be neutral, writing about Tree Tremont. I knew a lot of sportswriters who felt overmatched, covering him. The speed at which he won his first thirteen major championships and fifty-three PGA Tour victories had no precedent. A lot of us with no blueprint were lost. My take on him was that as easy as Tree could make the game look, he was a grinder at heart. He brought intensity to every shot, and he played in a controlled fury. On Friday, for the second round, it was humid, and his mocha skin was glistening by the first green. The golfing highlight of the day came on the fairway of the par-5 fifteenth. He stood dead still and assessed a thorny shot. He was standing on a tilted fairway, his ball below his feet. The pin was on the front left of the green. He'd have to hold a draw against a slice wind. The shot required strength, nerve, and superior skill. Most players would have chosen the safety of laying up. Tree pulled out a 1-iron, a club so unforgiving that only he carried one. I once asked him when he'd replace it with its modern, easy-to-hit equivalent, the 15-degree hybrid. "When Hogan does," he said. The long-dead Ben Hogan.

Tree took a few purposeful practice swings. Many golf swings on Tour, clinging to old models of gentlemanliness, were long and graceful and artistic. Tree's action was blunt and forceful and scientific. I had seen him play tens of thousands of shots, but the violence of his action still awed me. He lashed at the ball on fifteen at Kapalua and drove it through the heavy air with an audible sizzle. The TV cameras and spectators followed the ball, as they always did. I watched Tree. From his cocky twirl of the club, I knew it was a superb shot and that he knew it, too. That twirl move was a rare move for him. The ball came to rest twenty feet from the hole.

He stalked the eagle putt, missed it, but went on to shoot a second-round 64. He was leading by five with two rounds to play. The tournament was all but over. Stepping from the scorer's tent behind the eighteenth green, Tree was greeted by tiny Bill McNabb from Golf Channel. Tree took one look at him and couldn't stop laughing. "Jee-zus, did you microwave your face? You're gonna be the reddest Irishman in Orlando."

McNabb laughed heartily, flattered by Tree's putdowns.

Tree resented that Golf Channel monopolized so much of the Tour programming. The cable outfit was costing him money. CBS and NBC and ESPN gave him so much more exposure. Richard Fenimore, the commissioner of the PGA Tour, lived in fear that Tree would someday criticize their TV contracts, and negotiating the TV contracts was the commissioner's most important job. But Tree never did. He always played his part in all things. After every round, regardless of his score, he answered questions from Golf Channel stand-up guys and everybody else. Back when Tree turned pro, Big Herb told him, "You play golf for free. You get paid to promote." Tree understood that TV made myths and that myths made people rich. After the twins were born, Tree did spots for Saturn about the importance of car safety. He talked over footage that showed him strapping his kids into their car seats. Nobody I knew had ever seen Tree Tremont driving a Saturn. He was a Bugatti guy, a Maybach guy, a Range Rover guy. A tricked-out Hummer now and again. He did not drive Saturns. I knew that; the general population did not. Another thing I never wrote up.

Tree pretended to treat McNabb's questions with great earnestness. On-camera, he was always thoughtful but careful, sometimes amusing, occasionally funny. Never sarcastic, never cutting, never off-message. His discipline was astounding. He told McNabb how refreshed he was from having spent the holidays with his family. He told a story about his daughter asking Santa for a green jacket. He imitated her high voice: " 'I want one just like the one you got for winning the Masters, Daddy.' "

He credited his good play to his new 5.75-degree driver made by Arrow Golf, the manufacturer, which paid him $30 million a year. He owned a piece of the company, too. "That new Arrow driver is giving me another fifteen yards, and I love how I'm flighting it," he told McNabb. *Flighting it*. That was one of Tree's ways of letting people in, by using the terms of his craft in ways other people did not. No duffer ever talks about how he flights his driver.

When the interview was over, Tree hopped in a golf cart that raced up a steep hill toward the press room. (Pete rejected the phrase *media center*, and I followed his example.) I jogged up the hill and arrived winded, just as the press conference was beginning. I settled in my seat and Tree gave me a nod.

Up on a little stage were two oversize armchairs, one for Tree and one for a young PGA Tour media official, Tom Delaney. The scrim behind them was dotted with corporate logos.

"We are joined by Tree Tremont," Delaney said. He was excitable and nervous. "Tree followed his course-record-tying sixty-three with a sensational sixty-four, giving him a four-stroke lead."

Tree whispered something to him.

"Excuse me, five-stroke lead," Delaney said. "Five shots clear. So, Tree, even for you, this is a pretty nice way to start a new year. Why don't you give us a few thoughts on the round, and we'll open it up for questions."

I waited for what I knew would be Tree Tremont's first witticism of the year.

"Well, I broke eighty, so that was pretty good," he said.

He had decided to go with old reliable, trotting out a line that was familiar to me and other veterans but likely new material to most of the local media and the tournament volunteers who had crowded the back of the room. They laughed on cue and a little too loudly.

"You know, I drove it on a string today. I really controlled my traj with the irons, flighted the driver beautifully, and I was very happy with how I putted," Tree said. "Yesterday I made a bunch of putts, but I didn't like how the ball was going in the hole. It was kind of tumbling in a little off-center. Today my ball was hugging the ground and diving into the hole like a scared gopher. That was satisfying. That's what I like to see."

Tree was the only player on Tour who complained about the way he made putts. Other players, after a couple of pints, would tell you that if they could putt like Tree, they'd *be* Tree. It wasn't true, not for any of them. Not for Vijay Singh, not for Sergio García, not even for Rickie Fowler.

There were a dozen or so questions about specific things in the round. I knew or could account for every reporter in the room. Nobody looked to be from *Eye of the World*. I looked at the photographers in the back. About them I could be less sure. Just thinking about the *Eye* made my feet itchy. The *Eye* could turn everything I knew upside down. Unless we did it ourselves first.

A woman in a straw hat from a Honolulu golf magazine said, "Tree, I have to ask you this: Do you think you can win?"

The four or five regular golf-beat guys cringed at her question and its wording, but Tree just flashed his famous smile, showing off his orderly, Crest-sponsored teeth. He had a warm, happy, easy smile. A killer smile, really. "Well, I'm not here to work on my tan, ma'am," he said. That was one of his regular jokes, too, and the closest he ever came to acknowledging his racial lineage. People laughed. "Do I think I can win? Yes, but there's a lot of golf still to be played."

I put a finger in the air and waited for Delaney to make eye contact. He pointed my way, and a volunteer scurried over and handed me a wireless microphone.

"Tree, as you know, the U.S. Open is at Pebble Beach this year, and the British Open is at St. Andrews, two of your favorite venues." After all these years, it was still jarring for me to hear my amplified voice. I sounded nervous and absurd. I plowed on. "The only thing you haven't done in your career is win all four majors in one year. Is this the year you do it?"

"Well, Joshie," Tree said. I have to admit that it was a little thrill every time he called me by name in a press conference. "It's interesting you would bring that up, because I was ruminating on that during the flight over."

Ruminating. Tree loved fifty-cent words. His mother was a stickler for grammar, syntax, SAT-vocab words. She came to tournaments with pocket dictionaries. Big Herb once told me, "In the boardroom and the press room, Tree's gotta sound white. Only place he gets to be black is the bedroom."

Tree looked at me and said, "I do believe a calendar Slam is well within reason. I've won all four majors in a row, just spread across two seasons. No reason I can't win 'em all again. That's my intention for this year. You know, this is the year I turn thirty. I'm getting to be an old man. Not old like you, but old. Better do it while I can, right?"

The room buzzed. This was news. Nobody had ever won the four professional majors in the same calendar year. It was an audacious thing to say—not that it was his goal but that to win all four this year was his *intention*. When any normal citizen of the world wants to make news, he has to make all sorts of effort, using Twitter and Facebook and publicists. All Tree had to do was open his mouth. Typically, his ambitions were locked in the well-guarded fortress of his inner self. On this occasion, he was standing up and saying he was in open pursuit of golf's holiest grail, the Grand Slam.

At the end of the session, I was sitting in my seat when he walked by. He tapped me on the shoulder with a scorecard pencil, which meant he wanted me to walk with him.

"You haven't been here in years," Tree said. "They make you swim over?"

It was like a reminder that he really did know me. We had a shared history.

"And what do you do?" I said. "Give my Grand Slam scoop to everybody."

Tree smiled. I wondered if he somehow knew why I was actually there.

We reached the front door of the clubhouse, where his car was waiting. Tree had a bag with his golf shoes in one hand and a cell phone in the other, useful props in his ongoing war against autograph signing. There were maybe a hundred people leaning against barricades, chanting his name.

He asked, "Your son still playing that Nicklaus power fade?" When he focused on you, Tree made you feel like you were the only person in the world, even with strangers calling out for him.

A few years earlier, I had taken Josh to the PGA Merchandise Show Demo Day at a massive driving range in Orlando, where manufacturers put out their wares for writers and other lucky souls to try. We were whacking balls side by side when Tree, paid by Arrow to be there, materialized behind us. "Let's see who's in the slump now," he said, chiding me.

I made a flailing, breathless swing and hit an ugly duck hook.

"Put that in your fuckin' paper!" Tree said.

My son, ten or eleven then, hit a couple of smooth drives with a gentle left-to-right bend. Tree gave him a look of approval. "The Nicklaus power fade—very old-school," he said. Tree Tremont knew more golf history than anybody, me included. Jack Nicklaus became Jack Nicklaus by perfecting the power fade in the late 1960s. "Good thing you got your mom's athletic genes," he said to Josh.

That's what conversation was like with Tree, everything in code, indirect, the needle always out. He was often playfully profane, unless he was in public or his mother was around.

Back in the parking lot, the crowd had grown to maybe two hundred. Four hundred eyes staring at Tree. He blocked them out.

I said, "Josh plays a real sport."

"I know, lacrosse," Tree said. "Tell him lacrosse is gonna cost him teeth, and golf is gonna get him girls."

With that, he ducked into his courtesy car, a sleek black Mercedes, and drove off. His caddie, Mac McCausland, was in the passenger seat. Mac was a smart, tough Glasgow native who had moved to the United States as a teenager. He'd been on Tour since the tail end of the Nicklaus era. Other players would have their caddies drive them off the course and to the hotel. For Tree and Mac, it was the opposite.

I got out my phone and texted my parking-lot exchange with Tree to Josh. He responded with two smiley-face emoticons, to use a word he taught me. Then I settled in front of my Toshiba and banged out a game story, leading—like everybody else writing for a paper or website—with the bit about the Grand Slam. Only I used the phrase "responding to a question posed by *The Review-American.*" I didn't want to put it in, but if I didn't, Pete would. He always wanted his paper out in front. The idea of facing Pete if the *Eye* broke news on Tree actually scared me. "Tree is ours," he once told me. "If he has a hangnail, our readers need to know."

Kapalua is the most intimate venue on Tour. Down the hill from the course is the Ritz-Carlton, where the players stay, along with the TV people and the few out-of-town reporters. The resort's PR staff arranges a hundred-dollar-per-night media rate with the implicit expectation that the scribes will be so grateful, we'll rave about the resort in print. Which we do. Pretty corrupt, when you think about it.

Usually, nobody knew where Tree stayed during any given tournament. You'd see other players at dinner, at the mall, at movie theaters, but you never saw Tree. At Kapalua, he was known to stay at the Ritz. I couldn't imagine how the mysterious Amanda could be there, unless she was in her own room or deep in Tree's suite. I knew I had to try to find her. That's why I was there. On Saturday, when Tree was on the course playing his third round, I decided to call his room just to see what might happen. I didn't feel comfortable about it, but I had to make the effort.

Years earlier, Big Herb had told me that Tree culled old Chicago Bulls rosters when looking for pseudonyms for hotel check-ins. Until that afternoon at Kapalua, I'd never had any reason to use that unusual piece of information. I called the hotel operator from my room and asked to be connected to Scottie Pippen. No such guest. Was there a Horace Grant in the house? There was not. Steve Kerr, maybe? No Steve Kerr. The nice young lady on the phone was trying her best to hide her exasperation.

One last gasp: Bill Wennington, a tall, slow, gangly Canadian. Tree would find that amusing.

There was a pause, and then the operator startled me by saying, "I'll be happy to connect you to Mr. Wennington's room."

After three rings, no one picked up. Relief washed over me. I was searching for the end button on the cordless phone when a woman asked in a sleepy voice, "Yes?"

"Amanda?" I asked.

I could feel my heart pounding in my neck. Up until then the whole Amanda-in-Hawaii thing had not been real to me. Now it was too real.

"No, this is not Amanda."

In my nervousness, I couldn't immediately place the wonderful, accented voice. "I'm sorry," I said.

"You have Belinda. Is this the room service?"

I really should have hung up. But right there on the phone, I had Belinda DeCarlo Tremont, the beautiful wife of the most famous athlete in the world, who had never been quoted in any American publication except *People*. I wasn't going to be the one who ended the conversation.

"No, no," I said. "Not room service. This is Josh Dutra, golf writer for *The St. Petersburg Review-American*."

"Oh, I know you, Josh," Belinda said. She really didn't. "I read your newspaper. I read all the papers. I remember when you couldn't write enough about Tree's slump, yes? You feel maybe a little stupid when he wins the PGA that year?" *Stoo-peed*. She made it sound lovely.

"I didn't think you were making the trip this week," I said.

"I wasn't. But the twins were bored at home, so why not?" For some reason, she giggled. It was a girly giggle at odds with her sexpot image. "Okay, Josh, so I go now. I hope you find your Amanda. *Ciao*."

Tree shot a 68 on Saturday, extending his lead to seven shots. After doing a deadline tap-dance, I decided to head to the beach for a late-afternoon swim.

The beach at Kapalua is exposed and windblown, so I drove toward Lahaina. Just before the village, there's a residential area, and in it there's a small, hard-to-see sign pointing the way to coastal access. That leads to a footpath between a couple of houses and then to a glorious, protected, secluded spot that locals call Baby Beach. A reef just offshore produces excellent snorkeling and small, tidy waves. It's a perfect beach for mellow bodysurfing, one of my surviving childhood sports.

As I strolled onto the beach, my eyes immediately went to the perfect bottom of a deeply tanned, dark-haired woman in a white string bikini, knee-deep in the ocean. I heard the accent again. I pulled down my *Gilligan's Island* bucket hat and, from my knapsack, produced my David Goodis novel to hide behind. Belinda Tremont in the Pacific Ocean. What a sight.

Within splashing distance, standing in waist-high water with a giddy kid in each muscular arm, was her husband. Every few seconds Tree would let his legs buckle, and the twins would be plunged into the warm water, squealing with delight. Belinda was calling and waving to them and recording the whole thing on a tiny video camera. Eventually, she went back to the beach chairs, but Tree stayed in the water for another twenty minutes, splashing with the kids. It was hard to tell who was enjoying it more, the twins or their dad. When they got out, Tree peeled tangerines for them and smeared sunblock on their little noses.

Watching this charming family scene left me thoroughly confused. Pete had been giddy about breaking the story of Tree's infidelities, but I was starting to think it couldn't possibly be true. Even if Emerson had been telling the truth—that Tree did go to Gents—having a few drinks at a nightclub is not a violation of one's marital vows. As for Amanda, she seemed to be an apparition.

And even if the whole story was true, why should I care, and why should our readers? If Tree was fooling around on the side, wasn't that an issue for Belinda and Tree and not the rest of the world? You couldn't make the case that it was affecting his performance on the course, so what made the item newsworthy? Maybe by filming all those TV commercials and cashing all those checks, he forfeited some of his rights to privacy. But did he give up *all* of them? It wasn't as if we had elected him to anything. It wasn't like he was our minister. He was an athletic god. That was all.

The next day, Tree won his fifty-fourth career tournament. The twins raced onto the final green, wrapping themselves around their dad's legs. The whole world was tuned in. People couldn't get enough of Tree Tremont winning. With the Pacific glimmering behind them, Tree embraced Belinda and gave her a kiss that lasted a beat longer than normal. Later, in the champion's press conference, he was asked what it meant to share the victory with his wife and kids.

"That's always special," Tree said. "Family is everything to me." It sounded sincere to me.

My mind kept going back to the beach scene. I thought I had seen a photographer sneaking around high up on a cliff, her long lens poking out of a bush. I wasn't sure. I wasn't sure of anything anymore.

5

"What are you doing here?" Tree asked me.

It was the day after the win at Kapalua, and he was touring one of Maui's last massive pineapple plantations. Tree was the public face for a consortium of Chinese investors who wanted to convert the plantation into a golf course and luxury homes. The original plantation mansion was to be turned into a boutique hotel. A dozen people were trailing Tree, including the developers and the bankers and their PR flaks, a local TV crew, the lady in the straw hat from the Honolulu golf magazine, Tree's manager, Andrew Finkelman—and me. Tree was not happy to see me.

"At Kapalua, they had a thing in the press—" I started.

Finkelman, built like a jockey, cut me off. "They invited local media," he said in his oddly high-pitched voice. He turned to me and said, "You're a long way from home, Josh."

Prior to working for Tree, Finkelman was a senior agent with a reputation for ruthless efficiency at IGM—Intergalactic Golf Marketing. Tree Corp hired him away to be devoted to one lone client.

Finkelman was not an easy person to develop rapport with. In the press tent, we called him "Dr. No." Any request for Tree's time always got the same answer, delivered via e-mail: "Tree appreciates the thought, but he's too pressed for time. The answer is no. I hope you can understand what I'm saying." As if *no* were somehow complicated. The answer was always no. After a while, a lot of reporters just gave up. Which was exactly how Dr. No wanted it. He wanted one version of the Tree Tremont story going out, the one Tree himself told by playing amazing shots on TV. The official commentary was Tree's careful post-round press sessions or occasional postings on his website.

The group carried on, caravanning in camouflage golf carts on dirt trails. I sat in a backward-facing rear seat in the last cart, looking at tire tracks and feeling ridiculous. I wanted to call Lily, but it would be the middle of the night for her back home in St. Pete. Loneliness washed over me.

And then I started stewing. First off, it was not like they had invited "local media," as Finkelman had said, on this glorified plantation tour. There was a sign-up sheet in the press tent at Kapalua for anybody who wanted to come. They just hadn't expected any of the handful of reporters from the mainland to stick around for a staged event with no news value. I'd signed up. It wasn't as if I had sneaked in. Second, Tree had asked me the question. Why couldn't Finkelman, that type-A, marathon-running neurotic asshole, let me answer it?

The caravan of carts made it to the plantation's manor house. It was a beautiful, sprawling brown-shingled building with a porch running along the entire front. Inside, it was completely empty but in perfect condition, with planked floors and baronial fireplaces and dark chandeliers.

"Oh, I love those," a woman said, pointing to the chandeliers. "Are they gas? Oh, no—they're candle. Absolutely gorgeous." She reached for a tiny tape recorder from a striped canvas bag over her shoulder. *She* was absolutely gorgeous, with long, flowing, shiny hair, impossibly high cheekbones, and piercing blue eyes. She had only one flaw: the left side of her lower lip drooped. You could overlook it.

She talked into her tiny recorder. "Lobby treatment: dark floral drapes for bay windows, greens and browns. Need uplighting for giant palms at entranceway. Do not let anybody touch the six ballroom chandeliers."

Tree smiled at her. The woman's cell phone rang from deep in her colorful canvas bag. Fumbling to answer it, she accidently put it in on speakerphone.

"Amanda?" It was a deep voice with a New York accent. "This is Donnie Blassingame. I'm a reporter with the—"

She clicked off the speakerphone and pressed the phone tight against her ear. As she listened, her face went white. She clicked off the phone, marched over to Finkelman, and urgently whispered something to him. Without ever changing expression, he took Amanda by the arm and led her out of the room. Tree followed them with his eyes.

The group carried on with its tour. I found a bathroom and called Pete. He picked up on the fourth ring. "It's three in the morning, Josh."

"I'm still in Maui," I said. "It's Monday morning here. I didn't think Amanda was here, but she is. I didn't think there was anybody here from the *Eye*, but now I don't know. They might've had a photographer trailing Tree at the beach, and I think one of their reporters just called Amanda. I think they've got something."

"Good," Pete said.

"Good?" I asked.

"We want them to break it," Pete said.

"We want them to break it?" I didn't get it. This was potentially the biggest sports story in forever. Pete had sent me to Hawaii to chase it.

"If they break it, we can follow," Pete said. "We'll sort out the fact from the fiction. Look, it's probably a one-off thing. People will forgive and forget it. It'll be a two-week story."

I was perplexed. I had thought Pete wanted to reveal Tree Tremont as the biggest fraud in the history of sports. Now his voice had all the urgency of an undertaker's.

"One-off?" I said. "There's Emerson. There's Amanda. That's two already."

Pete asked, "Did Emerson sign an affidavit for you? Show you any pictures? Play any tapes? You know, not everything a source says is actually true." Maybe Salty Morton, esteemed publisher of *The Review-American*, had ordered Pete to back off. Something had to explain Pete's sudden caution. "This is a story where we can't get too far out front. The *Eye* is used to fending off litigation. That's not our game. We need to take this slow and get it right."

Where was the Pete who delighted in getting softball coaches pissed off at him?

"What do you want me to do?" I asked.

"Stay as close to Tree as you can. Let's see what the *Eye* does. If they post something, try to get a reaction from Tree. If he won't give you anything, write what you know to be true."

"What, that he's got a decorator named Amanda?"

"That's a start."

Something was up. Something was not right.

"Quick question for you about Emerson," I said. "How'd you find her?"

"I didn't. She called the sports department cold. I picked up the phone is all."

"You didn't meet her at Gents?" I asked.

"Gents? Josh, you think my game plays at Gents? I'm going back to sleep."

I needed a break from the weirdness. I had a few hours before my flight home, so I went into Lahaina. On my road trips I always sent Josh a postcard telling him about where I'd been, even if I was just in Jacksonville to cover a football game. He would tape the postcards to the walls in his closet of a bedroom, and he and I would look at maps to see where they were from. He was a geography whiz; at teacher-parent conferences, which Meg and I amicably attended together, Josh's teachers always commented on that.

I wanted to find something for Lily, too, something that said (not literally) Hawaii. *The Rev-Am* gives reporters on the road thirty-one dollars a day in meal money. What we don't spend, we pocket. Thanks to free hotel breakfasts and free pressroom lunches and a couple of fast-food dinners, I was about a hundred in the black on this trip. Lily, a Northern California girl by upbringing and temperament, had no interest in expensive jewelry or expensive anything, but the colorful shell necklace I was looking at was just her sort of thing. Except for my mother, I'd never known anybody to take such interest in my reporting. Lily was always trying to expand my notion of the golf beat. Had I ever written about the lives of illegal-immigrant golf-course workers? Had I written about public golf in Soweto? She wanted to save the world. And me. And the special-needs kids she taught. Anybody and everybody. We met—should I admit this?—on an obscure dating site called whatdoyouhavetolose.com. We didn't do so well on the various check-lists. For one thing, her politics, unlike my own, were generous and progressive. But some person or computer had the good sense to put us together.

I called her while driving to the little open-air airport on Maui. It was late afternoon in Hawaii and near bedtime for her.

"What color is the water?" she asked.

"The color of your eyes."

"Oh, you should be a writer."

"What are you doing?" I asked.

"I'm reading your story."

"Where'd they play it?"

"I'm reading it on the laptop in bed."

Really, I was hopelessly out of it.

"It has a happy ending," I said.

"I like that," Lily said.

Another call came in. I saw it on my caller ID: TREE CORP. My heart raced. Nobody from Tree Corp had ever initiated a call to me. Nobody from Tree Corp ever even returned my calls.

"Lily, I'm really sorry. I gotta grab this." I clicked off, and the new call came on.

"Josh. Hey, man. It's Finky." I couldn't recall ever talking to Andrew Finkelman on a phone. He certainly had never referred to himself as Finky with me. That was Tree's name for him. "Listen, I was kind of short with you on the walk-through at the plantation."

Finkelman had fancy names for everything. *Walk-through.* A walk-through in carts.

"No problem, Andrew."

"No, I should apologize. Things have been a little tense. Listen, can I go off the record with you?"

"Sure," I said too quickly.

"Nothing that I want to talk about on the phone. I know Tree wants to talk to you, too. We're flying home tonight on *Flying Tree.* You want to catch a ride? We can talk on the plane."

I thought about four flights, three connections, middle seats, one-on-one time with Tree Tremont. "That'd be fine," I said.

"Good. But listen, the whole thing has to be off the record."

Sometimes you start off the record and later get the guy on the record. I remembered what Pete said: Stay close to Tree.

"Yeah, that's fine."

We met at the Maui airport, at a small terminal reserved for private aircraft. Nobody even patted me down. It was just Tree, Finkelman, and me. No Amanda. Belinda and the kids, Finkelman told me, had flown home after Sunday's win. Apparently, Belinda didn't want them to miss their water-aerobics class.

"Joshie, you got kids," Tree said.

"Just one."

"Right. Answer me this. This water thing Belinda has the twins do, it's taught by a guy who works full-time for us. Like, couldn't she just reschedule it? I mean, they're five years old. Am I right?" Tree was talking to me as if I could relate to his logistical problems. It was absurd. A logistical problem for me was finding a helmet at our local Sports Authority for some large-headed kid on Josh's Little League team. "Doesn't sound too hard to reschedule," I said. Tree nodded.

I had seen Tree's planes, though only from the outside. For shorter flights, he used what he referred to as his starter wings, a Gulfstream GV called *The Sapling.* For water landings near his yacht, he had a prop seaplane with giant pontoons called *Floating Tree.* For anything over four hours, he used his 737, *Flying Tree.* It was painted Masters green.

I climbed aboard, and a stewardess said, "Welcome to *Flying Tree.* What size slippers do you wear?"

You could smell the leather seats. Draped over every one was a cashmere throw with Tree's sequoia logo. I gave myself a little tour. There were enormous TVs, a full bar, a fully stocked kitchen, a foosball table, a full gym setup, two showers, and four cabins with queen-size beds. There were two attractive flight attendants, one chef/bartender, and two pilots. For three passengers.

Somewhere over the Pacific, Tree and Finkelman and I sat down for dinner. Cloth napkins, heavy silverware, mojitos. Tree drank his quickly, and another one silently appeared.

We talked about Tree's Kapalua win and all the attention over his comment about his *intention* to win the Grand Slam. We made forced small talk for a while. Then Finkelman put down his fork and looked right at me. "Some crazy shit is happening, Josh," he said. "*Eye of the World*—"

"*Eye of the Asshole,*" Tree said.

"Yeah, you got that right," Finkelman said. "Anyway, they've been sniffing around. We don't know what they're doing—bribing chambermaids, tapping phones, taking surveillance pictures—but we know they're trying to find dirt on Tree. They think they got a story on Tree and that girl you saw this morning—Amanda, our designer—and we don't know when they're going to run it, or if they're going to run it, or what."

Finkelman gave me a long look. I kept quiet. I was taught that reporters should listen, not talk. When you don't talk, people will fill up the silence.

"Belinda told us you called the room looking for Amanda," Finkelman said. "We'll forgive that little invasion of privacy and give you a chance to explain."

"I was following up on a tip, hoping to disprove a rumor," I said.

Finkelman looked at Tree. After a few seconds, Tree spoke. "That Amanda," he said. "For a while there, yeah, I was fucking her." It sounded so harsh. "It's over now. Belinda doesn't have a clue about any of it. Belinda and me—I know I can trust you, Josh—we were having some, shall we say, private problems, and Amanda, you could term it, filled a void."

Shall we say. You could term it. Classic Treeisms. He struggled with *me* and *I* and *good* and *well*, but you never knew when he'd drop in an *as it were* and make things sound all dressed up.

Listening to him talk about his marriage was unbearably uncomfortable. Naturally, I couldn't get enough of it. Finkelman, of course, ruined the moment. "So we've spoken to some friends," he said, taking over. "Karl Rove took my call. Some others. They all said the same thing: Get in front of the story. Define them before they define us. Our position is, what Tree does in his private life is none of your goddamn business."

"Look at Mickey Mantle," Tree said. "Look at JFK. Martin Luther King. Those guys rolled, am I right? I mean, all night long. Kobe, man. Look at Kobe. And they're gonna nail me? No fucking way."

He downed his second drink. Another appeared. I had never heard him so angry.

He stretched out his leg, massaged his right ankle, and grimaced. Everybody in golf knew he had a problem with his Achilles tendon, but it was treated like FDR's polio, something nobody ever talked about. Now I was seeing it as never before. He reached into the pocket of his Brooks Brothers workout pants, retrieved a Ziploc bag with a half-dozen pills in different shapes and colors, and swallowed them all with one big sip from his third mojito.

Finkelman said, "What Rove and those guys told us was, 'You're going to take a hit, mostly from people who were never buying your clothes and your clubs in the first place. Nothing you can do about that. What you can't do is lose your constituency.' And that got us thinking. We decided we need a media professional in-house, a media professional who knows golf, knows Tree, knows the men who cover the game. You've known Tree a long time. What we'd like to do, Josh, is bring you in, make you director of communications for Tree Corp. You'd oversee our website, write Tree's instruction pieces and tweets, work on our relationships with other writers. Ultimately, we'd want you to write Tree's book for him. Needless to say, we'll pay you generously. Whatever you're making from the paper and your freelance work, just double it, and that'll be your base salary. We'll give you a signing bonus, and there's more where that came from. We reward good work. We really think you'd be value-added."

I couldn't let Andrew Finkelman see my surprise. "What about the girls?" I asked. I watched him tilt his head at a weird angle. "You said 'the men who cover the game.' " I have something like a photographic memory for words. It sometimes got me in trouble with Lily but was always useful in my job. "What about the women who write golf?"

Finkelman's eyes locked on mine, as if he were literally trying to read me. It seemed like something you might learn in one of those management self-help books. "Good one, man," he finally said. "You had me for a second there. What about the girls. Geesh. Anyway, listen, don't answer us now. Take some time to think about it. Friday night, Belinda's throwing a party on *Off Course*. It's for the new Rolex deal." Tree had signed an unprecedented endorsement deal: three years, $100 million, every dollar of it going to his charitable foundation, Plant a Tree. "You should come. Let us know by then that you're taking the job, okay?"

I took a look at Tree. He was fast asleep, a spoonful of chocolate mousse still in his hand.

6

Lily was waiting for me at the St. Pete private airport. I climbed into her tinny Toyota truck with the pencil-thin manual-transmission stick. I wanted to tell her everything, but I couldn't. I made some semi-vague reference to Tree's sex life and quickly moved on to the job offer. I already hated the position they had put me in.

"They'd double my salary," I said. "I could be debt-free in six months."

We were driving by Ace Wimples pawnshop, on Central. I fished out a melted, mushy piece of wrapped Godiva chocolate from the plane for her. She ignored it.

"Tree Tremont fooling around," she said. "It's actually kind of shocking." Even Lily went straight to Tree's sex life. I shouldn't have been surprised. It was the way of the world. "You'd think sex with Belinda might be enough."

"Would be for me," I said.

Lily raised a fist and made a gurgling sound. I was Curly to her

Moe. She said, "How do you know this offer is even legit? Maybe they're just trying to stall you from publishing something."

She was the smart one in the family. That idea had never even occurred to me.

"Maybe they are," I said. "But I'll tell you, I've never seen Finkelman so rattled. Even Tree seemed pretty shaken up. He was doped up on something. He was swallowing these pills like they were Tic Tacs."

"Right in front of you," Lily said. "They must think they have you already. Did they talk about a title?"

I said, "Director of communications, Tree Corp."

Lily thought for a moment and said, "I like staff reporter, *Review-American*, better. You know, if you take it, you're gonna have to buy yourself some ties."

Lily knew my only ties were polyester freebies given to me and all the other male writers by the Royal and Ancient Golf Club of St. Andrews, the folks who run the British Open.

"I'm probably gonna take it," I said quietly.

Lily took her eyes off the road long enough to give me a disbelieving look.

I said, "The paper could go out of business any day. I'm one of the last dinosaurs on the beat. I have no other marketable skills. What am I gonna do if I get axed, become a blogger in my bathrobe?"

Lily heard me. She always heard me. "You are Josh freakin' Dutra," she said, borrowing Jennifer Aniston's line from *Marley & Me*, when Owen Wilson wonders if he has the stuff to make it as a columnist. Lily used that line every couple of weeks to build me up. "Don't forget it."

We got home. She pulled off my sticky Arrow Golf shirt. "Talk to Pete," she said. "But not now."

Pete Hough was all I'd ever wanted to be—a newspaperman. He had enjoyed long stints as both reporter and editor in news and business and sports, and he loved it all. I knew what would happen: I'd tell him about the job offer, and he'd talk me out of it and maybe even make me feel good about saying no.

It was a weekday morning, and the sports department was empty. Pete was at his desk, which was in shambles, as always. I told him the news. He asked, "What are they gonna pay you?"

"Double what I'm making now."

Pete stood up and extended a hand in my direction. "Nice knowing you, Mr. Dutra."

"What does that mean?"

"It means you're taking the fucking job, is what it means. Are you crazy? This is a life raft. A presidential pardon. You want to end up like me, serving out a life sentence with no hope of parole? Or a pension? You got a son. An ex-wife. A girlfriend. A mortgage. Tuition payments. Aging parents. Retirement. Don't be dumb."

My legs trembled. Pete opened his arms and engulfed me. I thought of Meg, eight months pregnant, when her water broke and she was a wreck. We went to St. Pete General, and a nurse—a massive black woman, a total stranger—swallowed my beautiful sobbing wife in her arms. A half day of hard labor later, Josh arrived.

"I'm gonna miss you, you little son of a bitch," Pete said. "Don't forget how to write."

I packed up twenty-four years of memories. A rectangular fake-wood plaque from my first Golf Writers Association award, which Pete used to carry pizza slices from the cafeteria to his desk. A signed glossy of Tree when he was a rookie, all legs and promise. One big box full of press passes I had hoarded for no good reason. Many shoe boxes crammed with saved notebooks, just in case. Four logoed duffel bags from different PGA Championships. A chunk of bone-dry sod, one of Tree's divots, that Big Herb had given me during my first visit to the sod farm in Brooksville. Twenty-four years at the paper. The only job I'd ever had. All I had to show for it: a few thousand stories in the morgue and a savings account running on empty.

In the parking lot, I put the key in the ignition. Two guys on the radio were talking about local high school basketball. *Little Land*

O'Lakes looks like a surprise contender. I say they make it to states. What say you, Jimbo? As a boy, all I'd ever wanted to do was make a living with a typewriter. At age forty-seven, I felt like my boyhood was over. I saw myself in the rearview mirror, leaned my head against the steering wheel, and sobbed.

7

Off Course was a floating mansion, 301 feet, stern to bow. Tree had bought the yacht for $61 million from a Russian oligarch looking for something bigger. The living space was walled off by bulletproof glass. The deck was outfitted with retractable shields that emitted blinding flashes of light to thwart the paparazzi, whether in helicopters or in boats. There were six decks, eight staterooms, three pools, a gym, a movie theater, a bowling alley, a ballroom, a putting green, and a helipad. It cost $8 million a year to maintain and operate, and that didn't include the $600,000 bill every time Tree's captain filled the fuel tank. Any time the PGA Tour was playing on either coast, Tree would stay on *Off Course* and commute to work via helicopter. It was an awesome display of conspicuous consumption, and Tree knew that it helped to reinforce every other player's feelings of inferiority, financial and otherwise.

I pulled into the marina parking lot, eager to see Tree and Finkelman again. I had spent several days at Tree Corp's law firm, hammering out the terms of my employment. It had taken most of a day just to complete the seven-page confidentiality agreement. Tree had three lawyers working on it. I had me.

At the launch, there was a series of security checkpoints and check-in tables. All the security people knew my name. I wondered how that was possible. *Off Course* was shoulder to shoulder with expensive suits and expensive-looking women. I was underdressed, still in my sportswriter costume. I wandered aimlessly around the yacht until I detected a different energy in the air, signaling that I was close to Tree and Belinda. I saw her before I saw him. She was wearing a skintight minidress with a plunging neckline, nicely displaying what a couple of the other Tour wives referred to as her "moneymakers." And there was Tree, holding her hand as he chatted with a conclave of CEOs.

When I went to shake Tree's hand, he gave me a warm bro hug and said, "Welcome to Team Tree, Joshie. You made the right call. This is going to be good for all of us. You and me, we'll finally be able to talk again. There's a lot of things I've wanted to tell you but couldn't. You were the enemy."

The enemy? I could see him saying *Eye of the World* was the enemy. Even I thought of the *Eye* as the enemy. (I had been checking its website addictively, paranoid about what it might post.) But Tree saw me as the enemy? That was disturbing.

"It wasn't anything personal, man," Tree said. "Our thing is, anyone who's not wearing the team uni is the enemy."

Then came a startling sight: Amanda in a white leather miniskirt, walking in our direction. Tree put a hand on the small of her back and guided her next to me.

"Amanda, this is Josh, the new PR guy I was telling you about. He knows what the *X* stands for, but he'll never give it up. Josh, Amanda is our designer."

"Yes, didn't we meet in Hawaii?" Amanda said.

"Oh, that's right," Tree said, not innocently. He grabbed Belinda's hand. "Time to—what's that word?—schmooze with our new friends." He whispered to me, "Motherfuckers give you a hundred million, turns out they want something in return."

Belinda turned to Amanda and said, "I don't care for that new chair in the bedroom salon. Maybe you can shoot me an e-mail with some other suggestions?" It wasn't icy, but it certainly wasn't warm. She pivoted on her spiky heels and was gone. She and Tree both were.

Amanda seemed annoyed. "I understand you've been trying to reach me," she said. Even with the drooping lip, her face was so captivating that I found it hard to focus. I was at a loss for words. "Let me give you a tour," she said. "You should know my work. I did the interior design of every room on this vessel." *Vessel*. She must have picked that up from Tree.

She led me into a library that looked like it belonged in a Brahmin town house in Back Bay, Boston. There was nobody in it. She closed the door.

"Here's what you need to know, *Josh*." My name came out with utter contempt. "I'm his fuck. His personal, private, on-demand fuck. I know you've been talking to Emmy. She's so doped up, she doesn't know what end is up. *Eye of the Asshole* doesn't have shit on us, and they won't. Belinda doesn't know anything, and she's not going to. There's something you should know about your new boss: I give him what he needs." She walked out, Belinda-style, all heels and hair and attitude.

At midnight, everybody was called into the boat's grand ballroom. Tree and Belinda stood in the center, each with a microphone in hand. The chairman of Rolex stood beside them.

"Okay, those of you who know me know that I like to let my clubs do the talking," Tree said. "But we're gathered here for a special purpose. And since we're five miles out to sea, if ever you want to see Florida again, I suggest you get out your checkbooks and credit cards. 'Cause this is a fund-raiser."

The lights went low. On every wall and on the ceiling, an elaborate slide show started to play, beautiful photographs of kids, many of them black and Hispanic, in classrooms, climbing rocks, hitting golf balls, playing at the beach, visiting the Oval Office, shaking hands with the president, shaking hands with Tree, with his perfect teeth and $5-million-a-year Crest smile. On every picture were the words PLANT A TREE. START A LIFE. A guitar-heavy sound track backed the whole thing.

"You like the music?" Belinda asked the crowd. A chorus of cheers went up. "It's the first new song Hootie and the Blowfish have done in years. Tree's favorite. It's our new personal—how do you say that?"

"Anthem," Tree said.

"Anthem!" repeated Belinda.

More cheering.

The show finished. The lights went up.

"Monsieur Andre LeGrande, chairman of Rolex, has something he'd like to say," Belinda said. She handed the towering Frenchman a microphone.

"Merci, Madame Tremont, Monsieur Tree," the Rolex man said. "We at Rolex are so delighted that you have joined our family and we yours. This is an extraordinary arrangement we have made, to be supporting your foundation with this new relationship, and we are honored to do so. The children you help educate, we hope they will grow up, make a lot of money, and buy Rolexes themselves! Seriously, you are doing a great thing for the children, and as a small token of our appreciation, we want you to have these."

LeGrande handed Belinda a Rolex Cosmograph Daytona covered in sapphires and rubies, an eighty-thousand-dollar watch. She showed it to the crowd. There were oohs and ahs. He handed a much smaller watch to Tree. Tree held it up and said, "It's a Timex! No, really, it is!"

I watched the guests laugh, and as they did, I noticed Amanda slip out of the ballroom through a swinging door by the galley.

"We also have this for you, Tree," the Frenchman said, handing Tree an oversize cardboard check. It was made out to the Plant a Tree Foundation in the amount of $100 million.

"I'm overwhelmed, Andy," Tree said. "I truly am. I promise I will work hard each and every day to make this a win-win for everybody.

On behalf of the kids and everybody at Plant a Tree, thank you, Andy, and thank you, Rolex. We're gonna do a lot of good with this."

"The night is young," Belinda said. "We want you to dance, have a good time, and leave us a big check!"

The music started up again, and I watched Tree slip out of the ballroom through Amanda's swinging door.

8

In January and February, I made four separate trips out west with Tree as he played in four different tournaments. It didn't go well. Tree was, for him, short and crooked off the tee. The CBS golf analyst Peter Kostis said on TV that it looked like Tree wasn't pushing off his right ankle. Tree had top-ten finishes in all four events but contended only once. Lousy, by his standards. Tree knew about the comment from Kostis, and he hated it. He didn't want any injuries, real or imagined, discussed in public. He said he wanted something done. He sounded like a TV mob boss.

"I mean, he spouts this bullshit, and he doesn't even talk to me first?" Tree said.

"I know," Finkelman said. "Total bullshit. Josh, talk to Kostis. Talk to him, talk to the writers. Tell 'em the truth—that if Tree didn't think he could win, he wouldn't be playing, and he wouldn't be playing if his ankle was any kind of serious problem."

There was nothing I could do about Kostis. If I tried to prevent him from talking about Tree's ankle, that would make him more eager to do it. I had a better chance with the writers. When I first showed up on Tour as Tree's new PR guy, most of my friends on the beat gave me the stink-eye. I was sure they resented me for the move I had made. I was the side man to Dr. No, the man who had been cruelly holding them down! I tried to be an actual ally to the regular beat writers. I couldn't deliver any meaningful time with Tree, but I did get him to respond by e-mail to questions for their Masters preview pieces. I gave them some details about *Flying Tree* and *Off Course,* two off-limits inner sanctums. I offered details about Tree's practice sessions and the specs on his clubs—not much, but more than they were accustomed to getting. When I couldn't answer a question, I said so, and when I could, I did. I FedExed the writers his-and-her invitations to the grand opening of Tree's first golf-course-design project, a reworked public track in Miami Beach to be rechristened Tree Links on the Beach. I avoided at all costs using the word *branding,* at least with a straight face.

During those four West Coast tournaments, I had thirty-eight meals with Tree (I kept track). Breakfast very early in the morning. Dinner very late at night. I talked to him about letting fans into his life more. I made the case that they paid his salary, stopped his golf balls from going into ponds and bushes, and could be there for him in times of need. He allowed me to take a picture of him grinning over his twenty-four-ounce T-bone steak at Donovan's Steakhouse in San Diego and put it on his Twitter page. Within days there were over seven hundred thousand views. I'd slip innocent personal things into his blogs and tweets, like movies he had seen and what he thought about them. Finkelman, always undermining me, called them "leaks," but Tree enjoyed the reader feedback. One reader tweeted to Tree, "I can't believe you can't get tickets for the Lakers! If you don't mind sitting with my mother-in-law, you're welcome to go with us in the nosebleeds." Tree wrote back, "Count me in!" In a column, the media critic at *USA Today* noticed "the new Tree, who seems almost human."

He seemed to get by on no sleep. He had marathon sessions on the practice range and in the gym. He went for long runs. He spent hours on the phone doing business for profit and for his charity. He spent nearly as much time talking to Belinda about home stuff. He'd Skype with the kids and play video games and study tape of his swing and then rehearse it in front of hotel-room mirrors. Sometimes I'd ride a bike alongside him while he ran eight or ten miles at a seven-minute-mile pace. No other golfer was doing anything like Tree's running or lifting or practicing with such intensity. I couldn't see how a person could cram so much into every day, not without pharmacological help.

His nights were busy, too. Amanda would be there, and then she'd be gone. (Emerson was nowhere in sight.) A sultry blonde, an aspiring rapper, was hanging around for a couple of evenings early in one of the tournaments. She went by the name Lady B. Tree called her Plan B. In other weeks, there were other girls. Tree's late-night friends were always gone when Belinda and the kids flew in for three of the four West Coast weekends, but their existence was an open secret among the very few true insiders: Finkelman. Big Herb. Norman Henley, Tree's swing coach. Mac, Tree's caddie. And maybe me.

Mac and Big Herb and Norm all had nicknames for Tree—nicknames for a nickname. Herb called Tree Bo. Norm called him Pardsy. Mac called him C. They were rugged men from another generation. They reminded me of my father's older friends, men who had fought in Europe or served in Korea, men for whom Ted Williams and Sophia Loren captured their ideals of manliness (The Splinter) and sexuality (Miss Loren). One of the charming things about Tree was that he could talk about icons of the 1950s and '60s as if he had lived through those years. He'd seen all the great World War II movies: *The Caine Mutiny, The Dirty Dozen, Patton*. He knew the real-life battles and heroes.

Mac had been a prisoner of war in Vietnam. None of the writers could get him to talk. That didn't stop them from portraying golfer and caddie as being exceptionally close.

At dinner, Tree and I never talked about Amanda or Emerson or any of his late-night visitors. But we talked about everything else.

We talked about his parents, other players, Tour officials, press people, Belinda, the twins, Finkelman and Norm Henley and Mac.

"You know what Mac calls me, don't you?" Tree said one night.

I told him I did: C.

We were in a Cheesecake Factory, facing the kitchen door, as he preferred. Nobody bothered him there.

"That's right," Tree said. "Do you know where it comes from?"

I didn't. Tree could see I was almost tingly with anticipation.

"Chosen One," Tree said. "My first Masters win. I'm on eighteen. Sunday, last group. Trailing by a shot." He buttered his bread and took a long, slow bite. He was dragging it out and enjoying it.

Anybody with an interest in golf knew what had happened at Tree's first Masters, Sunday on eighteen. Tree hit a shot from the fairway bunker at the final hole to a foot. His birdie there got Tree in a playoff with Will Martinsen, which he won.

"I was standing near Palmer and Nicklaus when you hit that shot into eighteen," I said as Tree chewed. "Arnie says to Jack, 'This kid can golf his ball.' "

Tree loved hearing inside chitchat, what Arnie said to Jack, things like that. He said, "That's cool. Okay, so right before I step into the bunker, Mac goes, 'Hole this shot, motherfucker. You're the goddamn chosen one.' Ever since, whenever I'm up against it, Mac's like, 'Jar it, motherfucker. You're the chosen one.' "

"And in public, you're C."

Tree nodded appreciatively. Then he said, "That'll sell us some books, will it not?"

Motherfucker. Will it not. From minute to minute, you never knew which Tree you were going to get.

Lily would never get this, but Pete would: Hanging out with Tree Tremont was as intoxicating as anything I'd ever done. I'd spent a decade writing about him. Now I was getting to know him.

The fourth of the West Coast tournaments was the Match Play Championship. In match play, a golfer competes against just the person he is playing with, not the entire field, and each hole is a separate contest. Tree made it to the final match, where he faced Luke Donald, a precise, tidy Englishman.

Match play is a head game, and Tree played it well. At the driving range, he greeted Donald warmly and needled him about Manchester United's recent struggles. (Tree followed Premier League soccer. He followed anything that had winners and losers.) A half hour later, Donald bounded up to the first tee with a big smile and said to Tree, "Let's have a great time out there. Play well." He didn't realize small-talk time was over. Tree didn't make eye contact with him, he said only "Arrow One," identifying his ball. Donald slinked away, rattled. He hit a giant push off the first tee into the desert. His ball came to rest at the base of a cactus bush that poked tiny bloody holes in the pale white skin of his arms.

On the greens, Tree had an elaborate program in intimidation. Reading his longer putts, he was often annoyingly slow, practically forcing Donald to watch as he prowled around in all his athletic superiority, seeing breaks in the ground that only he could see. Every time he had a chance to hole out and finish ahead of Donald, he did so. Eight times, according to my notes, I heard Tree say to him, "Mind if I finish?" Technically, he had to ask, though there wasn't much of a question mark. Tree would knock in the short putt, and a mob of spectators would bolt to the next tee. Poor Donald repeatedly had to block out the noise and excessive movement while facing his own crucial short putts, one of which he missed. In the end, it didn't matter. Tree, off his game, could not match the Englishman's straight driving and methodical ball-striking and beautiful putting. He lost two down on the seventeenth green. It was never even that close, really.

Tree's take for the week was $850,000. Donald made $1.4 million. Tree hated to lose, and he hated giving away $550,000 every bit as much.

"Little English twit was driving it a hundred yards past me," Tree said an hour after it was all over. Tree, Finkelman, and I were on

Flying Tree, going to Fargo, where Arrow Golf had its headquarters. "How does *that* shit happen?"

In truth, Donald was driving it ten or fifteen yards past Tree. Usually, Tree was twenty-five to thirty-five yards ahead of Donald.

Tree had an ice pack on his ankle. "How's it feeling?" Finkelman asked him.

"Fine."

Tree lived to be in the thick of competition, like he had been on that Sunday. Losing on Sundays was something he knew little about. The Luke Donalds of the world, all the guys Tree called "nice little players," were supposed to fold in the face of his greatness. They nearly always did.

Abruptly, Tree ripped the ice pack off his ankle and flung it against the airplane wall. "Fuck!"

The ice exploded all over the inside of the cabin. Tree didn't even acknowledge it. He just reached into his Brooks Brothers workout pants and retrieved his plastic Ziploc bag of pills.

Turner Darlington, the founder of Arrow Golf, greeted us in his office. In the 1970s, he had been a counterculture pioneer in cross-country skiing. He still had the ZZ Top beard. The Reagan era had turned him into an entrepreneur. The Clinton years had turned him into a corporate maverick. His office was loaded with stacks of *MAD* magazine, *National Geographic*, and *Runner's World*. His office smelled of weed. Medicinal, he claimed. He was dressed in the sleekest high-performance materials a branch of his company made. He still had the body for it, all sinewy muscle. He was a billionaire.

"You're coming out with me tonight, right?" Darlington asked Tree.

"You know it, dude."

"But work first. We've got a great day planned for you."

Darlington led us into an enormous theater. He and Tree sat on stools in the center of a stage, behind a curtain. A throaty woman's voice came over the PA system. "Ladies and gentlemen of Arrow Golf, presenting two legends of our time, Mr. Tree Tremont and Mr. Turner Darlington!"

The curtain went up, and there was pandemonium. People stood and shrieked and held signs. These were happy employees. *Fortune* had called Arrow the single best company in America to work for. Secretaries made ninety grand a year. Top shoe designers made five times that. Seven out of every ten golf clubs sold across the world were made by Arrow. The stock price was $1,023 per share, and the guy on *Mad Money* was still pushing it. A parade of young female models crossed the stage, wearing clothes that were far too seductive for golf, although that was how they were being billed.

"Folks, we're having a thirteenth day of Christmas here at Arrow," Darlington told the crowd. "After much serious negotiation with the incomparable Andrew Finkelman—shout-out to Finky!—and some special enticements sent to our man of the hour, Tree has made a big decision. Starting at this year's Masters, not only will Tree have fourteen Arrow Golf clubs in his bag, he'll be dressed head to toe in Arrow Golf apparel. We're calling this fashion-forward line of clothes Tree Trunk. Ladies and gentlemen, the inspiration for the collection and so much more: Tree Tremont!"

Tree stood and waved. The parading models were taking off their golf duds, revealing a layer of après-golf lounging and (in theory) exercise clothing. Togs were being thrown into the crowd. The models then took off the workout layer to reveal the skimpiest swimsuits I'd ever seen. High heels dropped from the ceiling, and the models scurried to put them on. A dozen other women came out and oiled them up. It was like a Vegas show. I learned later that it actually was a Vegas show.

"Hook me up with that one," Tree said to Darlington, nodding in the direction of a girl in her early twenties in a tangerine bikini. He was shouting over the music. I was fifteen feet away and could hear him. "And that one," he said, nodding to a young double-D brunette with a colt's legs.

"Tits on a stick," Darlington said. "How 'bout a third?"

Tree pointed to a girl with green eyes and blond hair and muscular thighs.

"Good choice," Darlington said. "*Exceedingly* limber."

An assistant director handed Darlington a microphone. He said, "Everybody is welcome at the indoor range, where Tree is going to put on an exhibition of an athletic talent the likes of which the world has never seen! What this man can do with a wedge!"

I imagined Darlington narrating that night's bedroom action.

9

I had to talk to somebody. Lily was out of the question. It was painful for me to admit that, but it was true. If she knew the scale of Tree's sexcapades and my silence about them, she'd make me quit. I certainly couldn't talk to Pete or any of the beat writers; it was the kind of story that could make a career. On various unreliable blogs, there were hints that the *Eye* was looking to break a "major" story about a "leading sports celebrity." In the modern-media echo chamber, I saw those phrases again and again, and each time I came across them, my skin would go clammy. But the days would pass, and there would be . . . nothing. I sometimes tried to bring up the prospect of an *Eye* story with Finkelman, but he gave me his classic talk-to-the-hand response. He didn't want to hear anything about it, and the implication was that it was my job to make sure nothing got into print. Really, there was only one guy I could go to: Big Herb. When I returned from the West Coast swing, we met at the Great American Diner.

Herb sipped his black coffee, and I got right to the point. "I'm sure you know Tree's got girls everywhere," I said. "He can't keep them all quiet forever. If just one of them ever talks, it's going to be awful. For his marriage. For his relationship with his kids. For his deals with sponsors. For everything. It's gonna kill him."

Herb looked like he was more worried about me than he was about Tree. "Josh, Josh, Josh. These girls he sees, you think they want to keep seeing Tree? They do. If they talk, the whole party comes to an end. They know that. Some of 'em, you know, get paid. Expensive gifts. Nice hotels. They're pros. I'm not saying hookers. But pros. It's just sex, Josh. It's not love."

"I don't think *Eye of the World* is going to care whether it's love or not," I said.

"Don't worry about the *Eye*, Josh. If it gets to where they're looking to do something, don't you think we can convince them not to?" Herb slid the tips of his thumb and index fingers together, rapid-fire. It looked like he was starting a fire. "Believe me, we've been there."

I suddenly felt like a child. Like I had no idea how the world worked.

"The president of the United States has Tree on speed dial," Herb said. "Tree was on that *Time* list of the hundred most important philanthropists in the country. There are a hundred thousand kids in Tree's schools. You want to be the editor of the rag that brings that to a screaming halt? Believe me, that editor has a boss, and we know him. And if we don't, we can get to know him."

The food arrived. Herb had ordered a massive burger with bacon and American cheese, a side order of mashed potatoes, a thirty-two-ounce sweet tea. How he remained so skinny was a wonder of the world.

"What about Belinda?" I asked.

"Be-lin-da," Herb said, enjoying each syllable. "Don't you think she's got it good? C'mon, Josh. I spent three years in Vietnam. Do you think I remember all the hookers? Not a one. You think I remember the names of the men I held in my arms with their legs blown off? Every last man. You think I felt any guilt with Tree's mother? Hell no. I sent her my paycheck. I carried her picture in my boot. But I was fighting a war for this country. I got by on adrenaline and uppers. I needed an outlet, you know? That's all it was. Stress. Boredom. Like a doper getting a quick fix. A release. And let me tell you, it wasn't any different for Mickey Mantle. Or JFK. Or Martin Luther King. Or Keith what's-his-name. And it ain't no different for Tree."

He loaded a cheap diner fork with fluffy diner potatoes. He ate. I sat there.

"Tree's in a war," Herb said. "You think this Frenchman from Rolex wants to hand over that hundred million to some black kid? Hell no. You think all those country-club kids on Tour would give up their left one to have half the drive and talent Tree's got? They'd say yes, but you know what? They'd never have enough heart to bring knife to skin. Tree's leaving his blood and guts all over those pretty greens, taking their money, and going home. Ain't that a shame."

The aggressiveness of his words and tone didn't match up. His words had so much anger in them, but he sounded like James Earl Jones in *Field of Dreams* when he does his baseball-has-marked-time speech.

Lily would have called bullshit on every last thing Herb had said, from *Vietnam* to *ain't that a shame*. I was mesmerized. I believed him. Metallica's "Mama Said" started playing on the jukebox. I thought of Mrs. Tremont and her pink lemonade. Herb and I were at the last diner in St. Pete with a jukebox on every table.

I asked, "Don't you worry that Tree's road life is going to show up in his home life?"

"Josh, you watch too much TV. Is there anything in human nature that makes you think that monogamy is a realistic goal? Or that it should be?" Herb now sounded not like the career army man but like Professor Tremont, the one who had done grad work in political science. "Do you know what Belinda is like behind closed doors? I don't. Do you know how she spends those hundred twenty nights a year when she's not with Tree? I don't." He paused, sipped from his tea, and continued. "You've been married, Josh, right?" I nodded. "You stood in the front of a church in front of all those nice people and said you'd be faithful for the rest of your life. How'd that go for you?"

I thought of our wedding day. Meg was so young. "It didn't," I said.

"Yeah, I thought I heard something about that. That high school swim coach, right?"

It was scary to think how much Team Tree knew about me. I wondered if Finkelman had detectives on the payroll. Probably. Maybe that was how the security guys knew me when I boarded *Off Course* for the first time.

"We lost a baby after Josh," I said. "Meg and I had a really rough time. I went elsewhere."

"I'm sorry," Herb said.

"Me, too. I fucked up."

"Really?" he said. "Is that what you think? I think you had a tragedy. Your wife lost interest in sex. What were you supposed to do, be celibate for the rest of your life? Let me ask you something. Is Meg all right? Is your son? They're living their lives, and you are, too. You got a good thing with that hippie girl. Lily, right? You got a good job. Hasn't it worked out all right?"

He gave me the time to consider his questions. I did have a good thing with that hippie girl. I wondered if I was blowing it with my new job.

"Tree, you know, is not just my son. He's my best friend. We can talk about anything. But do I presume to understand everything that goes on his life? I do not. The great reverend doctor, M. L. King himself, fucked around an awful lot, Josh. Loved those four kids. Loved Coretta. But he loved pussy, too. And what'd he do? Won a Nobel Peace Prize. Changed the world. Tree can, too. He's not even thirty. Think of what he can do. With his wealth? His popularity? His skin color? He's the goddamn chosen one. Makes me pinch myself."

10

The books were the first clue that the carefully cultivated artificial reality of Masters week extended well beyond the gates of Augusta National Golf Club. A few steps into the vast living room of my rental house were floor-to-ceiling bookshelves with row after row of classic titles, their shiny bindings embossed with gold lettering. I went to a Steinbeck novel, and three other volumes came down with it. They were not actual books but hollow shells that had been glued together, mere filler in a giant house devoid of life.

Augusta has many motels but few hotels. By long-standing tradition, home owners rent out their houses to fans, players, and reporters. Tree Corp and Arrow Golf rented a half-dozen homes in the newish West Lake development, where the streets were named for famous golf courses. Tree insisted on staying on Pebble Beach Lane, because Pebble was his favorite course in the world. (He was partial to public courses, even those with five-hundred-dollar green fees.) He had the house to himself for most of the week; Belinda and the kids weren't due to arrive until Saturday night. Finkelman and I were in the pile of bricks next door. To avoid the indignity of fake books and Thomas Kinkade prints, Tree rented his house for an extra week prior to the Masters, allowing Amanda and an army of movers to redo the interior to his exact specifications. At the end of the tournament, all the furniture would be donated to local charities, a tax write-off for Tree that also made for a nice annual feature in *The Augusta Chronicle.*

In the simpler times of Tree's early trips to the Masters, I had been invited to his rental house for dinner, which had allowed me to chat with Big Herb and to watch Tree play video games. In more recent years, I hadn't made it across the moat. Now I literally had a key to Tree's castle. I walked across the big lawn, over its dormant Bermuda grass, to Tree's. I rang the bell and rapped on the knocker. No answer. I let myself in. It was early afternoon on the day before the start of the tournament, and everyone else was at Augusta National.

I was writing a piece for Tree's website, in Tree's voice, about the new Tree Trunk apparel he was unveiling at the Masters. It never failed to amuse me how people obsessed over Tree's clothes. Once, when he turned up with the lead on a Sunday in a charcoal-gray polo—not his usual Sunday black polo with the red armbands—it was news in China. An entire bedroom in Tree's house had been turned into a staging ground for his outfits. For my story, I needed to examine the clothes. Finkelman had said to get the story to him by noon for approval, and I was already running late.

Walking through Tree's rental house, I was amused to discover that the sleek, modern furniture, in shades of red and black, recalled the decor at Gents. He had ordered big TVs and well-stocked bars. I was examining the large photographs of Tree winning major championships adorning every wall when I heard noises from another wing of the vast house. I thought at first it was a TV, but then I realized that the voice sounded something like Tree's. I tiptoed down a long hallway on the mushy carpet, toward the source. The door to the master bedroom was not quite closed. Against my better instincts, I peeked in.

Tree was on his knees on the bed, wearing his green Augusta National sport coat and nothing else. Facedown in front of him was a slender brunette. He was yanking on a handful of her hair while spanking her bottom so hard there were welts on her skin. When Tree spoke to her, it was in a growl. "Bite the pillow, bitch, I'm taking the dirt road home."

I turned and ran. I would have bolted out of the house altogether but for that goddamn apparel story I had to write. I found the Tree Trunk room, with each day's outfits all laid out. The piles of clothes—short- and long-sleeved polos, coordinated sweaters, vests, raingear, socks, and shoes—mocked me. I scribbled notes for a few minutes and was almost done when Tree appeared in the doorway. The green jacket was nowhere to be seen. He was wearing shorts and nothing else. A few steps behind him was the brunette. She couldn't have been over twenty-one. She was smoothing her hair.

"Hey, Josh, I didn't know you were here," Tree said. He was unnervingly relaxed.

"Just working on that Tree Trunk story. You know, the new duds."

"Right. If you have any questions, ask Cindy here. She works for Arrow. She's been helping me with my fittings."

He grinned in code. I nodded without looking at her.

"No Par-3 Tournament for you this afternoon?" I asked Tree. The Par-3 Tournament was a Wednesday warm-up act before the actual event.

"Nah. Big distraction, that whole thing. Besides, those greens Stimp a half-yard slower than the greens on the big course, and I'm stroking it so good." The doorbell rang. "Josh, will you walk Cindy out? That's my one-thirty massage. Tell her how to get to my room. I'm gonna grab a quick shower."

Cindy and I walked through the house in silence. At the front door was a bottle blonde in jeans and a tank top. She did not have a fold-up massage bed with her, or any other tools of the trade.

"Come on in," I said to her. "Tree's expecting you."

• • •

During the first round, Amanda hiked up and down Augusta's hills with Mr. Tremont and me, all of us engulfed in Tree's enormous gallery. People were checking her out. They couldn't help themselves. I even saw the wife of an Augusta National member spying through little opera glasses. Amanda didn't exactly blend, with her knee-high black boots and eight inches of exposed thigh before you got to the hem of her slinky skirt.

I wasn't worried about her presence. Between Mr. Tremont's lecture at the Great American Diner and the casualness of the bimbo parade in Tree's suburban Augusta palace, I was starting to become more relaxed about the whole thing. I distinguished between Tree's sex life and home life and his home life and public life. I focused on my job, trying to manage Tree's media life. Nobody was talking about his ankle. Everybody was talking about his new deal with Arrow, his public course in Miami Beach, his chance to become the first player ever to threepeat, as the writers called it.

Tree was playing that first round with Luke Donald and Hyung Young, the twenty-year-old Asian amateur champion, a Texan with Korean parents and a wildly unorthodox swing. Tree's ankle was far more than a nuisance, but with his meds, he could block out the pain and make good swings. At the Masters, he was driving it thirty yards past the little Englishman. Hyung Young, though, was driving it thirty yards past Tree.

"Nice to be young," Tree said to the writers after the round. They were gathered around the old oak beside the clubhouse entrance. "If I may use that homonym." He looked to find his mother in the crowd. She would never miss Masters week. There was no place lovelier to be in mid-April than the Masters, a coming-out party for spring in a little oasis in the heart of working-class Georgia. "Am I saying that word right, Mom? *Hom*-onym. Not *hon*-omym."

"You're saying it *correctly,* Herbert," Mrs. Tremont said.

They had a comedy routine. Once, appearing together on David Letterman's show, Tree used *ain't,* and Mrs. Tremont said, "Don't make me whack you with my thesaurus again." Letterman giggled and invited them back.

"Well, at least I played good today," Tree said under the shade of the oak. Mrs. Tremont shook her knuckley left fist at him. She was wearing shoes with Velcro straps. I had never seen her in shoes like that. I took it for arthritis.

Tree had shot 70, a good score given his afternoon tee time, with the wind up and the greens crispy. It was by two shots the best of the afternoon scores. But the players in the morning, catching a dead-calm course, had killed it. Three guys had shot 67 and were leading.

On Friday morning, when Tree headed out for his second round, it was humid, overcast, and still—perfect scoring weather. Tree shot 29 on the front nine, a record. He didn't come close to missing a shot and played the two par-5s in a total of six shots. No player had ever shot lower than 63 in any major championship, and now Tree was in position to do it. By the ninth green, virtually everybody at Augusta National was watching Tree, to the degree that you could see him at all.

On his way to the tenth tee, Tree stopped and put on his new Arrow rain gear. His whole body was unusually sensitive. He could feel wind on his cheeks in ways others could not, and a minor scar on his right forearm told him about incoming weather systems with uncanny accuracy. Within minutes of his wardrobe change, the wind kicked up, the air cooled down, and a heavy, cold rain started to fall. Big Herb and I decided to watch the back nine on TV. Tree's mother and her friend Barbara Nicklaus were eating at a nearby table.

Suddenly, Tree's swing was out of sequence. His hips were unwinding faster than his shoulders—a tendency he had been fighting forever—which led to some wild shots. He made a bogey on ten (drove it into the left rough), eleven (three putts from eighty feet), and twelve (tee shot spun off the green and into the water). He wasn't going to shoot 62. It was starting to look like he'd struggle to break 70.

Then came thirteen, a short par-5, shaped like a left-turning banana. A narrow creek runs down the left side of the fairway before making a right-hand turn and running in front of the green. On the right side of the fairway is a grove of perfectly placed pine trees. It's a gorgeous hole where things can go very right or very wrong. With a strong, swirly wind in their faces, the players—even the longest of them—knew they had no chance to reach the green in two shots, as they typically do. Hyung Young had the honor and hit an eighteen-degree hybrid off the tee. He smashed it into the wind, and it went maybe two hundred yards dead straight. A smart shot. Luke Donald did the same thing with a 3-wood. His went maybe one ninety.

Tree played last. He teed up his ball low and on the extreme left side of the teeing area, so the freshly cut pine bough that served as a tee marker was between his ball and feet. He had a driver in hand. Nick Faldo, the CBS golf broadcaster and three-time winner at Augusta, said in his working-class English accent, "I don't understand this club choice at all." Tree went under Mac's giant umbrella and dried his grip for a second time with a towel. He then hit a low, hooking drive that flew past Young's ball and skipped along the fairway for another forty yards. "Well, he got away with it," Faldo said.

"The thing with Sir Nick," Big Herb said, "is that he couldn't play like Tree, so he can't think like Tree."

At the table next to us, Helene said to Barbara Nicklaus, "I wish that Nick Faldo would put a sock in it."

Tree sized up his second shot. The wind was even stronger. "What do we got?" Tree asked Mac. You could hear him on the broadcast.

Faldo said, "He got away with the driver, but to what end? He's got to lay up here anyhow."

"Two-thirty-two to carry, plus twenty-eight, two-sixty total, five off the left," the caddie said. Tree had 232 yards to carry the creek that guarded the green. The flagstick was another twenty-eight yards from there and five yards from the green's left border. Tree handed his water bottle to Mac and took the head cover off his driver.

"Driver off the deck?" Faldo said. "On these fairways? They're like a pool table!"

"Kind of makes you wonder what Tree's got in that water bottle, doesn't it?" said David Feherty, a CBS reporter. "But if there are two men in the world I wouldn't bet against, it's this guy and his friend Bill Gates."

Tree closed his stance, hooded the driver's face, took it back inside, and hit the single most amazing shot I've ever seen. The ball landed on the front right of the green and started heading for the hole. It climbed one hill and went down another and had slowed to almost a dead halt when it kissed the fiberglass flagstick and fell in for a double eagle, three under par on a hole. The old clubhouse, steamy with people, roared. I thought the nearby portrait of Dwight Eisenhower might fall off the wall. Tree had undone the damage of ten, eleven, and twelve. He was seven under par for the round and finished with a 64. By Friday night, at the end of play, Tree had the lead and the attention of the sporting world.

When he came in from his Friday round, the first thing Tree said to me was "What'd Sir Nick say about that one?" Tree played his best golf when he was feeling defiant. Augusta National brought out that mood in him more than anyplace else.

"Belinda's coming—stall her!"

It was a few hours after the 64, and Tree was screaming at me via cell phone. He was in his house on Pebble Beach Lane in the West Lake development, doing God knows what with God knows whom. I was next door at a small client party Finkelman was hosting. Belinda had changed her plans, as she often did, without warning. Tree's double eagle had generated much excitement, and Belinda had decided she wanted to be part of the action. She hadn't bothered to tell Tree until she was in a limo headed to the house from Daniel Field, the Augusta airstrip for small private planes.

I ran to Tree's house. The first person I saw was Emerson, in the kitchen, trying to zip up an overstuffed shoulder bag, laughing at her ineptitude. She had been way overserved. "Josh, help me with this," she said, as if I saw her every day. I hadn't seen her since our meeting at the Great American Diner. She handed me the bag. I zipped it up.

Amanda—her hair wet, combed, and conditioned, wearing jeans and a T-shirt and no bra—was at the top of the steps. It was almost overwhelming, to be in the same house as Amanda and Emerson, two women who could destroy Tree and Tree Corp.

"Poor little Tree," she said, twisting his nipples with her fingers. "Afraid to take away wifey's keys to the jet."

"Very fucking funny," Tree said.

Emerson and Amanda made it out the kitchen door and into the back of a waiting Lincoln Navigator. I couldn't see who was driving. On a small TV in the kitchen, ESPN was showing a replay of Tree's shot on thirteen. The doorbell rang. Things were going fast. The kitchen smelled like popcorn fresh out of the microwave.

"Hey, babe," I heard Tree say. Husband and wife kissed. I was in another room, thirty or so feet away. "Where are the kids?"

"They'll come up on Saturday after their football," Belinda said. "After all your hard work today, I thought Mr. Tree might need a little attention." She stripped Tree's belt from his jeans and dropped it on the floor.

"Hey, Joshie, you still here?" Tree called out.

"Josh is here?" Belinda asked.

I approached them and said, "Hi, Belinda." I gave her a peck on the cheek. She held out the other one to complete the European double.

"Your breathing is so heavy," Belinda said to me.

"Hot water's out in the Finkelman-Dutra estate next door," Tree said. I was amazed at how quickly and well he could lie on the spot.

"We must take care of our Josh," Belinda said.

My phone rang. "Josh, listen to me very carefully." It was Amanda. "Can she hear me?"

"No," I said. "The tee times are not out yet."

"Good. Can she see you?" Amanda asked.

"Yes, he's wearing the blue on blue on Saturday," I said.

"Then you must be very, very discreet," Amanda said. Her voice was low and urgent, like that of Mrs. Robinson in *The Graduate*. "Go to the bar in the living room. There is an open bottle of Cristal there and three glasses. Remove them. There is a DVD in the movie player. Remove it immediately. There's a flannel sheet on the floor by the sofa. Let me be blunt here, Josh. It's soiled. Get rid of it."

I hung up and headed over to the living room. I didn't have time to think of the indignity of it all; I was just trying to do a job. I took the Cristal bottle and shoved it in a giant ice chest. I ran the three fluted glasses straight into the kitchen dishwasher. Belinda, trusting by nature, could see me scurrying around but couldn't know exactly what I was doing and didn't seem to particularly care.

"You are a good house guest," Belinda said. "You must know Tree is—how do you call that?—a neat freak."

I darted back to the living room and pushed one button after another, trying to find the tiny eject button on the DVD player. Where were my goddamn reading glasses? Belinda followed me in. I got the DVD out and shoved it in my back pocket. Belinda was making her way over to the flannel sheet.

She started to kick the sheet with her open-toed sandal into a corner of the room. I fell to my knees in front of her and scooped it into a ball and held it against my chest. "My bad," I said. I looked at my shirt. There was now a gooey stain on it.

The DVD, precariously lodged in my back pocket, fell out, faceup on the carpeted floor. On the disk was an image of two semi-dressed women pointing dildos at each other as if they were .38 Specials. I saw Belinda get a good look at the title: *Pulp Friction*. I snatched it up and put it under the sheet. My face was hot and red.

"Do not be embarrassed, Joshie," Belinda said. "In Italy, we are much more open about these things. You have been away from your Lily for a long time. You can get—how does Tree say this?—all backed up."

Tree came in, waving his cell phone. "I got the pizza guy. You want the usual, Bel? Pepperoni, mushroom, red peppers not green, little onion in the middle, super well done?" His coolness was astonishing with all that was going on. He was the same way on the golf course in the heat of it. "JD, you staying?"

Belinda looked at me and said, "Joshie stays. He's part of the family now." I buried my cringe.

Belinda excused herself to unpack, and Tree went with her. I did a sweep of the entire house. Finkelman called. "Did they get out?" He was hopelessly behind.

I was at the kitchen sink cleaning my shirt when Tree wandered in. "Nice work, Joshie."

I raised a palm at him and said, "Don't even start." For once I had the upper hand.

"Hey, I'm trying to pay you a compliment," Tree said. "Don't go being a little bitch about it." He couldn't let me have my moment, not even under those conditions.

The doorbell rang.

"Pizza guy," Tree said. "It's twenty-nine dollars. Can you expense it?"

"My wallet's at the house. I kinda had to run out."

Tree frowned and removed from his pocket a stack of bills, folded in half and held together by a rubber band. He handed me a ten and a twenty. "You do it. I don't want to have to sign for him." Arnold Palmer and Will Martinsen loved signing autographs. Jack Nicklaus didn't but accepted that it came with the territory. Tree actively hated it, and he resented how some people tried to make money off his signature.

"What about the tip?" I asked.

"Included," he said. His cheapness knew no bounds.

On a table by the door was the hat Tree had worn during his second round. Big Herb was old-school about never wearing lids indoors, and Tree was the same way. I handed the pizza guy thirty bucks. And then the hat.

"Tree Tremont wore this today during his sixty-four," I said. "It's got his name embroidered on the back. Sell it on eBay. Don't take less than a grand." Tree would never miss that hat. Arrow gave him hats by the dozen.

The kid was still examining the hat like a winning lottery ticket when I closed the door.

Belinda, Tree, and I sat down at a table in the kitchen. She had a postcoital glow and was as beautiful as a woman could be. It was hard to imagine how she could not meet any man's needs. She said to Tree, "Tell me all about your big shot! The pilots couldn't stop talking about it."

Tree leaned back in his chair, took a long sip of beer, and made sure we were both focused on him. "You ever have that thing where you're *almost* in a car accident?" he said. "You swerve away at the last second, and your body gets flooded with adrenaline, right? That's how I felt walking up thirteen. I'm looking at a shot that'll make or break my Masters. All my senses are going crazy. I can feel the grass under my feet. I can smell the magnolias. I can hear Rae's Creek. I can hear the rain falling on the umbrella. I'm taking my practice swings, and my heart's pounding so hard, I can see my chest heaving. Then I stand over the ball. Everything stops. Four seconds feels like an hour. My breathing's slow. I'm calm. I'm relaxed. I've already played the shot in my head. I already know the outcome.

"I'm not aiming at the pin; I'm looking at a branch on a pine tree twenty yards right of it, behind the green. That's my line. I look down. There's no ball there. All I see is the one dimple I want to strike. The swing is so tight, so strong. When I look up, the ball is exactly where I expect it to be. It's dead-on. Not just the right branch, the right goddamn *pinecone*. After that, I don't even watch it fly. When it went in, I wasn't surprised. That's how perfect it was. I'm sure the crowd went crazy, but I couldn't hear them. Mac said, 'Motherfucking Chosen One.' And I slapped his hand five so hard, my palm went pink. When I picked the ball out of the hole, it was actually warm."

The slice of pizza in my hand was stiff and cold. I had never heard Tree talk like that, about what golf felt like for him. He never talked about his feelings at all. He told jokes, and sometimes he told stories, but he didn't talk about his feelings. This was all new. It was gold.

I had to ask, "Can I use this for the website?"

"No. No way." He said it with a smile. "But it'll sell us some books, won't it? Joshie, you're my Keeler."

O. B. Keeler. The writer who chronicled the life and times of Bobby Jones, the great Ruth-era amateur golfer who had cofounded Augusta National. In the whole field, there could not have been another player who had even *heard* of O. B. Keeler. Not one. Just Tree.

• • •

The Saturday round was played on a brisk spring day. Belinda followed Tree on the course. Tree shot a third-round 71, and by nightfall he held a two-shot lead over his one true rival, Will Martinsen, who had the low round of the day, a 68. For the final round, Tree and Will would play together in the last group. A dream pairing for Masters Sunday. Tree had never wanted a win more. He had said in Hawaii at the start of the year that his intention was to win the four majors in one calendar year. To do so, he had to win the first one, and he'd have to do it over the one man who had his number.

Everyone knew Tree and Will had a complicated relationship. When we were on the West Coast during one of our late-night dinners, Tree gave me his take on how it had gone bad. "It all goes back to that U.S. Open at Shinnecock," he told me. "You know how at Shinny, there's nowhere to eat?"

Shinnecock Hills Golf Club is on the East End of Long Island, a land of plenty, with restaurants galore. But if you're Tree Tremont and you despise crowds and slow service, and you have a fear of getting stuck talking to people you don't want to talk to, there's nowhere to eat.

"So I hire this big-name chef for the week. The guy wants ten grand. I tell him I'll pay him two but mention him in my interviews. He says fine. I show up Monday. No chef. Turns out Martinsen has hired the dude away from me. For twelve K. Then Thursday morning, on the range, he says to me, 'Tree, you and Belinda need to come over for dinner on Saturday night. Missy and I got the best chef. I heard you guys have been eating out. Are you getting killed? That's brave. We figured, spend the money, eat great at home.' You know, he's riding me for being cheap with the chef. Where'd this guy get the balls to hire my chef away from me and then dis me on top of it?"

"Did you go to his house?" I asked.

"Hell no. And the worst part of the whole thing is I had to eat my mom's shitty cooking the whole week. You know that forty on the back nine on Sunday? Johnny, on TV, kept talking about how bad I was driving it? Malnutrition is what it was. Fucking Will Martinsen. Dude cost me a U.S. Open."

They could not have been more different, Will and Tree. Will was the Tour's most high-profile family man, his charming wife and children always by his side, not just on Sundays. They had five kids, all under eight, three of whom they had adopted: one from China, one from Bhutan, one from Mali. "Cute little accessories" was how Tree once described them. He claimed Will paid the kids to "entourage" him. He called him "Three-Dollar Will." My take was that Will was a real person and good for golf.

The rivalry was the best show in the game. During Tree's first few years on Tour, he owned Will Martinsen like he owned everyone else. After one playoff win in San Diego over Will, Helene Tremont, more competitive than the public knew, said to Barbara Nicklaus, "Herbert ate Martinsen's heart today." (Mrs. Nicklaus told it to Jack, Jack told it to Arnold, Arnold told it to a few writers he trusted. Nobody used it.)

After that U.S. Open at Shinnecock, after Chefgate, Will went crazy, matching Tree for majors won. From that Open on, Will wasn't buying the Tree mystique anymore.

Tree had Will on his mind on the Augusta driving range before the final round. Finkelman and I were silently watching Tree go through his choreographed warm-up session. When he was done, he walked over to us, nodded in Will's direction, and whispered, "Today I eat the motherfucker's heart." He then strutted to the first tee like a boxer approaching the ring for a title fight.

Despite his head problems with Will, Tree was the best thinker in golf, the most mentally tough. He was the one player who consistently controlled his emotions in a fickle sport. He was hyper-realistic about what he could do and what other players could do. He trained his mind to expect other players to do spectacular things, so that if and when they did do some amazing thing, it was never a surprise for him. He factored elements into his shot-making that others never considered. Was the bunker sand sticking to his cleats as he walked through it? What color was the rough, and how much water was in the grass? Which direction was the fairway grass cut? In match-play situations, he studied other players like a world-class actor. He could read neck sweat, water-drinking habits, caddie-golfer interplay, and he used it all to decide when to take a chance and when to hang back and wait for a mistake to happen. His golf IQ was in the genius range. The only person he could share this stuff with was Jack Nicklaus, and they did it in cryptic shorthand.

"You call that hanging back?" I once heard Nicklaus say to Tree.

"What do you call it?" Tree asked.

"I called it hanging around. I wanted the guy to know, we're both at six under, but I haven't done anything special. Yet," Nicklaus said

"Oh, that's the absolute best," Tree said. It was as if he were talking about sex. "What's that Sam Snead quote? 'When you go head to head against Nicklaus, he knows he's going to beat you, you know he's going to beat you, and he knows you know he's going to beat you.' "

"J. C. Snead," Nicklaus said.

"Oh, the nephew," Tree said. Sam Snead had a nephew who had played the Tour, J. C. Snead. "I love that quote."

"It's pretty cool," Jack said.

In the history of the game, only Nicklaus had a better head for golf than Tree. Still, Tree was human, and he made occasional golf-course mistakes, and one of them was on his first shot of the day on that Sunday at Augusta.

The first hole was playing downwind, so he tried to carry the fairway bunker with his drive. But the wind died with his ball in the air, and he came up a yard short. His ball buried under the lip. Bogey. Will made tap-in par, cutting Tree's lead from two shots to one.

On the short par-4 third hole, Martinsen laid up off the tee. When Tree unsheathed his drive—indicating he was going to try to drive the green—the crowd erupted in cheers, and this seemed to goad him, most unusually, into making an overly violent swing. Just before impact, Tree's bad right ankle gave way, and he sliced the ball wildly.

"Goddamn plastic spikes," Tree muttered, as if poor traction were to blame. Judging by the pronounced limp I saw in his first few steps as he left the third tee, it was more than that. By the time he reached his ball, he was walking slowly but without a limp. He made a bogey there and pulled his hat low on his forehead. He and Martinsen were tied for the lead. They matched each other from four to thirteen. Each made ten straight pars.

After a birdie to Tree's par on fourteen, Martinsen had a one-shot lead. The fifteenth at Augusta National is a short par-5 with a green guarded by a small pond. Tree pulled his drive left, behind a tall pine that blocked his path to the flagstick. Martinsen was in the fairway and, playing first, dropped his perfect second shot twenty feet from the hole. There were raised arms all around me. A year ago, I would have been thrilled. All I did was root for the story, especially on Sunday, when I'd be writing a game story off the winner. Now I felt dread.

Tree and Mac spent a long time conferring. It didn't look like Mac ever mouthed the words *Chosen One*. The obvious play was for Tree to knock his second shot down the fairway and then pitch over the pond to set up a putt for birdie. Tree, typically a more conservative player than Will, instead tried a shot Will had played unsuccessfully in his Friday round. (Tree watched endless hours of golf on TV at tournaments, making mental notes of what the other players were doing, how the greens were rolling, which bunkers held more sand. He was forever trying to get an edge.) I could guess what Tree was thinking: Pull off the shot Will could not, get in his head.

Tree must have had too much adrenaline. His ball went bounding over the green, and from there, he did well to make par. Will rolled in his putt for eagle. His lead was significant: three shots with three holes to play.

The world's greatest golfer was running out of holes. Standing on the sixteenth tee, looking at a cozy par-3 lined by fans, Tree knew he had to make his move then and there. The tilted green was guarded by a pond. (American golf went crazy for water hazards after World War II, largely because the golf-course architect Robert Trent Jones was so inspired by Augusta National.) Will played a tee shot designed to do one thing—keep his golf ball dry. Tree followed by stuffing his tee shot. He had a tap-in birdie to Will's par. Now my boss was two back.

On seventeen, from the right trees, Tree played a gorgeous low, running shot that quit twelve feet from the flagstick. Birdie to Will's par. Tree was one back with one hole to play.

As the two rivals walked to the eighteenth tee, I could feel the vibration of the applause right through the soles of my golf shoes. Will smiled sheepishly and gave his trademark thumbs-up. Tree was in his own world. He sat down on a bench, absently massaging his right ankle.

Both Tree and Will played the eighteenth hole out of a textbook, smashing drives down the middle within five yards of each other and following up with strong approaches to the heart of the green. In another era, when Jack Nicklaus and Tom Watson were having a similar mano a mano thing at a British Open, Watson turned to Nicklaus and said, "This is what it's all about, isn't it?" There was nothing similar on that Sunday in Augusta. Will charged up the hill, nodding here, waving there. Tree, his pace almost a crawl though with no sign of a limp, trailed behind by twenty yards, his eyes never leaving the flagstick.

Tree's mother was on one side of the eighteenth green; his father was on the other. There was nothing in life that made Tree's parents less compatible than tense golf. Belinda and the kids were behind the green, all of them wearing black polos with red armbands. Even as a member of Team Tree, I had to acknowledge the sheer awfulness of their matching getups. I stood behind the Tremont threesome. The mismatched Martinsen tribe was feet away. Nobody looked at anybody. Men in green coats were knotted in little groups, beaming. Their club was at the epicenter of the sporting universe, and their course was the best theater in sports. The grand finale was coming.

Tree was away, looking at a fifteen-footer with maybe two feet of break. Everybody knew he'd make it. He always made the putts he had to make. People were starting to take it for granted, even if Tree did not. He holed that fifteen-footer and clenched both fists as if he were shaking life into the hole, the veins in his neck looking like they might burst. If Will missed, he and Tree would be in a playoff. Tree was alive.

Tree Tremont could do something that was inexplicable: He had the ability to make guys miss putts. Players talked about it all the time. It wasn't enough that he made the putts you were likely to miss; he somehow made you miss the putts you should have been able to make. When guys said they thought he practiced putting voodoo, they weren't joking. Martinsen had a slick, breaking ten-footer to win the Masters. He had a ten-footer that would prevent his rival from winning a third straight green jacket. A ten-footer that could kill Tree's plan to win all four majors in a single year. He was also a three-putt away from giving Tree that green jacket. That was a possibility, too.

All over the country and all over the world, people were making bets as to whether Will Martinsen would make it. The rooting interest was in his favor. The betting interest was not.

And then he made it. Martinsen punctuated his winning putt with a low-flying jumping jack. Tree and Will shared an awkward handshake. On his way to the scorer's hut, Tree patted the twins on the head without ever breaking stride. When he emerged, Tree's mother wrapped him in a hug. When he was defeated, she was the only person who could get near him. Salty Morton, my old publisher, drove Tree to the press building in a golf cart in silence. When they reached the building, Salty—who had been a member of Augusta National before his passenger was born—put his right hand on Tree's left knee and said in a fatherly way, "You've been a great champion, old boy—better luck in your future endeavors."

Tree ignored Salty's well-meant bombast. He rose from the cart, spat on the walkway, and walked into the press building. He took his seat on the dais. An old member, acting as the press-conference moderator, sat beside him. I stood in the back. I'd never seen him so grim.

"Ladies and gentlemen, in keeping with the tradition of this tournament, Mr. Tree Tremont has graciously agreed to take some questions. As you all know, Mr. Tremont was trying to make Masters history today, seeking to become the first player ever to win three consecutive club coats, and he just missed that feat. A great performance. Tree, why don't you just tell us, for starters, your general sense of the day or anything else you might like to say."

"Let's just open it up for questions," Tree said.

"Okay, then, ladies and gentlemen, questions, please."

A reporter I did not know was standing next to me. He asked in a whisper, "What's with your guy?" I wondered if he was from the *Eye.*

"How's your right ankle, Tree?" came the first question from an *Augusta Chronicle* reporter.

"Fine. Nothing wrong with it." Tree almost never used a reporter's suggested words in his answer. There would be no quotes in which he referred to his ankle. "Just slipped on that tee shot on three. Wind died on my tee shot on one. That's golf. Bottom line, I didn't get it done."

The AP golf writer asked, "You said in Hawaii that your goal was to win all four majors this year. Now, of course, you can't do that. Do you have another goal?"

"That's your word," Tree said. "Don't put words in my mouth. I said it was my intention." He was done with that question.

Somebody asked, "What'd you think of Will Martinsen's round?"

"You saw it. I had my chances. Bottom line, like I said before, didn't get it done."

It went on like that for a while, and then, mercifully, the old member ended it.

Tree went to the Champions Room—the second-floor locker room for former winners—to clear out his locker. Big Herb, Finkelman, and I trailed him like pallbearers who had lost their casket. There were maybe fifty handwritten envelopes from fans and members on the top shelf of his locker. Tree couldn't be bothered with them.

"I ain't doing that fucking jacket thing," he said.

One of the quaint rituals of the Masters is that the previous year's winner helps the new winner into his green jacket in a ceremony on the eighteenth green shortly before sunset.

"Fuck it, don't do it," Finkelman said. "You don't owe this club anything."

"Let's not be childish here," Tree's father said. "You have to do it."

"You showed a lot of humanity, the way you put that coat on Will, that hug you gave him," Finkelman said.

Finkelman, Tree, and I were in an SUV, a Mercedes G550, heading back to West Lake. Tree was driving. There was a county sheriff in front of us and an unmarked sheriff's car behind us. Despite the police presence, Tree was drinking a double vodka and soda with a lime in an Augusta National glass. He responded to Finkelman's comment by turning up the music—old-school rap—even louder. A minute later, he turned it off and said, "You know what he says to me? 'It was an honor and a pleasure to compete with you out there.' " Tree started mimicking Will. " 'It was an honor and a pleasure. It was an honor and a pleasure.' Fucking Boy Scout."

We pulled into the driveway of the West Lake house. Inside, there were balloons and confetti. Belinda—lovely, spirited, hot Belinda—had planned a victory party, and why not? Prior to that day, Tree had never *not* won any tournament in which he had held the 54-hole lead.

She was waiting for her man in a teeny-tiny polka-dot dress with a tiara atop her head and a glass of champagne in each hand. "Come, Tree, have a drink," she said. "It is okay."

He grabbed the flute out of her hand and hurled it against the wall. Shards of glass exploded everywhere.

"Tree, please—the children are upstairs!"

He picked up a champagne bottle and raised it as if he might smash it against the fireplace mantel. Then he put it down and said, "Where're my fucking pills?"

Upstairs, I could hear the kids crying for their mother.

"My God," Belinda said, "it's just one round of golf."

"What the fuck do you know?" Tree said.

She started sobbing.

I stared at the living room floor, in the general vicinity where *Pulp Friction* had fallen days earlier.

"Andrew," Tree said to his agent. "Get me in to see that doctor."

11

Tree House was a temple of excess. As a bachelor, Tree bought a McMansion in a gated community in St. Petersburg, right on Boca Ciega Bay, where there was one vaguely Spanish suburban dream house after another. When he married Belinda, he was only twenty-two, but she was twenty-eight and thinking big. By their first anniversary, the house had nearly doubled in size through an expansion to the second floor and an addition on the third. In the second expansion project, to accommodate the twins, the house grew like a pink stucco blob until it took over almost the entire half-acre lot. Belinda fixed that. She had Tree buy and then raze six of the neighboring houses to create what she considered a suitable backyard. Tree House was 29,850 square feet (and growing) on over two acres when I got there on the Monday morning after the Masters.

Tree's sweatsuited majordomo insisted that I take "a quick house tour, orders from the boss." A quick house tour was not possible.

I saw the yoga room, the gift-wrapping room, the Ping-Pong room, the cardroom, the room for Tree's clubs, the room for Tree's trophies, the indoor driving range, the gym, the indoor pool separated from the outdoor pool by a retractable glass wall, the movie theater, the various bars, the many, many bedrooms (but not, of course, the one in which Belinda was still sleeping), the three kitchens—one for the caterers, one for Belinda, and one for the kids, where Tree was working over the stove, making perfect silver-dollar pancakes.

"Blueberries or chocolate chips?" he asked the twins. A matronly Spanish-speaking nanny was putting heavy silverware in front of their plastic sippy cups.

"Chocolate chips," they said in unison.

"And here's Josh," Tree said. "Guys, I want you to say hi to my friend Mr. Dutra."

They were still in their astronaut pajamas.

"Hello, space travelers," I said. "No school today?"

"No," Rocco said. "Mommy said no school for today."

I got it. Daddy loses the Masters, then loses his head, kids get the day off from kindergarten.

"Guys, Mr. Dutra is a writer. Do you know what a writer does?"

"Like George in *Seabiscuit*," said Isabella.

"No, George in *Seabiscuit* was a *rider*. Mr. Dutra writes stories."

They looked singularly unimpressed. I would have paid their father to change the subject.

"We do that with Miss Kathy," Rocco said.

"Do you have an iPad?" Isabella asked me.

I shook my head no. I was surely a technological disappointment to the Tremont kids.

"I asked Mr. Dutra to come by this morning so I could tell him what I told you guys before, that Daddy was in a very bad mood yesterday."

"Because of Will," the boy said.

"Because of his cook," the girl said.

"No, not because of Will. Because of me."

"Mom says it's only a game," Isabella said.

"And I want to say I'm sorry, to you guys and to Mr. Dutra, because I should not have said those things."

"And because you broke a glass," the boy said. "Mommy said you broke a glass."

"Marisol," Tree said to the nanny, "can you flip these? But wait for the bubbles."

Leaning against the side of the Sub-Zero was a metal hospital cane with a cushiony handle. Tree grabbed it and hobbled out of the kitchen, waving me along with him.

We sat by the outdoor pool. Tree pressed a button, and the retractable wall went up. The sweatsuited majordomo came out with fresh-squeezed orange juice. He had short, thick arms that barely moved.

"If you want to quit, you should quit now," Tree said to me. "I'll pay you for the rest of the year. Not that I want you to quit. I don't. I like having you around. I think you can write a hell of a book for me. When that will be, I don't know. Could be a year from now, could be ten years from now. But you know, you're going to see some crazy shit."

"I think I already have."

"Welcome to my world."

We sipped our orange juice. It was a perfect spring Florida morning, still and fragrant. Tree was wearing shorts and a T-shirt and rubber flip-flops, not a logo on any of it. He had the ankles of a ballerina. How they could support him, I couldn't imagine. His feet were the color of newsprint.

"My father said something interesting about you," Tree said. I was suddenly on high alert. The conversation was never about me. "Pops is talking about you, and he says, 'He's a good listener.' "

It was strange: The needle wasn't out. He was just talking.

"I don't have a lot of people I can trust. I trust Mom and Big Herb, but since they don't trust each other, it's not easy. I was raised in a bubble by parents who had only one thing in common: an obsession with me. I still live in a bubble, except now it's everywhere I go.

I scratch my balls, and somebody will snap a picture on their phone, and it'll get tweeted all over the world. I've got no space."

I was moved by his candor. "I'm not quitting," I said.

"Good," Tree said.

The breeze was starting to come up off the bay.

"I gotta talk to you about this one thing," I said. "*Eye of the Asshole*. I think Emerson's still talking to them. I don't know what they're sitting on, but it can't be good."

"Don't worry about that, Joshie," Tree said. "Finky gets paid to make crap like that go away."

We could hear the twins arguing over the last pancake. Marisol spoke to them in Spanish. Tree massaged his ankle. I asked, "What's with the cane?"

The helicopter was in Tree's backyard, on his regulation basketball court with the Tree Corp logo at its center. A half hour after taking off, we touched down on the roof of the Matteo Medical Center building in downtown Orlando. In the last few years, Dr. Antoine Matteo had become the sports world's most in-demand shaman, thanks to a pioneering procedure he developed and named after himself. In a front-page profile in *The Wall Street Journal*, he was described as "a first-class surgeon and an all-world egomaniac." The story explained the Matteo Method and its secret ingredient, performance-rejuvenating plasma.

In the method, Matteo—or the surgeons working under him—would draw blood from an injured athlete, add cod oil and blood from Brazilian calves, spin the mixture in a centrifuge, then re-inject the concoction into the injured area. It sounded like witchcraft to me. Its users swore by it. During spring training, a Dominican baseball star told Tree, "This PRP? It's like holy water. And this Dr. Matteo? He's like Jesus Christ himself." Well-heeled weekend warriors with torn muscles and ripped tendons lined up outside Matteo's office with the hope of getting seen. He ran a recovery factory.

Tree was taken for X-rays and led to a sterile examination room. The only thing to read was a *Golf* magazine with Will Martinsen on the cover. Tree studied the foldout swing-sequence pictures like a teenager in my day looked at a *Playboy* centerfold, except we saw unattainable perfection, and all Tree saw was flaws. "See how across the line he is?" Tree said. "Isn't that awful?" It looked pretty good to me, but I was a 92 shooter.

After a half-hour wait, Dr. Matteo finally arrived. No handshake, no greeting. He had X-rays in one hand and a folder in the other. He glanced at the folder to see the name of the lunch-break patient squeezed into his schedule. "Herbert Tremont?" He looked at both of us. Tree nodded at him. He didn't know Tree Tremont by sight. It was unusual.

"What was your height and weight when you were twenty years old?"

"Six even, buck-fifty." When I met Tree, he had the perfect build for golf, sinewy and supple. But he hated how skinny his neck and arms looked in polo shirts. He knew the public considered pro golfers to be second-rate athletes, just north of pro bowlers, and he wanted to be considered a true jock with a commanding physical presence. I felt that Tree's obsession with weight training was more about vanity than performance.

"And now?"

"Six-two, two-oh-four."

Dr. Matteo made some notes. Without looking up, he asked, "Who's your friend?"

"Josh," Tree said. "My adviser."

Dr. Matteo dropped the file on a low table and said, "You've outgrown your frame. You're at least twenty-five pounds too heavy. That it's all upper-body muscle makes it even worse. Your right Achilles is paying the price. In layman's terms, it's frayed like an old rope. There is a very significant tear. It's a surprise the tendon hasn't ruptured completely."

"Is that the good news?"

"The good news, Mr. Tremont, is that I can surgically repair your tendon and have you good to go in three to four months."

"How about two months?"

"Three months at a minimum."

Tree betrayed no emotion, but he spoke slowly, as if to a child. "Dr. Matteo, the U.S. Open is in eight weeks. It's at Pebble Beach."

Matteo looked at Tree in a different way. "You're the golfer," he said.

Tree nodded.

"Mr. Tremont, your timetable is unrealistic. Even if I could get you in next week."

"You can put me on the table today."

"Give me a minute here," Dr. Matteo said. He left the room.

I was still absorbing the news. Tree had already moved on. "You sure you don't want another opinion?" I asked.

"This is the guy," Tree said. "I can't waste any more time."

"How long has the Achilles been bothering you?"

Faced with such a direct question, Tree would typically lie, but with just the two of us in the room, I thought he might answer.

"Something happened last August, right before the PGA. I was trying to clean-and-jerk three-fifty. I could feel something tearing. Fraying, like he says. Couldn't even finish the lift."

"How could you keep playing like that?"

"How'd my father take two bullets in the thigh and walk for four days in the Vietnam jungle? My thing was nothing. Just pain. But on the third tee yesterday, I felt something go. Couldn't push off my right foot at all. No stability. I knew something was seriously wrong. Pain I can handle. But getting my ass handed to me by Will Martinsen? Something has to change."

His ass handed to him. He had lost by one shot.

Tree had a romantic view of his father's military service and three tours of duty in Vietnam. Once a year Tree went to Fort Polk, the army base in Louisiana, to do a week of training with special-ops troops. At the diner one day, Big Herb said to me, "I spent twenty years as an army grunt to give him a better life. And all he wants to do is play soldier." For years, I thought the Fort Polk week was an elaborate PR move for Tree to promote his charitable work with the armed services. I was starting to understand there was more to it than that.

Dr. Matteo returned. "We're going to get you in tomorrow morning. You'll be first. I'm going to do it myself. I'll need twenty-five thousand dollars from you right now. Black Card is fine. You'll be billed for the rest and for the post-operative treatments. The whole thing will run two fifty at a minimum. We don't take insurance."

"I'm in," Tree said. He started rummaging through his fat stack of bills, looking for the lone credit card in the middle.

"I want you to understand something, Mr. Tremont, so there's no confusion later. This tear is what I call MS-eight on the ten-point Matteo Scale, ten being complete rupture. You will never be ready to play by mid-June. Mid-July is the best-case scenario."

"You do the surgery, Doc," Tree said. "I'll take over from there."

"Go to Suite 100 on the first floor for your pre-surgery blood work," the doctor said. "Give the girl there a list of the meds you take, all of them. You can't walk on that ankle. You're in a wheelchair for the rest of the day."

Dr. Matteo left, and a male orderly with a wheelchair arrived. "Call Finky," Tree said as he was being pushed down a hallway in a wheelchair.

Finkelman was in New York for meetings. As I briefed him, I could hear his breathing become labored.

"I leave you unchaperoned for one morning, and he winds up in goddamn surgery? Are you fucking kidding me?" He started screaming about the millions Tree Corp would lose in bonus clauses and canceled appearance fees. It was a full-blown rant at somebody he thought was paid to take it.

"Andrew, can you shut up and let me say something here? The man's got a body that his ankles won't support. It's April, and he hasn't won a tournament all year. He's got a right Achilles that's frayed like an old rope. His career's in jeopardy. Wake the fuck up!" It felt great to talk to Dr. No that way.

I checked in on Tree. The "girl" taking his blood in Suite 100 was a voluptuous woman, maybe thirty, with green eyes, long streaked hair, and a shark tattoo on her left forearm.

"You know, there's a golfer called Shark," Tree told her.

"Greg Norman," the phlebotomist said.

"Very good," Tree said.

"What's he like?" she said coyly.

12

The surgery went off without a hitch, and for six weeks after it, Tree made biweekly trips by helicopter to Dr. Matteo's Orlando office. I joined him. Dr. Matteo would say that his recovery was on or slightly ahead of schedule, but Tree was frustrated by what he viewed as its glacial pace. Before long, there was a full-blown pissing match between two narcissists who were both accustomed to always being right.

"What can you do to speed things up?" Tree asked.

"I have accelerated recovery significantly," the doctor said.

I'd never seen anybody be so unaccommodating to Tree Tremont, except maybe a Tour rules official who wouldn't give him embedded ball relief when he wanted it. There were times when Tree would ask a question, and Dr. Matteo would have no response at all. He'd just stick another long needle in Tree's ankle and press down on the plunger until it reached the bottom of the plastic barrel and another fifty milliliters of Matteo magic would be in him.

By late May, Tree was putting, but he didn't feel stable over the ball. By early June, he was chipping, though without his customary authority. By mid-June, I was writing a press release.

> Tree Tremont announced today that he will not be playing in the U.S. Open at Pebble Beach Golf Links as he continues the final stages of recovery from his April ankle surgery by Dr. Antoine Matteo of Orlando, Fla., pioneer of the Matteo Method. It will mark the first time Tremont has missed a major championship since he made his golf debut at the U.S. Open, when the then-19-year-old finished ninth.
>
> "I'm heartbroken," Tremont said. "Pebble Beach is dear to me. I had dreams about winning where my hero Jack Nicklaus won back in 1972, when the U.S. Open was first contested at Pebble. I look forward to playing in the British Open next month on the Old Course in St. Andrews, Scotland."
>
> Tremont will attend this year's U.S. Open to introduce a new Arrow Golf rain gear line and to do limited guest color commentary for NBC Sports during the third and fourth rounds. He will also be making an appearance on behalf of his charity, the Plant a Tree Foundation.
>
> Tremont will be available to answer questions from credentialed media for 20 minutes on Thursday at 10 a.m. in the U.S. Open Media Center at Pebble Beach.

In a deal with Finkelman, Matteo agreed to take ten thousand dollars off Tree's total charges in exchange for the reference to him in the release, every word of it carefully negotiated.

Finkelman had been negotiating another deal, a more freighted one. A week before the Open, I flew with him to Little Rock and the headquarters of Omnivore Media, the parent company of the *Eye* and a dozen other down-market titles.

Omnivore was on the thirteenth floor of an old brick building. We were met at the elevator by a dowdy secretary. The carpet was dingy and the lighting was yellow. Along the walls were framed *Eye* front pages. The entire human condition was covered in a fifty-foot hallway: courtship, sex, teen pregnancy, birth, Child Protective Services, rehab, redemption, weight gain, weight loss, love, marriage, infidelity, divorce, death.

We were ushered into the corner office of Ray Rizzo, Omnivore's CEO. He was dark and rumpled. He greeted us with his arms wide open and said, "Welcome, my brothers from another mother." Finkelman looked disturbed.

We sat, and I looked around. One wall was covered with photos of Ray grinning next to B-list celebrities and politicians. Behind his desk in a gaudy gold frame was a diploma: a master's in journalism from Columbia. Rizzo asked, "Beer? Or something with a little more hair?" We settled for warm tap water and Fritos. Rizzo began pacing the room, talking and gesticulating.

"I've been doing this job for thirteen years," he said. "Hundreds and hundreds of flaks and managers and agents have called me. They beg for favors. They threaten me with lawsuits. They promise I will be visited with bodily harm. They offer me trips to Cancún, boxes of money, girls I wouldn't know what to do with. All over the phone or by e-mail. You two are the first people to ever get on a plane, come here, and do business in person. I cannot tell you how much I respect that. Or, for that matter, how much I respect what both of you do."

We muttered our thanks.

"Finky," Rizzo said, "you've taken one of the world's biggest pussy hounds and sold him as a family man. Absolutely fucking brilliant, man. And, Josh, with your excellent typing, you turned him into a deity. If I could write like that, I'd go straight. But the fact is, we all sell bullshit for a living. Isn't that right? The difference is, I'm up-front about it."

That was when I realized we were about to get ambushed. I hadn't see it coming before them, and I didn't think Finkelman had, either. He could not contain his agitation. He said, "Why don't you can your lecture and just offer us your goddamn deal?"

"Now, is that in the spirit of cooperation?" Rizzo said. "I think not." He twisted and cracked his neck and handed us a stack of papers. "You have had a chance to review the photos, text messages, and affidavits provided to us by Emerson Wright. We have more than enough to print a story. A very damaging story. A story that would expose Tree's hypocrisy and the hypocrisy of those around him. But Tree Tremont is worth more to us with his good name intact. He doesn't resonate with the *Eye*'s primary demographics. Housewives, college girls, and old biddies don't really care about golf. But the fourteen million readers of our leading men's fitness-and-lifestyle magazine love Tree. That magazine, of course, is *TEN! TEN!* readers want to know how Tree got so ripped. They want to see his gym at Tree House and the rest of the house. They want to see Tree's hot wife at the pool. For *TEN!* this is the story of the year."

Finkelman was ready for him. "You're asking for a lot—too much. We can get you a solid hour with Tree for an interview. Absolutely no Belinda. We get image approval. And you give us a guarantee in writing that the *Eye* will never publish a photo or story that conjoins Tree Tremont and Emerson Wright." He sounded lawyerly and impressive.

"Is there no honor among thieves?" Rizzo said. "None of us needs a paper trail. You have my word that unless he gets abducted by aliens, *Eye* will leave Tree's private life the fuck alone, as it should. He's an athlete, for crying out loud, not a rock star."

Rizzo stood in front of us, extended his hand, and Finkelman and I both shook it. We had a deal. Rizzo's palm was all moist. I walked straight to the restroom to wash my hands.

At Pebble, Tree picked up where he had left off in Augusta. In the English castle he rented on Del Ciervo Road in Pebble Beach, he made regular trips to the living room bar, to his Ziploc bag of meds, and to his lair in the turret, always accompanied by at least one fetching young lady, sometimes two, one time three. Belinda and the twins were in St. Pete. I was staying in the castle and seeing him and hearing him more than I cared to.

One night I was in the living room, watching Golf Channel,

while Tree was upstairs with his latest conquest. I was surprised to see his name appear on my caller ID.

"Tree?"

"Joshie, you gotta do me a favor. This is huge. Run out to my car and get the box of Altoids in the dashboard cubby. Leave the box outside my door up here. Thanks, bro."

At this point the humiliation didn't even register. I performed my errand and returned to the couch. Later Tree walked a young Asian woman, built like a gymnast, to the front door and sent her off with a halfhearted "I'll call you."

He sat down and watched the golf with me. Golf Channel was showing a replay of *Shell's Wonderful World of Golf,* Sam Snead versus Jack Nicklaus at Pebble, 1963.

"Oh, watch this three-finger five-iron Sam's gonna hit here," Tree said. "This is beautiful."

"Your friend not happy with your breath?" I asked.

"The Altoids were for *her,* dude. She popped five or six in her mouth and went to town. My dick's still tingling." Tree watched Snead's shot. "That is freaking perfect," he said. "That's as good as it gets, that swing, right there. That and maybe Mickey Wright. You know the famous Snead line? Guy asks him for his swing thought. Snead says, 'If you ain't thinking about pussy, you're thinking about the wrong thing.' "

"So you have that in common," I said.

Tree sort of giggled.

"I gotta ask you something. Don't you find it's all kind of the same after a while?"

"What, the tail?" Tree asked.

I nodded yes.

"Not at all, JD," Tree said. Now he sounded scholarly. "There's always something new. I mean, the Altoid B.J., that was an entirely new experience."

"Will you call her again?"

"Not likely. With rare exception, Joshie, the next time around is never as good. That first-time thrill, you get it only once. But there are exceptions. You've met one of them."

"Amanda," I said.

"Not Amanda."

"Emerson."

"Correct. Let me make this simple for you. Absolutely, hands down, without question, the single best fuck I've ever had. I actually dream about it."

He went to his iPhone and looked at pictures of Amanda and Emerson and him together, suggestive snaps that in the wrong hands could bring down an empire. He showed me one and it was enough. I went to the kitchen and poured myself a glass of cold milk.

Tree was frustrated to be at Pebble for an Open where he was not playing. But he was more relaxed than I had ever seen him, almost like he was on vacation. Tree felt that being home during off weeks was work. Being a father was work. Being a husband was work. Keeping his golf game sharp was work. Keeping his body tight was work. At least at tournaments, he could shed two of his jobs—husband and father—and fill the void with what I euphemistically thought of as his hobby.

He kept astounding hours. His bed would be shaking the floor at one in the morning, and five hours later, he'd be in the pool with a trainer as he did his tedious rehab workouts, sloshing through the shallow end like a fullback in a slow-motion replay. In the middle of the afternoon, he'd be in the castle's gym, screaming bizarrely profane things as he lifted weights that really should have stayed on the floor. He'd say, "You suck, you goddamnmotherfuckingcuntfacedasshole." Then you'd hear one final grunt, and in the silence, you'd know some obscene amount of weight was now north of his trembling head.

He stayed away from the golf course until Thursday morning, when he went for his press conference. He parked in the players' lot in a forest by the driving range. The first person he saw was Will Martinsen.

"Tree, my man," Martinsen said to him. He was perpetually cheerful. "How are the wheels?"

"Left's good," he said. "Right's better than ever."

"Very cool. See you at St. Andrews?" Will reached in for a bro hug. Tree went for the shake but quit before their shoulders made contact. "Good luck to you, man," Will said.

It struck me as a funny thing for the Masters champ to say, since he was playing in the U.S. Open and Tree was not. There was no way Tree was going to say good luck to Will. Larry David would have had a field day with it. *What, no good luck back? No return of service?* All Tree said was "Okay."

It wasn't much of surprise. He could be willfully socially inept. Plus, his competitive streak was unrelenting. That combination made him a disaster in team competitions like the Ryder Cup and the Presidents Cup, which brought a dozen American players together for a week. In the team room, he'd do his own thing and privately tell Big Herb how uncomfortable he was playing partner golf in a uniform. He'd tell his father, "Why would I want to be all cozy with a bunch of guys for one week when another twenty weeks a year, I'm trying to step on their dicks?" For his teammates, it was fun to take a break from the loneliness of Tour play.

Tree was closer to—or at least admired—a couple of players from Korea and Japan who seldom played in the U.S. and who pursued golf with military discipline. Whenever he saw the Japanese golfer Isao Aoki, Tree greeted him with a traditional bow and would say to anybody around, "Here's a man who had *game*." He meant it. He said Aoki had "great hands"—one of the highest compliments Tree could pay another golfer—and admired the small man's near-win over Big Jack in a long-ago U.S. Open. It was amazing what Tree knew. Aoki's heyday had come before Tree was born.

We arrived at the press tent, a white plastic haven of free ice cream and copy-and-paste quotes, at 9:59. That was typical of Tree. He was always punctual. Pete was waiting for me at the entrance, wearing stripes with stripes. It must have been a special day. All week he had been wearing his traditional plaid on plaid.

"Joshuamon," he said. "Can I borrow you for a sec?"

"Can we do it at eleven?" I asked. I hated that, sounding like a businessman with a schedule. Reporters don't have schedules, just deadlines. But I wasn't a reporter anymore.

Tree was engulfed by a slow-moving knot of USGA officials, Salty Morton among them. I trailed behind the group, all in blue short-sleeve button-downs.

Pete walked with me. "My damn boss is stalking me," he said.

"Salty Morton is the Forrest Gump of golf," I said. "He's everywhere."

For a minute there, I had again let down my guard with Pete.

Pete grabbed my elbow, got my full attention, and said, "Josh, I got something I got to ask your boss."

"He's right there," I said, pointing to Finkelman.

"Your other boss."

We stopped our shuffling walk.

"And you can't ask it on an open mike, right?" I asked.

My mind was churning quickly. I didn't think Pete's subject was Tree's sex life. I still couldn't see *The Review-American* breaking that story, not as long as Salty was signing the checks. Then a different story popped into my mind: cooked books at the Plant a Tree Foundation. I had no reason to think there was a problem, but Pete could talk about his 401(k) all through coffee, a muffin, and a refill. I could see him sinking his teeth into that kind of thing. My mind jumped to Tree and how shaken he'd been when Wesley Snipes went off to federal prison for tax evasion. Tree loved *White Men Can't Jump.* He once crushed Snipes in a celebrity one-on-one basketball tournament.

"I'll get you five minutes with him, Pete," I said. "I'm gonna have to chaperone."

That afternoon Tree did a clinic for kids on the driving range of a public course near Pebble Beach, the Pacific Grove muni. The clinic was sponsored by Plant a Tree, and five hundred children were bused in for it from Salinas, a farming town twenty miles east. Many of the kids were from working-class families, or families far poorer than that, all of them going to Plant a Tree afterschool programs in clean, bright buildings staffed by competent, well-educated teachers and counselors, all of it paid for with charitable donations that began with Tree's golf skill. The kids sat on the clumpy early-summer grass.

Tree said, "I never want any of you to think, *I can't do this. I'm too poor. My skin's the wrong color. My English is bad. I'm not smart enough or strong enough or whatever.*"

This was not boilerplate. This was the real Tree Tremont. I was reminded of the day I met him. Pete was standing behind the kids, taking notes.

"Young man, can you come up here?" Tree asked a boy with a small face and big ears. "What's your name?"

"Jose."

"'Hose?' Like I'm gonna water you?"

The kids giggled.

"Ho-ZAY," the kid said, this time with two syllables.

"That's what I figured. How old are you, José?"

"Eight. Tomorrow I make nine."

"Happy birthday. That's a good age to be. Can I ask you something, José? Do you trust me?"

The kid made a big nod.

"Really? I thought you were smarter than that."

The kids laughed.

"Okay. I want you to take this Hula-Hoop, walk out on the driving range, take a hundred steps, turn around, and hold it high in the air. You got all that?"

The boy nodded again, less sure of himself.

"You still trust me?" He nodded again.

José followed the instructions, and Tree tapped relaxed 4-irons right through the Hula-Hoop.

"How 'bout a hand for José?" he said. "Now let me tell you how I did that. You saw me stand behind the ball before I hit a shot? I closed my eyes and drew a picture in my mind of the ball going through the hoop. Picture it first, work at it, make it happen. Okay, guys? Work hard."

He walked off, and the kids spontaneously stood and cheered for him.

The four of us sat in a Lincoln Navigator in the golf course parking lot, Tree behind the wheel, Pete in the passenger seat, Finkelman and me in the back. Pete put a tape recorder on the dashboard and asked, "You mind if I tape this?" I grew more nervous. Like me, Pete would never use a tape recorder unless he thought his story had a strong chance of being challenged or winding up in court.

"Dr. Matteo's office was raided this morning," Pete said. He spoke in his comforting drawl, making steady eye contact with Tree all the while. "Nobody knows yet. He's being held right now by the feds. They're going to charge him with felony possession of cocaine and amphetamines, unlawful prescription of steroids and human growth hormone, practicing medicine without a license, and twelve other counts. The IRS will come next. They're going to have a field day with him.

"They've seized all his records. They got a list, thirty-three athletes he's been shooting up with every performance-enhancing drug known to mankind and some that aren't. Two guys from the Yankees, patients of his, failed drug tests. Those test results are going to be released tomorrow. The feds are going to ask you for a blood sample. They know from Dr. Matteo's records exactly what he shot you up with. He kept careful records of it all." Pete turned to me and said, "Like Nixon with his tapes." He returned to Tree. "They're gonna want you to testify as a federal witness, appear before the grand jury. If you won't cooperate, they're ready to indict you, too. They got a girl in his office who gave 'em everything. She filed sexual harassment charges against Matteo with the Orlando police, they dropped it, and she got mad and went to the feds, handed them everything."

"Who's that?" Tree asked.

"I don't know her name. She did the blood work for him."

"Fuck me," Tree said.

"Tree, don't talk," Finkelman said, "Pete, we thank you for this information. I assume you're writing tonight?"

"That's right, and I want to know if Tree has something to say, something I can use."

"He doesn't, and let me say something off the record," Finkelman said.

"I'd rather you not."

"Show me a little professional courtesy here," Finkelman said. It was almost comical, as Dr. No had never shown any courtesy to anybody with a notebook. "Listen, we would greatly appreciate it if you'd leave Tree out of it for now. I mean, he hasn't even been contacted by the authorities. Has Tree not been an exemplary athlete? Let's give him a break, Pete, shall we? And at the appropriate time, we'll make him available to you exclusively."

"That's very kind of you, Finky, but that ain't gonna work here," Pete said with utter confidence. He had the upper hand, and he knew it.

Tree looked at the blinking light on his BlackBerry and massaged his forehead with his fingertips. I wondered if Pete would describe the scene in the Navigator in his story. It was certainly fair game.

"Pete, I was with Tree pretty much every time he met with Dr. Matteo," I said. "There's no way he could know what Matteo was shooting him up with, and those treatments came in a period when he wasn't even competing."

"The Tour rules don't distinguish between what you do knowingly and unknowingly," Pete said. "A Tour player has to keep the PEDs out of his body whether he's playing or not. You know, they already suspended the one guy."

A little girl from the clinic walked through the parking lot, saw Tree through the windshield, and gave him a wave. On habit alone, he lifted an index finger and returned her greeting. I saw his face in the rearview mirror. He looked dead.

13

I felt Tree should stay for the weekend and do the NBC telecast, let Dan Hicks interview him about his inadvertent use of performance-enhancing drugs, and start to put the news behind him. Finkelman had the opposite view: Admit to nothing. He was a lawyer by training, and it showed. He was worried that Richard Fenimore, the Tour commissioner, would suspend Tree; that sportswriters and fans would start to question the legitimacy of his accomplishments; that sponsors would drop him. A triple crown of whammies.

We were in the English castle overlooking Pebble Beach. Finkelman said to Tree, "I think we should head home. What do you think?"

Tree, drink in hand, pointed east.

By Thursday night, the three of us were on the plane, flying from Pebble to St. Pete. Tree was trashed before the wheels were up. Friday morning, *The Review-American* had a screaming front-page headline:

FEDS SAY ORLANDO DOCTOR DRUGGING TREMONT, OTHERS

Pete's story was picked up by every wire service and website with even a passing interest in sports. Tree was named as a patient of Dr. Matteo's, somebody the feds wanted as a witness, and somebody who likely had been shot up with various performance-enhancing drugs, although possibly without knowing it. No matter, it was damning.

Friday, Saturday, and Sunday were a flurry of phone calls, text messages, and e-mails. I kept in touch with dozens of reporters, putting out Internet wildfires, fact-checking fiction-writing bloggers, and staunchly defending Tree. The *Eye* in particular was going crazy with the drug story, posting two or three updates a day on its website. I called Ray Rizzo to point out a handful of factual inaccuracies.

"Josh, your boy is amazing," Rizzo said. "Everywhere I go, people are talking about him. Housewives, Josh—*Eye* readers. I don't think he's a fit anymore for *TEN!* They don't even take ads from steroid dealers."

"What are you talking about?" I said. "We had a deal!"

"Yeah, but that was before I knew your boy was a druggie."

"He's not a druggie," I said.

Rizzo said, "Can I use that?"

I couldn't hang up quickly enough.

All weekend long, there was a woman from ESPN and a man from *USA Today* camped out at the entrance gate of Tree's development. Belinda played the indignant card. "It's an invasion of privacy!" she said. I had the feeling she enjoyed the excitement of the war room. Belinda was on fire. She looked great. She came up with a plan to "protect the children." She packed them up, put them in her low-slung Porsche Panamera (no Tour-wife Escalade for her), and drove straight across the state to the Breakers, the oceanfront five-star resort in Palm Beach, loaded with rich Europeans like her.

Finkelman arranged a Monday meeting between Tree and Richard Fenimose in the commissioner's office in Ponte Vedra Beach, Florida. But on Sunday night, Tree told Finkelman that he couldn't go. He might have gone, he might not have, but now he couldn't. Something much more important had come up.

At the conclusion of play on Sunday night, two players were tied for the lead in the U.S. Open. That meant on Monday there would be an eighteen-hole playoff. And that made it a holy day for Tree. The two guys were a veteran Korean golfer, Y. E. Yang, looking to win his second major championship, and a rising star from Japan, Ryo Ishikawa. It was the first U.S. Open playoff without an American player. Tree's plan was to watch every shot of it in the comfort of a cozy little den in Tree House. He invited me to join him.

"The kid, Ryo, he's almost the exact age I was when I played in my first Open at Pebble," Tree said. The federal investigation seemed to be of no concern to him. If the steroid charges stuck, he would be suspended and his reputation trashed. He never mentioned anything about it.

Finkelman, unhappy that I was developing something like a friendship with his client and meal ticket, was texting and calling me every half hour. He wanted to know what Tree was doing and saying. He wanted me to respond to every claim on the Internet that Tree had been using steroids since he turned pro. His body had changed so markedly that you could understand why people were suspicious. Still, I buried every typist who made such a claim with the same response: "Your article is irresponsible and potentially libelous. Remove it immediately or legal action will be brought against you." Finkelman wanted to know if I had learned anything more about Tree and the girl with the shark tattoo. "You know what he's like after sex," Finkelman said, "how he gets all talky and confessiony."

Tree was consumed with the playoff. He watched with a tilted head as Yang and Ishikawa arrived at Pebble's eighteenth tee, a small peninsula of green grass with the Pacific gleaming behind it. Ryo had a one-shot lead. Yang, after a par to Ryo's double bogey on seventeen, had the honor. Tree turned off the volume. He took a final swig from his tenth Bud and put the empty bottle on the mantel, all the labels lined up in a perfect row.

"Yang has got to hit driver here," Tree said. "After that double, this Ryo kid's gotta be scared shitless. You hit driver, get the kid thinking, get him confused, and from there you don't know what he might do. He could snap one in the ocean! Oh, man. This is too painful to watch. If I'm Y. E. Yang here? If I could hit driver as straight as that dude? I'd have the dog *out*, I'd be toweling down that grip, making sure the kid gets a good look at it."

On the TV, we could see Yang taking out a smaller club, leaving his driver in the bag.

"What is that, Joshie?" Tree asked. "Is that a fucking three-wood? No—don't do it, Yangski! I can't even look." He covered his face as if he were watching a horror movie.

The phone rang. The caller ID said H. TREMONT.

Tree pressed the speakerphone button and said, "Pops, you watching this shit? Do you believe this guy is hitting that little three-wood here?"

"Tree, I have bad news," Mr. Tremont said. There was a gravity in his voice that brought me out of my slouch on the recliner. "Your mother's had a heart attack. She's at St. Pete General, on life support. You should get yourself down there right away."

I closed my eyes and saw a picture of the thank-you note Mrs. Tremont had sent me after my first story on Tree. It was written on sky-blue stationery, in her perfect cursive script with a black pen.

Tree was hunched over, his face in his knees, vertebrae protruding through his T-shirt, shoulders heaving up and down, up and down. His body started to shiver.

I put a blanket over his shoulders and asked him if he wanted me to drive.

The timing could not have been worse. But even with Tree's name in the middle of a federal drug investigation, the golf establishment showed up for Mrs. Tremont's funeral at the First United Methodist Church in St. Petersburg. The church was formal and imposing. There was muted light coming through the stained-glass windows. The closed mahogany casket was in the front. The organist played "Hymn of Promise."

Salty Morton was there, representing the USGA, Augusta National, and *The St. Petersburg Review-American.* Will and Missy Martinsen flew all night from San Francisco to be there. Richard Fenimore arrived early and sat in the middle of the church with one of his Tour lieutenants. Turner Darlington from Arrow Golf sat beside Tommy Roy from NBC Sports. Norman Henley, Tree's teacher, was not there, which surprised me; but his caddie, Mac McCausland, was sitting near the back with Arnold Palmer. Lily and I sat behind Palmer, eightysomething and oozing vitality. We had an excellent view of his leathery neck and fine, silvery hair. Tree had grown up surrounded by older men, and he had an easy comfort with the older past winners of the Masters, like Palmer. They liked Tree. Bob Goalby and Doug Ford, former Augusta winners, had driven to the funeral together from South Florida in Ford's gleaming white Cadillac. Barbara and Jack Nicklaus sat near the front.

The first two or three rows were filled with Mrs. Tremont's relatives from Chicago, the women in their Marshall Field dresses, hair stiff with super-hold spray, balled baby-blue tissues in their pink hands.

Barbara Nicklaus was called to the pulpit. "I only knew Mrs. Tremont for ten years—many of you knew her far longer," she said. "We met at Augusta, on Tree's first trip there. Helene and I both had fathers who were midwestern schoolteachers, and we hit it off right away. When Tree won that year, Helene and I sat together at the club's Sunday-night winner's dinner. I said, 'Helene, you must be very proud.' She said, 'Oh, my hair's on fire. I especially liked his victory speech, the way he used the word *commiserate.*' "

Mrs. Nicklaus went on in that vein for a while. Near the end, she turned to Tree and said, "Tree, you honor your mother's memory not just with the shots you hit but with your words, your deeds, and your thoughts. I'm lucky enough to have called your mom a friend and to know how much she loved Belinda and the twins—and you."

Lily whispered in my ear, "True class."

Tree was the final speaker. "When people talk about my start in golf, Big Herb is always the star," he said, speaking without notes. "They talk about the day I whacked my father in—how do I put this?—a sensitive area with my driver when I was two, or how he tried to hustle loose change off me on the putting green when I was six. How'd that go for you, Pops?"

There was a ripple of modest laughter through the church.

"But there's a lot that people don't know," Tree said. "They don't know that Mom had more competitive drive in her than Pops and me together. Pops and I, Pops and I. When I finished ninth in that first U.S. Open, she said, 'Well done, Herbert, but you need to work on your lag putting.'

"What people don't know is that Mom bought me every great golf book ever written, started reading them to me before I knew my ABC's, and instilled in me my love of golf history that inspires me to this day.

"They don't know how Mom sewed those Tree logos on my shirts herself when I started out. We had no money. A few years ago, when I bought the big jet, Mom said, 'The important thing to me is that it'll give you more nights home with Belinda and the twins.' Her first time on the plane, she gave me a gift for it, one of those deluxe Scrabble sets where the pieces stay right in place even if there's turbulence.

"Mom was the one who had the vision of what Plant a Tree could do, to help the lives of kids in need. Mom was the one who instilled in me the idea that playing golf was great but that golf alone was not enough.

"I'll never know how much the stress of the last week contributed to Mom's heart attack. I will suffer with that each and every day for the rest of my life. When I saw her in the hospital shortly before she died, Mom could barely talk. It took all of her strength just to whisper to me. She said, 'Do good.' And that's what I plan to do. In her memory. Goodbye, Mom. I will always—"

Grief overwhelmed him. Tree came off the steps of the pulpit and fell into Belinda's arms.

14

"Between now and St. Andrews, the only thing I'll be doing is hanging with Belinda and the kids," Tree told me after the funeral.

He urged me to do the same thing with my threesome. And he urged me to bring Lily to the British Open. Actually, it was pushier than *urge*. Tree wanted us to fly over with him and Belinda on *Flying Tree*. He wanted us to stay with them, at the swanky Old Course Hotel. He wanted us at their big communal dinners. He wanted everybody together: Tree and Belinda and the twins, Finkelman, Big Herb, Norm, Mac, Turner Darlington, me, and all of our significant others. He was paying for everything. He wanted one big happy family.

For nearly two weeks after the funeral, I heard from Tree only the few times he called or texted me. He and Belinda and the kids were swimming. They were waterskiing. They were visiting family in Chicago. They were going to the movies. They were playing mini golf. It was like Tree was making up for lost time—and escaping the pressing realities of his life.

Finkelman, citing Tree's "period of mourning," persuaded the federal prosecutors working the Matteo case to wait until he returned from the Open before getting testimony from him. I had a sell job of my own with Lily. She loved the part about us going to Scotland but not the part about being a kept member of Team Tree. I reminded her that by joining me, she'd be helping Team *Dutra*. On that basis, she signed on.

The plane was like a walk-in refrigerator. You could almost see your breath. As Lily and I boarded, Rocco, crouched in *Flying Tree*'s wide aisle, shot Nerf arrows at us from a toy semi-automatic. Tree, wearing a 1960s-style argyle cardigan, said, "Little man's on alert for terrorists." He looked at his son and said, "These guys have been cleared."

Belinda gave Lily a warm hug, as if they'd known each other for years rather than meeting for the first time. "Tree has told me so much about the wonderful things you do with your students," Belinda said to Lily. "You are my hero." They sat together for the first hour or two and talked about special education, in which Belinda had a keen and particular interest. Walking up and down the plane, Tree was beaming. If he was troubled by anything—the Matteo investigation, his right ankle, his mother's sudden death—you could not tell.

Tree's caddie was sitting in an oversize seat near the emergency exit. I passed him on my way to the loo and asked, "You like the upgrade, Mac?"

He put down his Scotch and said, "This shit makes you soft."

About three hours into the flight, while Lily and I were under a blanket watching *Local Hero*, a stewardess tapped me on the shoulder and said, "Mr. Tremont asked that you join him."

Tree was all the way in the back of plane on a sofa. He motioned for me to sit next to him. "Couple of things I want to show you, Joshie," he said, rummaging around in his backpack. He pulled out a simple bronze urn.

"Is that your Western Open trophy?" I asked.

"It's Mom," he said. He pulled off the lid, and I could see the gray ash. "She loved St. Andrews."

"What about the casket?" I asked.

"For the Chicago relatives. They couldn't handle the idea of cremation."

Families are full of surprises.

"Let me read you something," Tree said.

From his backpack, he produced an unmarked envelope. He carefully removed a thick letter. It must have been five or six pages. I immediately recognized his mother's perfect penmanship. Tree read aloud.

Dear Herbert,

I'm writing this in the Augusta clubhouse. Come July, you'll be heading to the Old Course, trying to win a British Open at St. Andrews. I know that is an important goal for you, and a worthy one. I thought I'd share with you the story of my first and only trip to St. Andrews.

In June 1964 I boarded a bus in Chicago headed for New York. I flew from New York to London and took a train from London to Edinburgh. What a trip—my first time on a plane. It was my first time outside of Illinois!

Eventually I was deposited in front of an ivy-covered dormitory at St. Andrews University, for a summer program. On my first night in the old gray town I tasted ale for the first time, under duress, courtesy of my new roommates. Later that night, a group of us explored the cemetery at the tip of town, walking by candlelight among the old gravestones of the decaying cathedral. Seagulls shrieked in the night. I felt terrified—and alive.

Tree stopped reading. "Do you know that's exactly how I feel when I play in a major, like late on Sunday afternoon? Terrified and alive. I copied the whole letter for you. It's amazing. I just want to read you this one last part."

We spent most Sundays picnicking on a sprawling lawn at the center of town. This "lawn," naturally, was the Old Course, the double fairway of the first and last holes, closed for play on the Sabbath. That summer, as you know, the Open was played in St. Andrews. I saw Jack Nicklaus! My girlfriends and I walked the whole last round with Tony Lema, who won. On one hole, he looked at us. He was like a movie star! It was magical. I thought the course looked like the surface of the moon, but my friend Agnes was a keen golfer and she explained the intricacies of it all. I came to think of it not as a golf course but as an artist's canvas, and I look forward to returning there this summer to see how you decide to paint it.

Tree turned his head and looked out the window into the vast night. Everything raw in his life was starting to bubble up. I tapped him on his thigh to signal consolation and headed back to Lily.

The Old Course Hotel overlooks the seventeenth hole of the Old Course. It's the most American hotel in St. Andrews, with excellent water pressure, unlimited ice, and a wine cellar that rivals Augusta National's. The Tree party took the entire top floor. When I checked in, there was a large envelope waiting for me. At my request, a clipping service had collected all the front pages from the British tabloids since the Matteo story broke. The headlines were so bad they were good. Had I not been the director of communications for Tree Corp, I would have been amused.

The Daily Mail:

TREE FELLED IN DRUG SCANDAL

The Sun:

**AN IMAGE IN SPLINTERS,
A CAREER TURNS TO PULP**

The Daily Record:

TIIMMMBBBEEERRRR!

The Daily Herald:

THERE'S 'JUICE'
IN TREE'S SAP!

Tree was scheduled to have a press conference at noon on Monday, the day we arrived. (I advocated to get it over with early in the week so he could focus on the tournament.) After the press conference, Tree was on the docket to have his much delayed meeting with Richard Fenimore, over lunch. He also wanted to play a late-afternoon practice round, in the peculiar wind and light of a St. Andrews afternoon, when the contenders would be playing on Sunday. A crowded day, just as he liked it.

I feared the press tent would be a slaughterhouse. Every day the British tabloids seize the opportunity to show that the rich, the famous, and the royal aren't any better than the ordinary workingman or -woman, and I was worried that Tree was all teed up for them. I suggested that we have a dry run before his press conference. I didn't think he'd go for it, but his surprising response was "Whatever you say, boss." We made plans for me to come by his suite in the late morning.

I ate breakfast with Norman Henley. Tree paid Norm a nominal retainer, twenty-five grand a year. In the golf-teaching business, his pay was considered a joke. But Norm was the swing coach to the greatest talent in golf history, and he used that fact to promote himself as a golf entrepreneur. His latest thing was "Power of Oneness," a giant hot-pink rubber band that stretched from the top of the golfer's head to the bottom of his feet, to promote "the sensation of mono-oneness" and to cash in on the breast-cancer-awareness craze. Finkelman had come up with the marketing scheme and insisted on a cut of the sales for Tree Corp.

Norm loaded up on the hotel's full Scottish breakfast. Ringing his plate were mushrooms, tomatoes, and potatoes; at its center, fried eggs stared at him like giant squid eyes.

"What's your take on Tree's game?" I asked Norm as I dug into my bowl of Weetabix.

"Let's see," Norm said. "It's July eleventh. The last round of golf he played was on April tenth. I have no idea if this new right ankle can support his swing in the heat of battle. I have no idea how deep the steroid thing is in his head. I have no idea what his mother's death will do to his competitive urge. He hasn't had a good fuck in God knows how long. His practice sessions are half-assed. His back is out of whack. If I were you, I'd get myself to Ladbrokes and see what kind of action you can get on him missing the cut."

At half past ten, I rang the button at Tree's suite. About two minutes later, a chesty redhead with hypnotic hazel eyes answered the door. She was wearing a form-fitting uniform embroidered with the name of the company she worked for: Loving Hands Massage.

"Mr. Tremont's getting a rubdown in the bedroom," she said in an Irish accent. "He asked if you could wait in the living room until we're done?"

From a living room window, I could see a player attempting shots from the Road Hole Bunker, an ancient and celebrated greenside pit beside the seventeenth green where Opens have been often lost and sometimes won. I was writing an e-mail to the editor of *Golf Digest* on my BlackBerry when I heard a commotion inside the bedroom. The door opened, and there was Tree, wearing only a heavy white cotton towel, while his Irish masseuse hastily gathered her things.

"Mr. Tremont, this is all a terrible misunderstanding. Mandy told me she had taken care of you last time, and I thought you liked the full service."

"Just get out," Tree said.

"Please, *please*, don't report this to my supervisors."

"Believe me, I won't," Tree said. "But I'm not gonna pay for this massage, either."

The young woman ran out.

The door closed and Tree said, "She tried to give me a reach-around! My back's knotted up from the flight, I need a legitimate massage, and Kathy Ireland here starts in with the rub-and-tug!"

I tried to conceal my surprise and asked, "You actually stopped her?"

"Yes!" Tree said. "This is a brand-new day, Josh. It's like my mother's watching every move I make. It's creepy, but it's working." The urn with Mrs. Tremont's remains was on the mantel, right at eye level.

Tree's press conference took place in an enormous white tent that was the temporary work station for five hundred reporters from around the world. We caught a break. The first question was from a British reporter who asked about Tree's mother. The next several questions were all touchy-feely ones about Mrs. Tremont, too. One writer asked, "Can you summarize, in a sentence, what your mother gave you?"

Tree said, "If there's anything that's good about me, it's because Helene Tremont was my mom. She gave me what all mothers give. She gave me my life."

In response to another question, he talked about his mother's summer in St. Andrews. "Mom picnicked on the first fairway. She loved it here, and so do I. The Old Course is a grand old lady who still has all her teeth and all her marbles. My mom was that way, too."

Finally, a black-suited German TV reporter with a robotic voice broke the reverie by asking Tree the question that all the American writers had been eager to ask—about Tree's steroid use. Scores of reporters turned their heads to look at him. Tree said, "I wish I could answer your question, but I have to talk to the authorities in the U.S. first, which I'm going to do as soon as I return home. I'm going to tell them everything I know."

The German reporter followed with "You profess love for this course, but if you win, will your victory here not be tainted?"

Tree gave the man a careful look and said, "Lemme guess. You got that song 'Tainted Love' stuck in your head. Good luck with that, sir."

Four hundred and ninety-nine reporters laughed. Tree put the cap back on his water bottle, showed off his famous smile, and moved on to his next appointment.

The Royal and Ancient Golf Club was founded in 1754 and presided over the game everywhere in the world except the United States and Mexico. Its private headquarters, imposing and gray and built to last, was golf's ultimate inner sanctum, patrolled by fossils in tweed seemingly teleported from the nineteenth century. The club's ornate, musty interior did not offer the kind of atmosphere in which Tree could ever feel comfortable. In fact, he wouldn't even change his shoes in the place. Which was precisely why Richard Fenimore chose it for their lunch meeting. The room was drafty and wood-paneled, with an ornate crystal chandelier at its center. Colorless cold cuts, a slab of smoked trout, and six-ounce bottles of Schweppes ginger ale sat on a small buffet table. There was no ice.

"Gentlemen, partake, please," Fenimore said to Tree and Finkelman and me, sweeping an arm grandly toward the inedible spread.

He was a large man with dyed hair that did not move. He was, like Finkelman, trained as a lawyer, and at the Tour he was known as a boardroom warrior. He disguised his ruthlessness with a bland public manner and a vocabulary so pretentious it would have made Mrs. Tremont blush. He was flanked by two grim-looking Tour lieutenants. They handed us business cards. Nobody from our group made a move for the food.

"I'll get right to the point," Fenimore said. "This Matteo matter is problematic for all of us, and we need a resolution that will preserve your high standing, Tree, as well as the outstanding reputation of the PGA Tour and its affiliated properties. I give great credence to your statements that you did nothing more than trust your doctor. The hard truth, as you no doubt know, is that you are ultimately accountable for your person.

"Now—and you assuredly know this, too—our weekly testing for performance-enhancing drugs is done at random. From all available science, we know that any PEDs that might have been administered by your physician, with or without your knowledge, would be out of your system in three to four months."

Fenimore stopped just long enough to take a sip of water. "I understand that it is unlikely that you will be tested this week, at a co-sanctioned event overseas. Back home, I cannot say. A suspension is in the best interests of neither the Tour nor, I assume you might agree, yourself. Thus, my counsel to you: At the conclusion of the British Open, announce that you will not be playing for the rest of the year. Perhaps your Achilles will require more time to heal, I don't know. When you do return to the PGA Tour next year, you will no longer have any reason to worry about providing testers with urine samples. Without a positive test, you will be exonerated by the Tour and in the court of public opinion, and we can all start a new chapter."

Tree took a deep breath and said, "Richie, I gotta tell you." He knew how it infuriated the commissioner when his name was infantilized. "I am repulsed by your suggestion that I leave the Tour in such a disingenuous way. Your whole plot is rooted in mendacity." Helene, surely, was smiling. "I trusted my doctor, as people do. I'm going to testify for the feds, as it is the right—the proper—thing to do."

He looked out the window and saw the inviting links. The wind was up. Players were on the course, hard at work, getting ahead of him. His tone changed. "That fuckhead doctor belongs behind bars. I ain't running from this, Richie. Not only will I not fake an injury, I'm gonna play every damn event from here to the end of the year. The only way I won't is if you suspend me. Are you gonna suspend me?"

Tree then walked out. Finkelman and I were right behind him.

There was a fair amount of nonsense in what Tree had just said. The fact was, he should have been more diligent about Matteo. Tree's uppers and downers and some of his painkillers, for which he hadn't been caught, were on the Tour's banned list, too. Still, faced with the commissioner's bullshit and threats, he gave it right back, impressively.

I knew he was a good actor, but I was learning how good. For years there had been an Arrow TV spot in which Tree was dressed like a robed Moses crossing the Sinai, complete with beard. He tapped his staff against a rock and watched the staff turn into a driver and the surrounding desert into a golf course. Still in his Moses robe, he started hitting long, soaring drives. For the spot's kicker, he looked straight into the camera, arched an eyebrow, and said, "Don't get left behind. Arrow Golf." In the final frames, a gorgeous girl in a golf cart drove up and whisked Tree, smiling slyly, away. He was playing against type as the ultimate family man. People bought it and loved it. Really, he was a very skillful actor.

Golf will keep you honest. A golfer is responsible for keeping an accurate scorecard, but if he doesn't, his playing partners will make sure it's accurate for him. You shoot what you shoot. You can tell stories about your round or not. A Tour player can talk all day about how he hit sixteen greens, but at the end of the day, a 73 is a 73, no matter how well you struck it for all but two holes. Tree had always liked that about golf. How was your day? Sixty-eight. Sure, you could tell a much longer story. Every round of golf is *Canterbury Tales*. You start in one place, go out on some crazy-assed adventure, and come back alive to tell the tale. But the short answer is 68, with two attesting signatures right on the card. A professional's posted score is an accepted fact, like the weight of your apples at the supermarket.

In his first round at the British Open—his first round on his new right ankle, the first round since he was implicated in the Matteo arrest, the first round since his mother died—Tree was flat, and so was his golf. He played in the morning, shot an even-par 72, and was in the middle of the field.

He was moseying along at even par when he reached the twelfth tee in the second round. The twelfth at St. Andrews is miles from civilization, and there weren't many fans around, even for Tree Tremont. He was standing on the tee considering his line when a drunk spectator started railing at him. The man said, "You fookin' cheatah, Tremont, y'are. Ya canna pleh without the magic drugs, ken ya?"

"Shoot yer trap there, wouldya?" Mac McCausland said back. It was the first time I ever heard his Scottish boyhood in his voice.

"Ew, I'm so scared, I am, ya grown mon with a bib," the man said. It was true. The caddies were required to wear bibs. "I used to caddie when I was a wee boy, but then I got me a real job."

"Ignore him, Mac," Tree whispered to his caddie.

A bobby went over to the fan. "That's enoof, it is," the police officer said.

The man put up his hands. He was done.

It wasn't common for Tree to be heckled by fans, but it had happened before. Drunk racists, typically. He carried on, standing over his ball and making confident waggles.

What happened next occurred so fast that I could hardly take it all in, but later, describing it to Lily, I found I could replay it in my mind with every detail in place.

Tree made his backswing. Right in the middle of it, the man screamed, "Ah hoop ya miss the coot!" *I hope you miss the cut.* Tree smoked a chasing 1-iron right in front of the green. With the ball in the air, Mac walked off the tee in the direction of the man and hit him so hard with a single punch to the stomach that he fell to the ground, vomiting beer and spitting blood. Mac retrieved Tree's bag, put it on his shoulder, and gave a quick look at the bobby.

"He had it kooming, the bawbag did," the officer said to the caddie. Choice Scotsman's word for *scrotum*.

Tree put an arm around Mac's shoulder as they walked down the fairway. He made a birdie on twelve and three more before the day was over and shot 68. He shot 66 in the Saturday round and had a six-shot lead as he stood on the seventeenth tee on Sunday. It was a dominating performance, devastatingly so. The sports world was watching, enthralled.

Tree made a two-putt par on seventeen in the final round. He then walked over to his gigantic Arrow Golf bag, unzipped its biggest pocket, and removed the urn containing his mother's remains. He went over to the Road Hole Bunker and, standing on the green above it, looked up for a long moment. Then he looked down toward the heavy, coarse sand. He opened the urn, fell to his knees, and poured out its sandy contents.

When he holed out on the home hole—he was the winner by seven shots with rounds of 72, 68, 66, and 65-—he buried himself in two long hugs, Mac McCausland first, then Belinda. He was gulping for air and crying in the name of his mother. Waiting on the edge of the green was Big Herb with the twins, boy in one arm, girl in the other.

The victory party was subdued. Tree Tremont had the missing piece in his golfing résumé, a British Open win at the Old Course, "the home of golf," as he said so often. On Sunday night, everybody in the Tremont party, plus Jack and Barbara Nicklaus, gathered in Tree and Belinda's room, the Royal and Ancient Suite at the Old Course Hotel. There was smoked salmon and smoked trout and champagne and M&M's and hamburgers and pizza and Coke and Pepsi. Mac was praised over and over and the story of his knockout punch told again and again. Tree thanked his father for teaching him on the sod farm in Brooksville, Florida, how to hit low, into-the-wind British Open draw shots by moving his left thumb on the grip to the right "just a hair."

Big Herb, looking bemused, said, "Is that how I said it, Bo?"

"Something like that," Tree said. He was going through a list in his head. "I want to thank Jack," he said.

The great Nicklaus—in his orthopedic shoes, beer in hand—smiled impishly and asked, "What'd I do now?"

"C'mon, Jack. What didn't you do? How 'bout 1970? Right here. British Open, Old Course. Playoff with Doug Sanders. That argyle sweater. Jimmy Dickinson on your bag. Wind blowing, what, thirty to forty?"

"Fifty-six," Jack said, "in the gusts."

"You hit a three-wood over the green on eighteen," Tree said. "Amazing. With that itty-bitty persimmon head and the balata ball."

"The little ball."

"That's right, you were playing the little British ball back then. What was that ball like in the wind? Hold it, hold it. I'm gonna lose some people here. Anyway, Jack, the example you set, the eighteen majors, you and Barbara, the kids—all of it. You will always be a hero to me. Barbara, you, too. I thought about what you said at Mom's funeral when I was standing there over the Road Hole Bunker."

The room went silent for a moment. It was right on the edge of solemnity, and then Finkelman spoke. "I wanted to ask you about that, Tree. Did you get a permit for that? 'Cause, you know, we have enough legal problems."

Everybody laughed.

"Thank you, Finky. I want to thank Josh for being there before I played my first shot as a pro, and for being here today. Lily, I'm glad to finally meet you. I'd like to see you wear those Birkenstocks in the Augusta clubhouse next year at the Masters. Ideally, at the Sunday-night winner's dinner. Would you do that?"

Lily gave a shy nod.

"I want to give a shout-out to my little Rockman and the incredible Isabella," Tree said. The twins, wrapped up in their DVD (*Big Fat Liar*), paid no attention. Tree looked at them and said to us, "Let sleeping dogs lie, right?"

There were murmurs of agreement.

"But the person I most want to thank is Belinda. My beautiful, hot-blooded, one-of-a-kind Italian wife. Best decision I ever made, asking her to marry me. She keeps the house going, she keeps the kids going, she keeps me going. I hope I do the same for her. Everybody, please raise a glass, your bottle, your jug, whatever you got, and join me in saying to Belinda, *Salute*!"

"*Salute*!"

Tree guzzled from the old Claret Jug, the trophy you get for winning the Open. He passed it on to Belinda, who took a swig and gave it to Jack, whose name had been engraved on it three times.

"Next week, you know, I turn thirty, and we're going to have the biggest blowout party you've ever seen," Tree said. "Hootie's gonna play live. Tiffany Derry, from *Top Chef*? She's going to be cooking—"

"What the fuck?"

It was Belinda. She was reading something on her iPhone. I don't think she even realized she was speaking out loud.

"I don't fucking believe this," she said. "Is this some kind of joke?" Within a few seconds, she was almost hysterical. I was standing beside her and tried to read over her shoulder, but she ran off into the bathroom, locking the door behind her.

Barbara Nicklaus said to Tree, "Jack's hip is bothering him. Thank you for this evening." And they were gone. The party was over.

15

The story was posted on the *Eye of the World* website, which meant that the whole English-speaking world had access to it, and if you wanted to read it in Spanish or Chinese or Korean, all you had to do was click on a flag. Tree, Finkelman, Big Herb, and I read the story that night in the Royal and Ancient Suite right after Belinda stormed off with the twins. Finkelman said, "I will fry that motherfucking Ray Rizzo's balls in a skillet."

GOLFER'S GIRLFRIEND in *EYE* EXCLUSIVE:
MARRIED TREE TREMONT SWINGS AT NIGHT!

By H. H. Peters

(Special to *Eye*)

Married golf hero Tree Tremont has been carrying on a torrid two-year love affair with a Florida party girl, *Eye of the World* has uncovered in a worldwide exclusive. Tree's gal pal Emerson "Emmy" Wright has supplied *Eye* with irrefutable proof of the affair, including graphic audiotapes and raunchy "sext" messages. Tree has become the world's first billionaire athlete largely because of his wholesome family image, but "he is not the person the people think he is," Emmy said in her exclusive interview with *Eye.* "Sex is almost as important to him as golf—or more! He is an animal in bed. Very aggressive, very kinky."

The knockout blonde first met Tremont when she was working as a VIP hostess at the Sporting Gentleman, an upscale nightclub in St. Petersburg, Fla. That's the city where Tree lives what seems a fairy-tale life, with a $61 million yacht (*Off Course*) and a $22 million home (Tree House), his gorgeous Italian bikini-model wife, Belinda, and their two precious kids. They travel the world on their personal jet, *Flying Tree.* But all that wasn't enough for Tree!

Emmy says Tree pursued her relentlessly after their first encounter, sending as many as 20 text messages in a single day, many of them quite racy!

"He would say how much he missed me and needed me and how much he wanted, quote, to put his root in me," Emmy said. "I was young and naive, so I believed everything he told me." Emmy's all of 23.

Tree soon began flying Emmy around the globe for secret liaisons. She would stay in his five-star hotel or on his yacht. "I felt bad sometimes because he was married, but I got caught up in the excitement of the lifestyle and being with a celebrity," said Emmy, who has recently entered beauty school to pursue her lifelong dream of being a Hollywood stylist.

On many occasions Emmy would leave Tree's love nest just as his wife and children were arriving. "Yes, I've had to hide in closets. Once I had to hide in the trunk of his Maybach!" she said, referring to the luxury auto of the stars. "I think Tree got off on the danger of almost getting caught."

Why didn't Tree just leave his wife for his sensual mistress? Money. He makes $150 million a year through endorsements with corporate giants like Coca-Cola, Pepsi, Arrow Golf and Rolex. Tree's family-friendly image is the key to all his deals.

"He told me his wife was 'like an ice queen, in bed and out,' and that I was the one who made him 'feel like a real man,' " said the down-to-earth Emmy.

Those are just short examples of the juicy pillow talk Tree and Emmy shared. "It was much more than just sex, though there was tons of that," she said. "We were soul mates. He told me everything."

A loose-lipped Tree Tremont? "Oh, he loves to talk—when he's done!" the vivacious Emmy exclaimed.

Approached for an interview at the just-completed British Open, where Tree claimed the trophy and $1.4 million, the golfer denied the relationship to *Eye* but didn't elaborate.

Eventually, Emmy grew tired of all the deceit. After consulting with her astrologer/spiritual adviser, she felt compelled to tell his many fans around the world the harsh truth about their beloved hero. "People may think I'm some kind of bunny boiler who is doing this to hurt Tree, but that's not true," Emmy said. "I think I'm helping him. I've seen how stressful it is for him to lead this double life. I heard this in a movie the other night, and I want to share it with Tree and the whole wide world: 'The truth sets you free!' "

16

The flight home was grim. Belinda and the twins were not on it. Tree drank the entire time. When we got to the St. Pete airport, there was a young guy in a puffy coat, beyond a chain-link fence, shouting at Tree and taking pictures with a long lens. Tree was rattled. He said to me, "Don't leave me alone." Lily drove herself home.

It was startling to hear Tree talk like that. Six months earlier, I had been lucky to get him alone for five minutes in a parking lot in Hawaii. I wondered if he could even remember his life before the world was kneeling at his feet, checkbooks open and bra straps coming off. *Don't leave me alone*. He sounded desperate.

He drove slowly and silently from the airport home. I had no idea what he was thinking. When I asked if he knew about the *Eye* story before it was published, he mumbled, "Not really." He stopped the car near the front door. Tree House looked smaller than I remembered. Before getting out, he said, "You know what the worst part is?

I had turned the corner. If it wasn't for Emmy going public, I would have ridden this whole thing out."

Maybe he would have, maybe not. He *had* turned the corner at the British Open, and he might have stayed on Belinda Lane for a while. But his urges could have resurfaced at any moment.

"If you look at the *Eye* story, it's one girl," Tree said. "It's just her word, no real proof of anything, not even a picture."

The story ran with no art, no photo of Emerson and Tree together, which was odd. It was still pretty convincing.

"What about the other girls?" I asked Tree.

He said, "What other girls?"

Was he serious? He knew I knew.

He sat in the car for a long moment, staring at his front door.

The next morning, a Tuesday, Big Herb and I met for breakfast at the Great American Diner. We were in our regular booth. He came in with a Newark Bears hat perched high on his head and the New York and Florida papers under his left arm. He looked worn out. Belinda and the twins had been AWOL since Sunday night.

"I wonder how it happened," I said. "How does this story get published without us hearing about it first?"

I had been rereading the *Eye* story. Most of it rang true. The byline was weird. H. H. Peters. Man or woman? A woman, I guessed. British or American? Maybe an American trying to sound British.

"Somebody with more juice than Tree had to want this story out," Herb said.

"I should have seen it coming," I said.

"Hey, I'm the one who thought Tree could play by Mickey Mantle rules," Big Herb said. "Turns out he's just another celebrity, like some goddamn movie star."

Erratic behavior from movie stars was the *Eye*'s stock-in-trade. The paper could spend weeks on a famous actress throwing a cell phone at a hotel clerk, that sort of thing. They milked the stories so that reading it on the checkout line was a serial event, like watching an afternoon soap opera.

"That rag is gonna rip ten years of hard work right out from under him," Herb said. He looked at my copy of the *Eye,* which I had marked up with various notes. "Have you even heard of this fucking H. H. Peters?"

When he said the name, something suddenly became clear to me: H. H. Peters was a pseudonym.

"Mr. Tremont, I gotta go," I said. I rose and put down a twenty.

Big Herb picked up the bill with his long elegant brown fingers and put it back in my hand. He said, "Don't burn yourself out. We need you for the long run."

I drove straight to the *Review-American* building, got past the sleepy security guard with a casual wave, and walked into the sports department. The only person there was my old boss.

"Joshuamon," Pete said. "I was about to call you, and here you are."

"I read your story."

My cheeks were hot. Pete looked at me and didn't say a thing.

"Peter Henry Hough. Make the first name the last, add an *S,* use initials to make it sound gender-neutral but close enough to real so that those who should know would know."

Inspector Josh Dutra.

"I can neither confirm nor deny," Pete said. "How's your guy doing?"

How was my guy doing? What I wanted to say was *How the hell do you think he's doing?* But I needed information. I knew I'd have to give up something in order to get it.

"Belinda and the kids are out of the house," I said. It was a safe thing to tell him. They'd be spotted soon enough. "I got a question for you, Pete: How'd it land in the *Eye?*"

"Salty," Pete said. "*Eye* goes to Hawaii. They get bubkes. Emmy's photo, the one of her and Amanda with Tree? Photoshopped. *Eye* drops the story. I keep talking to Emmy. I tell the Salted One what she's saying. He's all ears, but he doesn't want the story. Then, after the Masters, he calls me into the big room and says, 'I observed Mr. Tree Tremont from close range at Augusta. If he is the proverbial loose grenade, that is not for *The Review-American* to say. We're a family paper. But if you want to write up your story for another publication, well, live free or die.' "

Pete had Salty Morton down cold. Of course, he had been Pete's publisher for nearly thirty years.

"So you were reporting Emmy and the Matteo story at the same time?"

"Emmy turned me *on* to Matteo. You work at Gents, you look like her, people tell you shit, and some of it's actually true."

Now Pete was giving to me so that I'd give to him. It was an arms race.

"Salty was happy to run the Matteo story," I said.

"More than happy."

"And happy to help you place the other one," I said.

"Delighted," Pete said.

There was a brief silence.

"You met her at Gents, didn't you," I said. I wasn't posing a question. "Emerson."

Pete shrugged.

"Why didn't you tell me the truth?" I asked.

"I had to protect my source," Pete said.

"From your own reporter?" I could feel my blood pressure rising. "There's something else I don't get, Pete. Six months after the Hawaii thing, why'd Emerson still want to go public?"

" 'Cause she was pissed," Pete said. "When Tree's mother died, she wanted to come to the funeral, and Tree wouldn't let her."

I could see Emerson Wright responding that way. I could see the whole thing. Salty Morton, by himself, was just a small-city Florida newspaper publisher with nice hair and a good golf game. Tree Corp could squash him. But Salty Morton linked arm in arm with his rich and powerful golf buddies? They chose governors. They could certainly teach a loose grenade of a golfer some manners. Morton surely knew somebody who could make one useful call to Ray Rizzo and get the lesson started.

I asked, "How'd you get Tree's denial?"

"*Eye* sent a stringer from London to the Open. The guy got Tree coming out of a Porta-John," Pete said. "Tenth tee, first round. Tree blew him off."

What a sleazy move. Still, Tree must have known the *Eye* story was coming. And he went on and won the Open. Talk about an ability to put things in boxes.

"It's a shame you didn't come talk to me first," I said. "Tree was turning things around at home. Might have been a better story for you."

"You're starting to sound like Finky," Pete said. "The guy was not what he said he was, Josh. That's the news here."

"That's bullshit, Pete," I said. "Did Tree ever stand up and say he was some sort of fucking god?"

"He didn't have to," Pete said. "His golf said it for him." That was the crux of it. People confused the perfect golfer for a perfect person.

"You think you broke an important story here," I said. "All you did was catch an athlete sleeping around. I don't even know why you care."

Pete's retort came instantly. "My readers care, Josh," he said. He sounded sympathetic, like he was talking to a lost child. "You've gotten so close to your boss and new best friend that you can't see the big picture anymore. When you were covering him, what was the question you got over and over?"

I knew where Pete was going. I wasn't going to play his game. I said nothing.

"It's always the same," Pete said. "They want to know what the dude is, quote, really like, right? So how good a job were we doing?"

Pete had a point.

He waved me over to his desktop computer. On the dirty plastic edges of his screen were taped photos of his daughters playing Little

League baseball. He went to the *Eye*'s internal website. "Lemme give you a heads-up on this," he said. "It's going live in an hour."

There was a bright red flashing icon on the screen with the message HEAR TREE IN HIS OWN WORDS.

Pete clicked on the red icon. Then came this message: *For mature audiences only. Authenticated audiotape of Emerson Wright and Tree Tremont in a private setting, the wine cellar at Augusta National, Sunday morning at the Masters.*

"What you do here is you click on this button, and for two-ninety-five on PayPal, you hear the two of them," Pete said, sounding like a website tour guide.

The clarity of the recording was fuzzy but understandable. You could hear Emerson saying, "Show me what you'll do to him."

Tree grunting and saying, "Take *that,* Will."

A moan. "Show me."

"Take it, Will."

"Show me!"

"Take it *all,* Will!"

I asked Pete to shut it off.

I drove back to Tree House. I couldn't pretend to be horrified. I hadn't learned anything about him that I didn't already know. What was horrifying was to think that the whole world would find out what Tree Tremont sounded like while having sex in a wine cellar with a woman who was not his wife on the morning before the last round of the Masters, complete with odd references to his afternoon playing partner and chief nemesis.

I briefed Tree and Finkelman about the Augusta audiotape. The vein across Tree's forehead started to pulse. "Fucking Martinsen," he said. "He got in my head when he hired my chef, and he was in my head at Augusta, too. I didn't feel good about my lead. That's the only reason I was saying that shit."

There was nothing to say to that.

"Josh, listen," Finkelman said. I hated when he said *listen.* "Karl

Rove took my call. He said, 'You got one girl claiming an affair. Bury her. Bring in the troops.' So that's what we're doing. We're gonna bury her bullshit *Eye* interview. Tree, that audiotape? It's a total fabrication. They did it with actors. We're gonna bury the tape, too. Turner Darlington's here. He's been talking to his crisis-management people at Arrow. Follow me."

I trailed Finkelman and Tree on the winding walk to the yoga room. Darlington was on the floor, being stretched out by a fetching young Indian woman in a skintight velour sweatsuit. His knees were in his stomach.

"Everyone sit, sit in a circle, hold hands," Darlington said.

We did as instructed. I had Tree to my left—his hand was cold—and the workout girl to my right. Darlington introduced his new assistant, Kamini, an Iyengar yoga master. One of her eyes was blue and the other green.

"I thought we'd start with a little group exercise," Darlington said. "I want everyone to complete this sentence. It begins with the words *I believe*. The question is, where will Tree go in his life? Conjure his greatness. I'll start." He took a dramatic breath and looked all around. "I believe that Tree will be bigger than ever before this is over."

Finkelman said, "I believe that Tree will win more majors than Nicklaus."

"I believe," Kamini said, "and that is enough for me."

I don't know why, but for some reason, my mind drifted to the old overnight police reporter on *The Review-American* from my early days there, a holdover from the '50s who worked in T-shirts on hot summer nights and could get the cops to tell him anything. I imagined him in Tree's yoga room, watching this scene, and waves of unstoppable laughter came over me.

"That's okay, Josh," Darlington said. "In times like these, it's good to be in touch with your inner mirth."

I got myself under control and said, "I believe that Belinda will come back." I didn't actually believe that, but I wanted to get through Darlington's stupid game.

"Tree?" Darlington said.

"I don't know," he said. "Same as Joshie, I guess."

"That's excellent," Darlington said. "Tree, picture Kobe. See him in your mind's eye? He's smiling and successful, right? Maybe he just buried a three. Think of Kobe. Michael Vick. Ben what's-his-name in Pittsburgh. Mike Tyson. So many others, athletes who became even *more* dominant after various peccadilloes. I don't know what your other sponsors will say. I cannot speak for Coke or Pepsi or Rolex or Crest.

"But Arrow? Arrow has never been afraid of controversy, and we will always be behind you, Tree Tremont. Controversy is free marketing but much, *much* more. Controversy humanizes people! You were almost too good, Tree. The reason the Moses spot worked so well is because it played against your perfect image. The American public has the biggest collective case of ADD in the history of humankind. This whole thing will come and go. In your next act, Tree, you will be the comeback kid, like Clinton after Lewinsky. Americans love a comeback story. The *world* loves a comeback story, and the world will *love* the Tree Tremont comeback story."

Darlington looked spent. Poor Tree was mesmerized. Darlington's bullshit did that to people.

"Thank you, Turner Darlington!" Finkelman said. "Thank you for being here, thank you for being *you*. Tree—and you, too, Josh—you should know that Turner and I have been talking about what we're calling Operation Emmy. Operation Emmy is rooted in the traditional good cop, bad cop model, if you will. Officially, we're keeping everything in-house. We want to be in control of the message. And the message is, *No comment.* Radio silence. Our position is that a decade of brand-building cannot and will not be disassembled in a week. We don't think golfers are going to care if Tree had one affair. Why should they? Our internal studies show that forty-eight percent of them have had at least one affair themselves.

"So publicly, we don't dignify anything with a response. Privately, that's a different story. Privately, we use the Arrow people in New York and around the world to undermine every single quote, tweet, text, audiotape, videotape, photo—anything and everything that comes out. Arrow has detectives, ex-cops, former *New York Post* reporters, political operators, people who know how to dig dirt and place it without a trace. We've already retained Emerson Wright's mother as a consultant. Mother and daughter, it turns out, hate each other. Isn't that lucky for us? Tree, Emerson Wright is gonna wish the only time she ever opened her mouth was to fill it with your big multiracial dick."

For a moment there, I saw a familiar expression on Tree's face, the expression you saw on Sunday afternoons when he was in contention, his eyes open wide, taking everything in. "I like where this is going," he said. You could see the fight had returned to his face. "Let's go get a little Florida sun." He led the way to a patio.

Before we even got outside, Nightingale took off his workout jacket and then, bizarrely, his polyester workout T-shirt underneath it. Tree said to me, "Joshie, let me use your phone. Belinda's blocked calls from my number."

He called and got his wife's voice mail. He stood by a door, sun lighting his face, and left a message. "Bel, I gotta talk to you. I'd give up everything to have the chance to make it right with you and the kids. I know you're humiliated. I am, too. Please. What can I do to get you and the kids to come home? I love you." He handed the phone back to me and said, "As long as I have the kids' passports in my safe-deposit box, she can't run off to Italy with them, can she?"

"I'd guess not," I said.

"Okay, bro." He did a little jock's jog, with a big shoulder bounce, and caught up with Turner and Finky, getting water bottles from an outdoor refrigerator.

Kamini approached me. I didn't know which eye to focus on. "The soul of a woman lives in her secrets," she said. "That is what we say in India. Maybe that will help you help your friend?"

I had no idea what it meant, but it sounded good.

The next few days passed in a blizzard of nothingness. Finkelman and I sat in the big living room at Tree House, and I listened to him droning on and on with federal prosecutors, trying to limit the scope of Tree's cooperation. I surfed the Internet for hours on end or furiously typed e-mails to reporters and editors and producers, looking busy but accomplishing nothing. Tree wandered in and out, doing sudoku puzzles out of a book, drinking Buds, stealing looks at his iPhone every few minutes. Belinda had not returned a single call or text, and he had sent her dozens. There were stories on websites about her interviewing divorce lawyers. Others had her partying with friends in Miami. The fight was gone again from Tree's face. In its place was three days' worth of stubble.

I was as lost as he was. What are you supposed to do when your boss, one of the most famous people in the world, is in a marital shit storm being watched by millions? The bloggers typed away, spewing judgment, some of it vilely racist. All through cyberspace, everyone had the same question: Was the *Eye* story true? Did Tree have a girlfriend? Singular. I tried to change the subject, reminding reporters of Tree's charitable works, the vastness of his athletic accomplishments, his relationships with serious people, such as the president of the United States. I asked them to respect his family's privacy. I got nowhere.

Tree House was normally immaculate, but by the third day, there were empty soda cans and liquor and beer bottles everywhere and trash bins piled high with Chinese-food cartons and pizza boxes. Darlington had told Finkelman to tell Tree to permit only "essential staff" in the house, for security reasons, so the housekeepers weren't coming in. Tree's majordomo was now the dog walker, too.

Things were piling up in every way. I had been struck by the same inertia as Tree. I felt powerless to stop the flood of rumor and innuendo and speculation that was being passed off as news. My callback list had eighty-four names on it, the most recent of which was Larry King.

"Don't call Larry King," Finkelman said. "He never did shit for us, and now he's finally in the old-age home."

"He says he's got marital advice for Tree," I said.

"Call him back," Tree said.

• • •

Lily was weirded out by my hours, by the *Eye* story, and particularly, by the wine-cellar audiotape. Everybody was.

"Look at you," she said during dinner one night.

Our dinner-at-home routine was barely a memory. I was practically living at Tree House. My time with Lily was on the fly and the flow of our conversation stilted. I was guarded. There were things I couldn't talk about.

"You look like you've been wearing the same pants for a week," she said. She was close to correct. "Can you say this work is more satisfying than what you used to do?"

I didn't know how to answer her. It was less satisfying but more involving. The inner turmoil of a celebrated man was on full display for me day after day. It was certainly interesting.

Josh Jr. was spending only one or two nights a week with me, if that. He'd bike to my house after swim practice, his hair soaking wet.

"How'd it go?" I asked him one night after practice.

"It's getting bad out there, Dad. On the starting block, kid next to me's going, 'Take *that,* Will.' " Josh did an Elvis-meets-Eminem pelvic thrust that was actually quite funny.

For a while I worried about how the scandal around Tree might affect Josh, but he was of the generation used to seeing its heroes torn down. To him, Tree was an amazing golfer. Nothing more.

The light on his phone started blinking, and Tree scrolled quickly through his latest text. "Unfuckingbelievable. This is from the boat captain—Belinda's trying to set sail!"

It was late afternoon. He was drinking a beer and wearing sweats. "She's on *Off Course* with the kids. It's still on its mooring. Roll out the wheels, Josh."

I went to the garage. For some reason, faced with many choices, I rolled out the camo-painted Hummer. I hated the Hummer, but I knew Tree liked it. He met me in the driveway, wearing an Arrow T-shirt, an Arrow baseball cap, board shorts, Oakley sunglasses, and a black Rolex Deepsea. He moved me over to the passenger seat with a nod.

We banked the mellow curves of the development and arrived at the guardhouse. There was a buzz of activity on the other side of the gate. I could see three motorcycles parked on the side of the road and a squadron of news vans, SUVs, and Hertz sedans. Emmy's wine-cellar audiotape was drawing them in like flies to horseshit. As the gate swung open, a dozen mangy-looking men surrounded our car and began pressing cameras against the windows. (On my worst day at the paper, that never would have been me.) The flashes were blinding. Tree leaned on the horn and then rolled down his window. "Fuck off, Di killers!" he shouted.

He'd surprise you sometimes with the things he knew. I had never heard him mention anything royal.

"You're gonna make it worse, Tree," I said.

"The fuck I am."

He stepped on the gas, scattering the paparazzi. We raced through the streets of downtown St. Petersburg toward the marina. I looked behind us. We were being trailed by a motorcade, swerving through traffic to keep up. We were approaching a green light at fifty miles an hour when Tree said, "Hang on."

He smashed on the brakes and brought his tank to a sudden screeching stop at Fourth Street and Fourth Avenue, right in the middle of the long green light.

Ptoop. Ptoop. Ptoop. It sounded like we were being hit on all sides. I could hear the awful sounds of crumbling glass and exploding air bags. I felt sick. The Hummer rocked but barely moved.

Within seconds, there was a rap on the driver's side window. It was a St. Petersburg patrolman using a night stick to get Tree's attention. He rolled down the window.

"Sir, I'm going to need your license and registration and ask you to step slowly out of the vehicle."

"I'm not trying to be an asshole here," Tree said, "but I've got an emergency. I'm trying to get to my wife, and I've got these goons with cameras chasing me."

With Tree's beard stubble and hat and glasses, the cop didn't recognize him. Or maybe he did and didn't let on.

"Sir, I'm going to ask you to refrain from using profanity. You've got an emergency, so you slam on your brakes in the middle of a green light?"

"Those guys were tailgaiting me," Tree said.

"So you thought you should take matters into your own hands?" the cop said. He looked at Tree's license. He pressed the button on the walkie-talkie on his shoulder epaulette and called in backup. Then he turned back to Tree. "Mr. Tremont, you're driving with an expired license. You're driving without shoes and without securing your safety restraint. You're operating your vehicle in a reckless manner, causing multiple accidents. Mr. Tremont, have you been drinking?"

"No."

"Mr. Tremont, have you had anything to drink in the past hour?"

"Yes."

"So when I asked you, Mr. Tremont, if you had been drinking and you said no, was that a lie?"

"I gotta get to my kids!"

"Sir, for the second time, on police orders: I'm going to need you to step out of the vehicle."

Then Tree did a dumb thing. And by that I mean the dumbest thing I've ever seen in my life. The light at Fourth and Fourth was red. A motorcycle, a sedan, and a van were semi-embedded in his Hummer. A police cruiser and a uniformed officer were beside it. Tree went for broke. He stepped on the gas pedal and roared away. My shoulders were thrown into the back of the seat. My life was in the hands of a man who was out of control. It wasn't exciting. It was terrifying. Tree's chin was almost on the top of the steering wheel, like a speed racer, with his head bopping up and down and the rapper Brotha Lynch Hung on the CD player. He turned up the volume to an ungodly level while flying down Fourth. The sirens behind us grew louder and louder until they were a screaming chorus, loud enough to drown out Brotha Lynch's crude chants.

• • •

Big Herb went to pick him up. He knew how to get to the police station. It was right near Tropicana Field, where Mr. Tremont often went to watch whomever the Tampa Bay Rays were playing. (He said he could never root for a team that "played at home under a dome.") There had to be fifty photographers at the entrance when Big Herb and Tree walked out to Herb's black Lexus. But the prize winner was the AP shot of Tree on his way in. With his flat-brimmed Arrow hat and stubble and hooded eyes and grim expression—and that great modern fashion accessory, handcuffs—Tree had done the unimaginable. The man who personified country-club values and middle-class aspirations had made himself look like a thug, albeit one with exquisite taste in watches. His Andre LeGrande–issued black Rolex Sea Dweller was nicely on display.

Tree was charged with leaving the scene of an accident, reckless endangerment, failure to obey police orders, and suspicion of driving under the influence of alcohol. Tree permitted the police to draw blood.

The police interrogated me about the drinking Tree had done that day, and I told nothing but the truth. I thought about asking for a lawyer but in the end asked for black coffee. I told them three different ways that Tree had not held me against my will, which led to a whole series of questions about whether I had aided and abetted him. In the end, they settled for my home, office, and cell phone numbers and my promise to make myself available.

Tree was all over CNN and FOX, the networks, Jon Stewart, Jay Leno, for the third time in under a week. First the British Open win and the *Eye* story. Then the audiotape. Now the joyride. In his monologue, David Letterman said, "How dumb is this Tree Tremont guy? He thinks green means stop and red means go, and when a police officer says get out of the car, it actually means floor it. The cops down there in St. Petersburg? They explain to him how it works. So Tree goes, 'Wow, thanks for telling me. Maybe you know this: Is it legal to make secret audiotapes of private sex acts in country-club wine cellars?'"

Tree's nod in his driveway, the one that moved me to the passenger seat, turned out to be costly though it was predictable. He always had to drive.

Lily picked me up from the police station. I had kept it together while in custody. I kept it together when she first saw me. She was in her Toyota truck with its pencil-thin stick shift. I didn't want to go to my house. I didn't want to go to Tree House. I didn't want to go to Lily's apartment. I didn't want to check my messages, my personal e-mail, my work e-mail, my texts, my Twitter account, my Facebook, the Tree Corp website. I just wanted to drive, see the Gulf, be with Lily. She got the truck in fourth and drove north on Gulf Boulevard with her hand on my leg.

We drove past the Don Cesar hotel, the proud old pink lady where Meg and I had spent our wedding night. We drove past the vacationing renters on their condo decks in Treasure Island. We drove past the crowded beach bars in Indian Shores, past old men on jetties fishing for porgies and kids on boogie boards in the warm Gulf water in Belleair Beach. If the life and times of Tree Tremont meant anything to any of them at that moment, it couldn't have been much more than a diversion from their everyday lives, another form of entertainment. I screamed to the roof, "Fuuuuuuck!"

"It's okay, Josh," Lily said, her fingers now on the back of my neck. "It's okay."

The attorneys wasted no time. Finkelman received a terse e-mail from a Rolex lawyer addressed to Tree before he even made it back from police headquarters. It read:

> Rolex appreciates our fruitful years together. Going forward, we will not be able to work together as you are in violation of the Morals Clause of your Contract (Section IX, Clause 2A, page 66). You are to cease and desist from making any public representation that you are associated with Rolex in any shape, manner, or form. To that

> end, we respectfully demand that you do not wear publically the Rolex watches loaned to you by Rolex while you were under your contract, as they were for promotional use only. (Belinda DeCarlo Tremont is welcome to continue to wear the Cosmograph Daytona presented to her should she so desire.) If you continue to wear promotional Rolex watches loaned to you by the Company, you can expect legal action.

When Turner Darlington heard about the arrest, he called Finkelman and said, "Time to lawyer up." He gave the name of an African-American woman in Orlando, Tulip Watkins, "who my people tell me is the best criminal lawyer in the state." *Criminal lawyer.* It sounded so harsh. Of course, it was apt. Tree Tremont had been charged with a crime. Ms. Watkins's nonrefundable retainer was $1 million. "She's expensive," Darlington said, "but she's got a chance of keeping him out of jail." I doubted that. My guess was that the authorities would go out of their way to show that a celebrity like Tree was not above the law.

He was already in a sort of jail. Finkelman had placed an order for four armed security guards to man the perimeter of Tree's property at all times. After Tree returned from police headquarters, he never left Tree House. He'd sleep until ten. He'd spend hours in or around the Jacuzzi. He'd watch *SportsCenter* and Golf Channel all afternoon. Sometimes he'd pop in old clunky videotapes of lessons on the sod farm in Brooksville. He wasn't shaving. He wasn't working out. He certainly wasn't hitting balls.

Meanwhile, the Tree Corp director of communications had pretty much given up on directing communication. The company website still featured stories about Tree's British Open triumph and the few new developments with Plant a Tree. Tree's Twitter feed hadn't been updated since the British Open. Tree had graduated from the sports page, and his scandals had become a global obsession. There wasn't a damn thing I could do to influence the coverage. My job had basically been reduced to hanging out at the house and offering support.

I'd ask Tree if there was anything I could do, anything he'd like to talk about. His answer was always the same: "I'm good." Herb told me he was getting no further with him.

Norm Henley wasn't calling. Jack Nicklaus wasn't calling. Arnold Palmer wasn't calling. Richard Fenimore certainly wasn't calling. Except for Mac McCausland, nobody was calling.

For a lot of the golf people, the problem was not that Tree had an affair with a bimbo. It was that he carried it out at a holy site, the Augusta National clubhouse, and on a holy day, Masters Sunday. One blogger wrote: "It'd be like Clinton taking that intern into the Oval Office on Easter." People were getting hysterical.

For the millions of non-golfers paying attention, the issue wasn't that Tree caused three stalkerazzis to crash into his Hummer. The thinking there was that they had it coming. (The injuries were minor. Still, a handful of civil suits had been filed against Tree Corp and Herbert X. Tremont, Jr.) I had the feeling that a caller on the Sports Animal, 620 AM in Tampa, got to the heart of what people were thinking in one sentence: "Where I got a problem is, you know, who does this guy think he is?" I was learning, in ways I had never known, the deep feelings of resentment people had for Tree Tremont. His fellow pros resented him, golf fans resented him, reporters resented him, people who had never even watched him hit a golf shot especially resented him. That puzzled me. There was much about Tree to like and admire. I truly believed that. I wondered: What did he ever do to them?

17

Belinda decided to come home. For some reason, she called me first.

"Enough is enough," she said. "He needs his wife. Tell him I am returning."

I asked if she thought she should tell him herself.

"No, I will know what to say when I see him. It is his birthday. I want to wish him happy birthday."

I knew it was his birthday. Tree said he'd fire anybody who mentioned it, including his father. The only thing he said he wanted to do for his thirtieth was hit balls alone at night, on the sod farm, by the light of his high beams, the exact way he spent the night of his eighteenth birthday. I was relieved to hear him say he wanted to do something involving a golf club.

On the Sports Animal, an announcer said, "Celebrating birthdays on this twenty-fourth day of July are Zelda Fitzgerald, wife of author F. Scott, who did a lot of drinking at the Don Cesar bar; Jennifer Lopez and her fabulous booty; disgraced slugger Barry Bonds, who hit nine tainted home runs in the Sunshine State; and the even *more* disgraced golfer, our own Tree Tremont, who turns thirty. Happy birthday, Tree."

Tree was convinced Belinda would not return to the house on his birthday or any time soon. "Her lawyers will never let her," he said. But around three P.M. the walkie-talkie from the security team crackled: "Mrs. Tremont and the children have arrived. Permission requested to grant entrance?"

Tree froze at the news. Big Herb snatched the walkie-talkie from the coffee table, pressed a button, and said, "Permission granted." He patted Tree gently on the back. "Go on, Bo. Open the door. Let 'em back in."

The twins bolted from the car with squeals of "Daddy!" They grabbed his legs, and Tree bent over so they couldn't see him sobbing. Rocco raised a hand to his father's cheek and said, "Daddy's got a beard!" Isabella reached for it and said, "It's Rip Van Winkle!"

Tree gave them gentle noogies through their soft hair. They giggled, squirmed away, and ran to their grandfather. Tree stood to face Belinda. When he began to say something, she pressed two perfectly manicured fingers to his lips.

"For better or for worse," she said. "That is what I told the priest, so I am here. I would never let you be away from your family on your birthday."

She looked ravishing. The matronly role of holding the family together suited her.

Belinda turned to Finkelman and me and said, "Thank you for watching over my Tree. Now we need some alone time. Go home. I'm sure your families miss you. Bring them tonight at eight for a birthday supper. We all need some wine and some laughs, no?"

Leaving Tree House on Tree's birthday, I drove at exactly the speed limit, used my turn signal, wore my seat belt, talked on a hands-free phone. I could not afford to get pulled over for anything. I arrived at Lily's apartment and told her about the birthday invitation.

"You have got to be joking, right?" she said. "He cheated on his wife. He could have killed you. Now you want me to be part of their whole charade?"

She was sick of thinking about Tree, looking at pictures of Tree, talking about Tree. My face was in the many Hummer shots all over the Internet. Lily had been fielding calls from worried and nosy friends and family for days.

There was one way to get her to the birthday dinner, and it had the advantage of being truthful. "Belinda likes you," I said. "She's asking you to come. You'd be supporting her."

At St. Andrews, Lily had been surprised to discover how much she enjoyed Belinda's company. She was impressed by Belinda's lack of pretense. (She had only one nanny.) Belinda told Lily about her older brother in Italy with Down syndrome, "the only uncle the twins have." She told Lily about her hope to start a Plant a Tree Foundation in Europe that would create schools across the continent to serve children with special needs.

"Fine," she said, not sounding happy about it.

In a matter of hours, Tree House and its owners underwent a total makeover. Belinda vetoed the security guys' concerns and brought in an army of maids. A team of florists arrived and filled the house with hundreds of white roses. When Lily and I arrived, Belinda was wearing a short skirt with tall boots and a button-front cashmere sweater with a plunging neckline. Tree looked like his old self, clean-shaven and wearing an elegant navy blue suit with a European cut. The twins, in colorful party clothes and freshly groomed, were running around. The house had a giddy energy, and so did Tree.

At dinner, Tree and Belinda and the twins all sat on one side of a long farm table that was intentionally distressed. Lily and I and Finkelman and his wife, Deb, sat on the other side. Big Herb was at the head of the table. The conversation was muted until Herb began telling stories of his courtship with Helene.

"Let me give you the list of all the restaurants in Louisiana where your mother and I could get a table for two, little white schoolteacher from Chicago and this backwoods brother." He held up his hand to start counting but never got to one. "I'm telling you, you guys don't know how good you got it. Your mother and I, what we had was picnics. Now the picnic has got to be about the most sorry thing man ever invented."

There was no staff. Belinda was topping off various wineglasses.

"You got ants and wild hogs in the woods, and you're on some scratchy blanket," Big Herb said. "Tree, I ever tell you where you were conceived?"

"Spare us, Pops, please, I beg you," Tree said.

For a while, I think, we all forgot about the tabloid maelstrom raging on the other side of the hedge. The nine of us sang "Happy Birthday" and ate a chocolate cake that had not a hint of golf in its decorating. Tree opened some gifts. Finkelman and his wife gave him a gift certificate to TJ Maxx "because we know you're such a bargain shopper," Finkelman said.

I gave Tree something he did not have from my bookshelf at home: a rare first-edition 1927 copy of *Down the Fairway*, by Bobby Jones and O. B. Keeler. I had bought it at a yard sale for two dollars. It was worth over a thousand. I imagine Tree knew that. The writing was exquisite, for those who cared about golf, or writing, for that matter.

"I'm touched," Tree said. "My mom read me this book at night when I was in kindergarten. Remember, Pops? When we were in the little house on Pondview? How 'bout that first page?" He closed the book and recited from memory. " 'You may take it from me that there are two kinds of golf; there is golf—and tournament golf. And they are not at all the same thing.' Thanks, Josh. Thank you, Lily. This means the world to me."

Big Herb gave him a copy of the Miles Davis album *Kind of Blue*. The actual record. "Listen to this on a turntable, and you'll never listen to that rap crap in your car again," he said.

"I guess I better buy a turntable," Tree said.

The twins gave him playful cards, pictures they had drawn themselves—a scene on a boat, a scene in a house.

Belinda's gift was last. She handed Tree a heavy beige envelope with nothing on it but an elegant handwritten *T.* Inside was a single sheet of folded paper with one handwritten word: *Later.*

"Okay, kids, time for bed," Tree said quickly, suddenly eager to move the evening along. He took the twins by the hand upstairs.

Belinda brought out Frangelico, Limoncello, Sambuca, some port wines. Everybody was getting pleasantly drunk.

"Let us speak of love," Belinda said.

You could hear the kids squealing upstairs as Tree splashed them with bathwater.

"Deb, what is love to you?" Belinda asked.

Mrs. Andrew Finkelman had hardly spoken all night, and I was curious to hear her.

"I don't know," she said haltingly. "That's so hard."

Her husband cut her off. "Love means never having to say you're sorry," Finkelman said without irony. It was obvious that he had never sat through one of those collegiate screenings of *Love Story* where the audience mocks the movie frame by frame.

Deb attempted to reclaim the floor. She said, "I don't know if this is going to sound corny, but maybe love is family?" She and her husband had two children together and two each from previous marriages. Their house was bedlam. It was no wonder Finkelman worked such long hours.

"How about you, Herb?" Belinda asked. "What is love to you?"

He was silent for a moment and then said, "Love is what you think about when you first wake up. Could be your spouse. Or your partner. Could be alcohol or drugs or whatever you do to escape the daytime world. Could be music, could be books. Could be a sport. Tree, growing up, he woke up and thought about golf. He loved golf. Loved it."

"And what's the first thing you think of when you wake up, Herb?" Belinda asked.

"Coffee," he said.

"After that?"

"Your husband," he said.

"Your son," she said. Belinda looked right at her father-in-law for a long moment. She then turned to Lily and me. "You two. Do you answer as one?"

"Yes," I said.

"No," Lily said.

Lily went first. She talked about the Don Cesar and the mad lengths F. Scott went to get Zelda interested in him, how their love survived the chaos of their lives. She talked about her parents in Northern California. They were in their seventies and went for a walk together every morning. Finally she said, "Maybe love is hope. The hope that two people can be happy together. The hope that a child will grow up, do good, be well. The hope that you can do something better next time than you did the last time, there's love in that. Love is a sort of devotion. It's like a prayer."

The room fell quiet.

"We came up with that together," I said.

Everyone laughed, and Belinda said, "Oh, Joshie, you are a very lucky man." She raised her glass, and everybody else did, too. She said, "To Lily, who has uncovered love."

We drank some more.

"And what about you, Belinda?" Lily asked. "Do you have an answer for your own question?"

"I don't know," Belinda said. "I have thought about it every minute since I left Scotland. You know—you all know—Tree hurt me. My mother, she is the old Italian. She said, 'It is just sex, it is not love.' Of course, that was before the tape in the wine cellar."

Herb, I noticed, responded with a sly smile. You could see how much he admired his daughter-in-law.

"But when I was away from Tree, I missed him. The children missed him. He is a good husband, a good father. A good provider, that goes without saying. He is cheap with himself but not with his good works and not with his love. I have always felt his love. So I have decided to forgive him for this thing with this Emmy woman. We will get through it. Love conquers all."

I wanted to stand and applaud. Herb raised a glass and said solemnly, "To love."

And then things went crazy.

Tree was still upstairs with the kids. He had left his phone on the dining room table. While Belinda spoke of love, it was vibrating again and again. The phone was crawling across the table, toward Belinda, motored by its vibration. When Herb said, "To love," we all emptied our glasses. Belinda returned hers to the table. It was a petite glass, a wineglass in miniature, very fine, streaked with old port. She picked up the phone. I think her intention was simply to remove the nuisance, but her eyes naturally went to the screen. I could see her lips moving as she read something in her adopted language.

She looked up at the grand staircase. Tree was coming down it triumphantly, having just bathed and read to and nighty-nighted the twins. His suit jacket was off, and so were his shoes. He was wearing his suit pants and a fine white shirt with gold cuff links and a gold Rolex President watch, the hours marked by diamonds. (I don't believe he was in violation of his cease-and-desist letter in his own home.)

Belinda dropped the phone, ran to the fireplace, grabbed a poker shaped like a 5-iron, and took a running swing at Tree, thwacking him across his upper thighs and, to use a choice Scottish word, bawbag.

Tree Tremont, one of the most physically imposing people in the world, fell to the floor, doubled over in pain, screaming hysterically. We ran over to try to stop her, but she was in such a rage that she had the strength of an ultimate fighter. She was kicking him in the face with the hard toe of her Christian Louboutin boots, drawing a ghastly amount of blood.

"*Che cazzo vuoi!*" she screamed with every new kick. *The fuck you will*, roughly, I learned later.

Herb came up from behind and grabbed her, pinning her arms against her sides. He tackled her to the ground and sat on her. Then he started shouting battlefield orders at Finkelman and me. "Get him to St. Pete General. Get towels on the wounds. Compress it hard. Keep a cool towel on his forehead. Keep him talking. Don't let him move. I'll tell them you're coming."

When Finkelman and I lifted Tree, he was barely moving. It was like carrying deadweight.

Later, I saw the exact contents of the text message. It was from Amanda.

> Hey birthday boy. Emmy and i are at the hotel. Ur late! I just shaved her. We r wet and waiting 4 u. Can you still go all night old man? Bring magic pills!

18

"Don't tell them a fucking thing," Finkelman said in the car.

He was barking like a mad dog. We were in the Suburban, heading to St. Pete General. Finkelman was driving. We had pushed down the second row of seats so the whole back section was like a makeshift ambulance. Tree was on his back, semiconscious but not talking, bleeding from his mouth and nose where Belinda had given him a particularly fierce kick.

It was a warm, humid summer night. The air-conditioning was blasting. The thick white bath towel in my hands was stained dark red. Tree's blood was under my fingernails. Big Herb called and Finkelman put him on speakerphone. Mr. Tremont asked if Tree was conscious. "He is," I said.

"Thank God," Herb said. I'd never heard him speak of God before. "They're waiting for you at the emergency room entrance. They're going to register him as John X. Smith. I told them I didn't know what happened. Don't say anything different. They'll know it's a domestic. After the joyride, who knows what the police will do."

"*Police?*" Finkelman said. He was screaming. "No police. This cannot get in the paper."

It was going to get in the paper, and it would be on the Internet long before that. Somebody would figure out the identity of John X. Smith, and quickly. Word would get out. Belinda would be interviewed by the authorities. She would either lie or not. You couldn't contain this kind of thing.

"Don't worry about it now," Herb said.

"I *am* worried about it," Finkelman said. "Nobody can see him like this. Nobody!"

"Calm down, Andrew!" Herb said. "Focus on the road. Get him to the hospital. That's what Tree needs right now." He must have been a good soldier. "Lily's going to spend the night at Tree House with the kids. Your wife's driving home. She saw nothing. We've got someone coming to the house for Belinda."

"*What?*" Finkelman said. "Like a fucking therapist? Absolutely not. They can be compelled to testify."

"She's an MD," Herb said. "A psychiatrist."

Medical doctors, as Finkelman knew, could cite doctor-patient privilege to evade police investigators and avoid giving court testimony.

"The hospital's got to understand that this cannot get out," Finkelman said. "We're getting killed on the Fourth and Fourth thing." That was what he called Tree's arrest. "Plus *Eye of the Asshole.* Plus Matteo. If he gets beat up by his wife on top of that, we're flat-out fucked. He's not Tree Tremont anymore, he's a fucking freak show!"

"Andrew, you're talking about my son. Do you know how much blood he's lost? Do you know what's ruptured internally? Is the retina detached? Have you taken his vitals? Is his nose broken? Just get him to the hospital."

I lifted the towel. The bleeding had slowed. I saw Tree roll his head and moan. I lifted the ice pack on his left eye. It was swollen shut. The flesh around it was every weird shade of purple and green. His right eye opened slightly. He said something. It was incomprehensible, but he said something.

"Mr. Tremont," I said. My mind was working fast. "We need to keep this private."

I've probably watched too many movies. At dinner, when Herb toasted, "To love," I thought of *Citizen Kane* and the scene where Orson Welles, as newspaper mogul Charles Foster Kane, says, "A toast, Jedediah, to love on my terms." Much later, when I finally closed my eyes and tried to sleep, I replayed the ride to the hospital in my head and thought of Al Pacino in *The Godfather,* when Michael Corleone returns to New York from Italy and says to Diane Keaton, "I'm working for my father now, Kay." He'd gone to the dark side. When I said to Herb, "We need to keep this private," I was doing about the same, even if the circumstances were far less grand. I'd entered the family business, jumped the border, violated my old principles.

I hadn't been drawn to newspapers to write about sports. Sportswriting was an accident along the way. I'd been drawn to newspapers to cover wars, to file Freedom of Information Act petitions, to right wrongs. To borrow the old newspapering credo, I wanted to comfort the afflicted and afflict the comfortable. I did some of that, modestly, as a young reporter. I settled into the golf beat in middle age because I liked the people, the game, the travel, and the stories, the ones you could print and the ones you couldn't. I joined Tree Corp because of twenty thousand dollars in credit-card debt and the fear that my job at the paper could be the next one cut. Before I knew it, I was inviting Lily, my do-gooder girlfriend, my Kay, to a dinner party where we would be window dressing at a reunion dinner not for an old friend but for my boss's boss and his wife. A dinner party in a house that had more kitchen space than my house had house. And later that night, at the stagey dinner party where we didn't belong in the first place, my do-the-right-thing girlfriend and I were witnesses to a definite crime, no matter how justified Belinda might have been, a crime that I could never mention to anybody, especially not the police, as it could bring down a man and his corporation, the corporation for which I worked.

And what was my deeply logical response to all this when I realized that my boss (Finkelman) was losing it and my boss's boss (Tree Tremont) was *not* going to die? I stood on my knees in the back of a makeshift ambulance, tending to the serious wounds of the most famous athlete in the world, and, via speakerphone, made the ridiculous suggestion that we forgo proper hospital care for a celebrity with a troubled marriage and a gashed face and go underground in the interest of pride and image and money. I'm not saying that I had turned into Michael Corleone, but the truth is, I had a certain power at that moment, and like a monster, I used it.

It was getting near midnight and we were still in the Suburban, driving not toward the hospital but in the opposite direction, to the airport. Tree was moaning and moving. I called Lily. She picked up on the first ring.

"You all right?" I asked.

"The twins are finally asleep. They're a wreck. Where are you?"

"I don't know."

"You're not at the hospital?"

"Lily, listen, this is crazy shit."

"Did you say *listen*?" she said.

"I'm sorry. Tree's okay. We're trying to figure out what to do."

"What are you talking about?" Lily said. "He's *not* okay. I saw him. He needs to be in a hospital."

"Don't talk about seeing him, especially on a cell phone," I said. Again, too many movies. But it was true. A cell phone was dangerous. "I'll call you in the morning. I know how much you must hate this. Belinda needs a friend. You can be her friend."

"I *have* friends! She is not my friend. She's a well-meaning person with too much time, too much money, a violent streak, and a husband with no penis control who signs your paycheck."

All excellent points.

"I'll call you," I said.

Herb felt we should go to Houston. He knew retired army medical doctors there. I didn't like the idea of retired doctors doing things the army way in Texas. I had heard Tree mention an über-rich surgeon in Southampton, on Long Island, whom Tree had met at Shinnecock during the Chefgate U.S. Open. The doctor had a large estate and access to the best people. It was a weekend in summer. They'd all be in their summer homes. Herb didn't hesitate. He said, "I'll tell the pilots to get a flight plan cleared." He met us at the airport.

Tree's wealth and celebrity opened doors with a single call. Dr. Lee Roy Jenkins III, the preppiest black doctor in America (Exeter, Harvard, Yale Medical School, Lenox Hill Hospital) was only too happy to help. He arranged for a Tampa doctor to be with Tree on the ride up on *Flying Tree*. He arranged for a private ambulance to meet us at Islip MacArthur Airport on Long Island. Dr. Jenkins was there, too, medical bag in hand. He was a small man with a shiny bald head and delicate fingers. He had invented a surgical stent that made him jet-rich. He was wearing a bow tie at midnight.

"How are you feeling?" Dr. Jenkins asked Tree on the drive to his house.

"I can't move."

"How many consecutive tournaments did Byron Nelson win in 1945?" Dr. Jenkins asked.

"Eleven."

"What's your mother's maiden name?"

"You trying to get my log-in password?"

"Brain function appears normal," Dr. Jenkins said.

We arrived at the doctor's estate. It was as tasteful as Tree House was opulent, though every bit as big. Tree was wheeled into a ballroom that had been converted into a giant operating room. The lighting was intensely bright, and there were two young doctors on hand, residents working for Dr. Jenkins, and a nurse, all in scrubs. Everybody was tending different wounds and inspecting different parts of the body. It was a flurry of hands. Tree was connected to an IV bag, given blood, and put under anesthetics. Dr. Jenkins gave one of the most famous faces in the world about eighty stitches across the lips and chin and right cheek. The nose, which was broken, was broken again and set. Tree's left eye remained shut and was compressed with ice. Dr. Jenkins said the retina had not detached.

"He's going to need plastic surgery in a week to ten days," he said. "He'll absolutely require it after so many facial stitches. He'll never look exactly the same. The nose will never be identical. He might look better but not the same. As the French say, 'You are never tomorrow who you are today.' Especially true in times like these. The tooth will be a complex cosmetic issue. I'm going to have to call in a specialist friend for that, a DDS/MD. Getting the shading correct is more art than science. But these are only the physiological problems. There will be other issues. Marriage, fatherhood, the fragile mind of the world-class athlete. He will need excellent psychiatric care, as many highly driven people do." He offered these intensely personal insights with deep austerity.

I took a look at Tree. He looked almost unfamiliar with the long line of stitches across his face and without his right front tooth. The man who was the greatest closer in sports history looked like the loser in a third-rate undercard welterweight fight.

Jenkins asked one of the residents to take some "patient photographs," and she started to take some close-ups of Tree's nasal cavity. Finkelman ran up to her and put his palm on the lens, which meant the back of his unsanitized right hand was about an inch from Dr. Jenkins's fresh work.

"Absolutely not," Finkelman said. "No pictures."

Jenkins looked furious.

"Andrew," I said. "Let the doctors do their job."

Finkelman stormed off.

Herb pulled me aside and said, "It's gonna be rough, this next stretch here. I'm telling you, as the chairman of Tree Corp, I want you to fill the void. Do what needs to be done. Tree needs you."

I'd never known that Tree's father was the chairman of Tree Corp. It had never come up in conversation. I'd never seen incorporation papers. But the second he said it, it made sense. He had always been the power behind the curtain, from the day I met him, when he was wandering around Legends Field looking for Mitch Albom, to the Sunday night at Augusta when he told Tree he had to go to Will Martinsen's green-coat ceremony.

Tree needs you. In my twenty-four years at the paper, nobody had ever said they needed me. Most people, I guess, don't hear that in their working lives. All hell was breaking loose, but I was strangely happy.

I woke up wearing new, never-washed creased pajamas in a twin bed in an austere guest cottage on the Jenkins estate. There were no shades in the bedroom, and the early-morning light was streaming in and lighting the planked floors. Finkelman was sleeping soundly in a twin bed on the other side of the room. He was snoring, almost comatose. There was estate stationery on a low plain wooden desk. I made a to-do list.

1. Call Tulip Watkins. So sorry, but Tree cannot make his Monday arraignment!
2. Call Richard Fenimore. Work out suspension deal over arrest/ steroid thing.
3. Call Greenbrier tournament chairman. Cite "personal issues" stemming from recent "legal matter" for withdrawal.
4. Call federal prosecutor on Matteo investigation. Tree wants to cooperate but cannot testify before the grand jury this week.
5. Get Turner Darlington up to speed.
6. Issue press release: Tree is taking "time off." Mention nothing about birthday "party."

My cell phone rang. It was 6:01 on a Sunday morning. It was Pete.

"I got a peculiar call last night," Pete said, drawling and slow. "Somebody at St. Pete Gen said Tree was coming in, but he never made it. Everything all right with you guys?"

"Everything's fine, Pete."

"Is Tree okay?"

The thing about Pete, the thing that made him a great newspaperman, was that he really did care. He cared about Tree. But he cared more about breaking news.

"Pete, I'm writing a press release about it now." It was my first lie since Herb had promoted me. "Can I call you back when I'm done?"

He said that would be fine. "But just so you know," he said, "because the last thing I'd want is for you to be caught unawares, I'm gonna tweet what I know now, that St. Pete Gen got a call from Big Herb, Tree was on his way in but never made it, and the rest is mystery theater."

"Can you give me twenty minutes here?"

"Hey, Josh—remember who you're talking to. I'll grab a shower and a muffin, give you a half hour, how's that?"

"I appreciate that."

"Hey, 'preciate *you*."

I knew Pete's Twitter account. He had maybe thirteen hundred followers. It was a small number but an influential audience. One of his followers was the AP golf writer, and the AP golf writer had access to the world.

I had no time. If the prosecutor in St. Petersburg found out from a *Review-American* reporter that Tree was going to miss his arraignment, he or she would swing back with a vengeance. I sent a text message to Tulip Watkins. (I could text like a teenager now.) I left messages on her cell, home, and office phones. From the guest house, I called the doctor observing Tree overnight. The resident told me Tree was under sedation and stable. His right eye was still shut. The lower part of his face was "swollen like a water balloon." Not what I was hoping to hear. Actual Tree quotes were out of the question. I started typing.

> Tree Tremont announced today that he will "take some private time" to address legal, personal and health issues.
>
> He sustained minor injuries after stumbling on a fireplace tool in his St. Petersburg, Fla., home last night.
>
> Mr. Tremont said he will play in next month's PGA Championship but has not decided which events he'll play leading up it.
>
> "I want to thank everybody for the good wishes they've sent me," Mr. Tremont said. "I guess I'm sort of in the rough here, but you guys know I can usually hack my way out of anything."

I read the press release to Pete before posting it on the Tree Corp website.

"That's it?" Pete said. "You got yourself a flying pig there, Josh, and without a YouTube video, ain't nobody gonna believe it. You got nothing on Herb's call to the hospital. Nothing on the arraignment. Nothing on the fed investigation. Nothing on the possible Tour suspension. Nothing on the state of the marriage. You're giving me pretty much nothing here, and nobody, and I mean *nobody,* is gonna believe that those are Tree quotes. 'Cause we know how he talks. And that ain't it."

"Pete, that's our statement."

Tulip Watkins, criminal attorney, was returning my call. I told Pete I had to go. I clicked over to talk to a total stranger about the criminal charges facing my boss. There was no time for niceties. I was on a deadline of a new sort. I jumped right in.

"What will happen if Tree doesn't make it to his arraignment tomorrow?" I asked.

"One of two things," she said. "They'll either issue a bench warrant for his arrest, or I can try to talk the prosecutor—the state attorney from the Sixth District assigned to the case—into taking a guilty plea. If it goes to trial, we'll win. He didn't leave the scene of an accident. He had a temporary psychotic reaction to the meds he was taking, compounded by acute strain over marital difficulties, complicated by post-euphoria stress disorder, his adrenaline overload from winning the British Open. It'll keep him out of prison, but the public will hate it. If we plea it out, he'll do prison time. Two months would be a guess. Fred Willoughby is the prosecutor. I know him well. His son is playing in the final of his club tennis championship this morning. Unfortunately for us, he's playing a kid he can't beat."

This was the trickle-down theory at work. The kid would lose, the father would be upset, Tree would get no break.

"But if you plea it out," I asked, "nobody sees Tree?"

"Not immediately. They could waive sentencing, but he'd have to surrender for his prison term. That would be the ultimate photo op."

I took a deep breath, exhaled, and said, "Plea it out."

"I'd have to hear that from Tree or Mr. Tremont," Tree's criminal lawyer said.

"Ms. Watkins, I'm a hundred percent certain of this: Tree wants you to plea it out."

We hung up.

I was still in my creased pajamas. Finkelman started stirring. "What's going on?" he asked.

"I put a press release about Tree's injury on the website."

"You put out *what?*"

I realized that Finkelman needed to hear about my promotion from Mr. Tremont and said, "There's breakfast in the big house. Herb wants to talk to you. I told Tulip Watkins to make her best deal with the DA."

Finkelman shot out of bed. "You told her *what*? Are you a complete fucking moron? You're sending him to jail!"

I saw a JENKINS ESTATE crest on his pajamas. He was swimming in his. I looked down. Mine had the crest, too—we were wearing matching pajamas. I ignored him. I could no longer treat Andrew Finkelman as my boss. We were in a crisis, and the chairman had told me to fill in the void.

I checked Pete's Twitter account. It said, *Click here for major Tree news. More trouble than I could possibly convey in 140 characters.*

The click took you to the paper's website. Pete's lede: "All signs point to a full-blown crisis in the life of celebrated golfer Tree Tremont. Last night his father, Herbert Tremont, Sr., made an urgent call to the emergency room at St. Petersburg General Hospital, alerting doctors there to Tremont's imminent arrival. But Tree never showed." And from there, he was off and running. Every fact was correct and every bit of speculation identified as such. It was the perfect modern news story, splashy, personal, and so easy on the eye that you could read it on your phone.

Now it was even more important for Tree to stay underground. In the short run, the media would go crazy. The manhunt for him, widespread since the Fourth and Fourth incident, would mushroom wildly.

I finally understood what Tree meant that day on the boat when he told me you're either on Team Tree or you're the enemy. That was how he had grown up. That was what he knew. No wonder Tree despised team golf, had no relationships with reporters, didn't want real friends on Tour. Everywhere he looked, he saw enemies. Nicklaus, in his day, wasn't like that, but that was a different era and Big Jack was a different kind of person. The Tremonts—father, mother, and son—had their own ideas about what Tree needed to do to be the best player in the world. *Us against the world.* That was their motto.

Finkelman, always looking to brand something, started calling the oceanfront Jenkins estate "the facility." The facility was about six acres, with a main house, a guest house, a barn, and an enormous trampoline on which Dr. Jenkins jumped for stress relief a half hour per day. There were golf carts to take you anywhere you wanted to go. The only access was on a narrow country road. I never even glimpsed the beach. By my fifth day at the compound, I was already worn out by this new life as Tree Corp's wartime consigliere. Every day, all day long, it was me, Big Herb, Finkelman, and a ghoulish-looking Tree, having the same conversations—about the secrecy of the facility, the length of the healing process, the length of the expected prison sentence, the length of the expected Tour suspension, Belinda's whereabouts, the lost income, blah, blah, blah. Had I been Michael Corleone, exiled to Italy after shooting Virgil Sollozzo and Captain McCluskey, I would not have lasted a month (he stayed for years). Before sunrise on Day 6 there, I got in a car, made the hundred-mile drive to LaGuardia Airport, flew to Tampa, rented a car, and drove home. I was desperate to see Lily and Josh.

They were at my house when I arrived, on an oppressively hot Sunday afternoon. It was awkward right from the start. I didn't know what was happening in their daily life, although I had at least an idea. They had no idea what was going on in mine, and there was nothing I could do about it. I started the charcoals, and we sat in the backyard drinking Dairy Inn root beers, a St. Pete specialty that quickly became watery with melted ice. Before long, we moved into the small dark living room, cooled by a loud, humming window unit.

"So you're not gonna tell us where you've been," Lily said.

I knew I couldn't and that Lily would not understand.

Josh said, "Every kid at school knows that you know where he is, and they think I'm lying when I tell them I don't."

"Josh, if I told you, I'd get fired."

"You don't trust me not to say anything."

"It's not that."

"Then what is it?"

"If you knew, people could put a lot of pressure on you. People would pay a lot of money to know where Tree is now."

Josh shook his head and turned his attention to a video game on the living room computer. "You know he's never gonna win again," he said. Then, more under his breath than aloud, "Can't even send me a fucking postcard."

I started to say something about his language but dropped it.

Outside, my charcoal fire was sending up plumes of gray smoke. Thunderstorm clouds were on the afternoon horizon. Why hadn't I just brought home a pizza? No, I had to turn it into an event, like all those other overcompensating asshole fathers who spent too much time away from home and then made some big showboat move to get to a youth-league soccer game that mattered to nobody but the coaches, and maybe not even them.

Lily signaled for me to follow her into the kitchen. It was not a house that offered much privacy. "If I were you, I'd be thinking hard about the costs of this job of yours," she said.

Her words were in my head for the next three hours I was home. While driving back to the airport in the summer dusk light, Finkelman called and asked, "When the fuck you getting back here?" Some day off.

• • •

The next week brought more of the same. One evening on the *NBC Nightly News*, Brian Williams concluded the broadcast with a sort of missing person report.

"Taking our inspiration from the popular children's book *Where's Waldo?*, tonight we ask, 'Where's Herbert?' Today marks the ninth consecutive day that golfing great Herbert 'Tree' Tremont has not been seen in public. Anywhere. Not by the literally hundreds of reporters trying to track him down. Not by legal authorities in St. Petersburg, Florida, where he faces a raft of criminal charges. Not by drug-testing officials from the PGA Tour. Not by his millions of fans. Calls and messages left with his management team, by us and other news organizations, have gone ignored. So if you see Mr. Tremont, log on to the 'Where's Herbert?' link on the NBC news website, and tell him to call home, would ya? I'm Brian Williams. Good night."

His humor was welcome, given what was out there. Internet conspiracy theorists had Tree on *Off Course* and the boat in the vicinity of Bora Bora. Others claimed that Belinda and Tree were in a villa in Tuscany, or that Richard Fenimore was holding him hostage in a drug-testing lab. One report claimed that Tree was at an ashram in India with Heather Graham. Some of the golf writers theorized that he was holed up in Arnold Palmer's house in Latrobe, in western Pennsylvania, or in the Crow's Nest, an attic suite in the Augusta National clubhouse. But there was not a single report anywhere on the Internet that placed Tree Tremont on the East End of Long Island. Dr. Lee Roy Jenkins III had either the most discreet or the most oblivious gardeners and housekeepers in America.

Tree watched the Williams report the next morning on the Internet and called me right away. "Did you see that shit? That's fucking hilarious. Are those the same guys who write *Saturday Night Live?*"

He was serious all the way around. He actually did find the Brian Williams report funny. And he actually did wonder whether *NBC News* and *SNL* shared a writing staff.

SNL was killing him. They had a bit that was oddly accurate, more so than anything I'd read by reporters. They had Tree (cast member Kenan Thompson) getting beaten up by Belinda (guest host Brooklyn Decker) and taking up full-time residence in the plush family doghouse, where Tree, living with a runty poodle named Mr. Martinsen, liked life so much that he didn't want to leave. "The bitch owns me," the Tree character said as Belinda put a leash on him. "But I got a bitch of my own." The final frames showed Tree sniffing underneath Mr. Martinsen's mangy tail—the actual tail of an actual dog. I thought it was gross. Tree loved it. He watched it over and over, laughing hysterically each time. Maybe he was making up for his lost childhood, I don't know. But in the last few days, he was looser than I had ever seen him.

One afternoon he called and said, "Dude, come up to the house, I got something to show you."

When I arrived, he had a big red piece of tape over his mouth. In a muffled voice, he said, "Pull it off." I did. He flashed his old, brilliant $5 million Crest smile.

"Congratulations," I said. "Maybe the reverse tooth fairy will visit you."

"It's better," Tree said. "It's stronger. It's fake."

The fact that Crest had pulled the plug on his contract didn't seem to bother him in the slightest. Half of his sponsors had dropped him. Finkelman was in a constant state of panic. He had lost maybe ten pounds since Tree's birthday, and he had been painfully skinny before it. But Tree, with his life unraveling, seemed liberated. Or unhinged. It was hard to tell.

I had noticed that Tree was becoming friendly with one of Dr. Jenkins's residents—Miles, a freckled young man who said he'd spent his summers as a teen caddying at Shinnecock Hills. Miles and Tree would regularly fall into discussions about the course.

"How 'bout that eighth hole?" Tree said to the young doctor.

"The eighth," the doctor said. He seemed to go through the course hole by hole in his head.

Tree didn't have to do anything like that. He could close his eyes and picture every hole he had ever played, right down to the positions of the bunkers and the slope of the green. He had thousands of holes cataloged mentally. He was a savant. He'd talk about course architects like foodies talked about chefs. He talked about William Flynn as if the great designer of Shinecock Hills were still alive.

"What Flynn wants on the eighth is to get in your head," Tree said. "You've just come off that little itty-bitty seventh, with that teensy-weensy green, and you're feeling all delicate and mellow, but then you get on that eighth tee and you got to rev your engine, you know?"

It was a pleasure just to hear Tree talking about golf, acknowledging the game that had made him.

"And that's one of the hardest things to do in golf, switch gears. But on that number eight hole, you gotta smash one off the tee. And if you do it right, you can attack the green, and that's critical, because how many legitimate birdie chances are you gonna have at Shinny? Four if you're lucky, right?"

"I couldn't say," Miles said, trying to answer Tree's rhetorical question. "I've never broken a hundred there. In the caddie tournament one year, me and another guy, we had to walk in from sixteen because we ran out of balls."

Tree laughed. They were buddies of a sort. Early one morning at breakfast, I saw Miles give Tree a little brown glass bottle of pills. I didn't think much of it. Miles was his doctor. After breakfast, Finkelman and Big Herb departed for Manhattan. They were heading in for a series of meetings with sponsors who wanted their endorsement money back, citing breach of contract. Over the preceding days, the expedition had been planned with military rigor.

My job was to keep an eye on Tree. They were barely down the driveway when he put an arm around me. "Joshie, I got a surprise for you. I know you're going a little crazy here at the facility, so I've arranged for you to play Shinnecock Hills today. Miles has a buddy who's a member. He told this guy your name is Josh Dent and that you're the sports editor of *The St. Petersburg Review-American* and you're here on vacation. Just go with it. You're teeing off in an hour. Miles brought his clubs for you to use."

I had a bad feeling about leaving Tree unsupervised, but I was going stir crazy, and more to the point, I'd been dying to play Shinnecock for years. A perk of my beat was that I often got to play America's best courses, usually on the Monday after a tournament. That was how I'd been able to play Augusta National, Oakmont, and other super-private, venerated courses that made people sick with envy when they learned I had hacked my way around them. But I had never sniffed Shinny. I couldn't pass it up. I ran to the guesthouse to try to find a clean shirt.

I was peppering the driving range with excited slices when my cell phone bleated. Under normal circumstances, I would have left it in the car. A ringing phone on a golf course is as welcome as a burping choirmaster in church. But these were not ordinary times. It was Tulip Watkins, criminal attorney.

She said, "Fred Willoughby, the prosecutor, wants to make a deal in your so-called Fourth and Fourth incident. I need to talk to Tree immediately. No intermediaries. He's not answering his phone."

"Let me try," I said. "I'll call you back."

I left two voice mails for Tree and sent him two texts that went unanswered. Miles wasn't answering. No one at the house was, including Dr. Jenkins. I bid adieu to my Shinnecock host, a genial pink-cheeked Wall Street banker. He said I could meet him later on the tenth tee, but I doubted that was going to happen. I drove back to the estate, furious.

There was a white Town Car parked in front of the main entrance, with a Middle Eastern driver behind the wheel. I knocked on the window and said, "Excuse me, sir, can I help you?"

"I wait here for the womens, yes?"

I bolted into the house. It was deserted. Tree must have sent all the staff home. I barged into his room without knocking. He was on the bed with Emmy and Amanda. They were dressed like strippers near the end of a show. Tree was wearing one of his Sunday victory shirts—the black shirt with the ridiculous red armbands—in a most unconventional way, his erection sticking out of one of the armholes. Emmy was the first to see me. No surprise, no modesty, just a naughty smile. "Play that Funky Music" was blaring from Tree's MacBook. Emerson did that curling index-finger thing at me and sang, "To disco down and check out the show / Yeah, and they was dancing—"

There were lighted candles and bottles of oil and lotion on a nightstand. Tree said, "That was fast. You run out of balls?" He laughed at his own joke. He seemed stoned or drunk or something.

"Tree, listen—Tulip Watkins needs to speak to you. Right away."

"What about?"

"I don't exactly know—maybe the length of your potential prison sentence?"

Amanda and Emmy slid off the bed, their perfect bodies glistening with oil. I tried not to look. "We're gonna get in the bath, give you two a little space," Emmy said. "Join us when you can."

I was sure she was talking to Tree, but for a moment I fantasized otherwise. The bathroom door closed. I looked at Tree.

"Hey," he said. "I needed girls I could trust."

I thought he was trying to be funny, although I wasn't certain. I said, "Have you completely lost it? You're gonna trust Emerson Wright? After she sold you out to the *Eye*?"

It was not easy, trying to have a serious conversation with a man wearing a golf shirt as underwear.

"Like she says, I had the *Eye* thing coming to me," Tree said. "I should have invited her to Mom's funeral." He shrugged. "What can I tell you, Joshie? You know my thing for her. And with Amanda caddying for her? Who could say no?"

On a coffee table beside me was the brown glass bottle Miles had slipped him at breakfast. When Tree saw me looking at it, he said, "You'll never guess what that shit is. Cialis! Maybe you and Finky can lock down an endorsement deal for me?"

He had turned into a comedian.

"Tree, you gotta stop thinking with your dick," I said. " 'Who could say no?' This is incredibly serious. We're one leak away from the tabs knocking the walls down here."

His face was still puffy, healing from the plastic surgery. He didn't look quite real.

"I know this is serious," Tree said. "Very serious. Doc's people are due back in a couple of hours. Finky and Pops, too. Me and the girls are not quite done. Go play some golf, Josh." He strolled into the bathroom.

"What about Watkins?" I yelled after him.

The only thing I heard was the sound of splashing water.

19

I was Googling "sex addiction" in my temporary office in the facility when Dr. Jenkins's main housekeeper delivered a letter sent by FedEx. This was an unwelcome and surprising development, since nobody was supposed to know where we were.

Naturally, the letter was from Amanda and Emerson. It was handwritten and addressed to Tree. Copies had been sent to Big Herb, Finkelman, and me.

Dear Tree,

Great seeing you last week! Your face looks fine and we can tell you've still got your "A game!"

We have some super "action shots" of our "threesome" at the "facility." Just wanted to know what you'd like us to do with them. (See sample photos, attached.) We know certain Publications would be interested in them. But maybe you'd prefer to have them for your private collection? Let us know what's best for YOU.

If Southampton turns out to be our "last round" together what a way to go out! Your call—we'd love to "play" again sometime. Maybe in a "foursome"? We hope you like all our golf references! We worked hard on them and now we're going to "sign our card!"

Hugs & kisses,
A & E

"A lawyer wrote that letter," I said to Finkelman.

We were in the war room (Finkelman's phrase), a sunny living room with silk drapes and plush sofas in pastel colors. By then I knew every single item of clothing Finkelman owned, right down to his socks. We were beyond sick of each other's company, and my newly elevated status with Herb wasn't helping matters.

"You think a lawyer wrote that?" Finkelman said. "You find me any law school grad who writes that bad, I'll show you a loser who never passed the bar."

"This is fake bad writing, not authentic bad writing," I said. "There's not a comma in it, except in that sentence in parentheses. *See sample photos, comma, attached.* That sentence from those two? No way. That's a lawyer, slipping up."

In his silence, I could tell that Finkelman saw my point and understood its implications. Amanda and Emerson on their own could do a lot of damage. Amanda and Emerson backed by a ruthless extortionist lawyer? No good could come from that.

In the backyard, I saw Tree in a chaise longue, a Sony PlayStation on his lap, a bottle of Hawaiian Tropic suntan lotion at his side. He was living out one of his oldest jokes: He was actually working on his tan.

The next morning brought another FedEx delivery. Same deal as the previous day: the package contained a letter to Tree, with copies sent to Finkelman, Herb, and me. This one was typed.

Dear Mr. Tremont:

My name is Daisy Slauter. We met in Dr. Matteo's Orlando office. I was his phlebotomist. I did your pre-surgical blood work. You noted the shark tattoo on my inside left forearm. You asked me if I was interested in joining you for drinks at Thee Doll House during my afternoon break. I told you that would not be possible. You may recall that we visited the basement custodian's room instead.

As you have not responded to my calls or e-mails, I have been unable to discuss with you the results of your blood work, which revealed inconsistencies with the boxes you checked on your pre-surgical "med list."

Before your first treatment by Dr. Matteo, your readings for the following drugs exceeded the normal safe maximum by 100 to 300 percent:

- *Tetrahydrogestrinone, the steroid cream commonly known as the Clear;*
- *Methylenedioxymethamphetamine, commonly known as Ecstasy;*
- *Zolpidem, a sleep aid;*
- *Dutasteride, used in the treatment of baldness;*
- *Dopamine, a stimulant;*
- *Sildenafil, used to treat erectile dysfunction.*

Your human growth hormone (HGH) and testosterone results were also cause for concern. The normal HGH range for a healthy, active 30-year-old male is 40–110 nanograms per milliliter. Your HGH level measured 875 ngs/ml.

Likewise, normal testosterone readings are 250 to 1,000 ngs/deciliter. Weight lifters and athletes often have elevated readings. Your result, 2,605 ngs/dl, is by far the highest ever recorded in Dr. Matteo's office.

Your midday blood alcohol level was .04 percent.

You or your designated representative (requiring a signed release) are welcome to call me at your convenience to discuss these results and what you would like me to do with them.

I didn't think two FedExed letters in as many days (as the AP always configures such things) could be a coincidence. Something evil was at work.

Another day, another FedEx package sent to our supposedly secret location. All the packages, I was able to determine by calling FedEx, had been dropped in the same box in downtown Los Angeles.

The third delivery contained just one letter, for Tree, who brought it to Finkelman, his father, and me. I had never seen such a distressed look on his face, not even after he lost the Masters to Will Martinsen. The letter was from Norm Henley, Tree's golf teacher.

Dear Tree,

Sorry to be out of touch. But with you not playing, there didn't seem like much for me to do.

Just wanted you to know I'm doing good with the Power of Oneness band. I sold four or five myself last week. I'm saving up for a Golf Channel infomercial. Oneness could probably help you from firing that left hip too early on the downswing. But we can talk about that another time.

One quick thing. Remember the second round at the Masters this year? Best I've seen you swing. Ever. Even with the ankle "injury." With the driver, you're just a hair short of parallel at the top, right where I want you.

Anyways, Finkelman called me over to the house that night, said you had some lady friends who needed a lift out of town. So I come over in the Navigator.

While I'm waiting on them, I'm taping some notes into that little tape recorder you gave me, about the 29 on the front nine, the double eagle on thirteen, knee flex, head dip, all the usual stuff. The two girls get in the car.

The Brunette says to the Blonde, "Can you believe that thing he said?" And then she imitates your voice and says, "Have you guys ever done a group thing with an Asian dude?"

And the Blonde goes, "You know he hangs with these Asian guys at Gents."

And the Brunette nods and she's still doing your voice and she says, "With a skinny little Asian dude, probably wouldn't hurt that bad. Not that I'm gay or nothing. Just curious." And the two girls start laughing like monkeys.

Reason I know this so accurate is because it all got recorded by accident on that little tape recorder. I can't hardly find the on/off switch. I just figured you'd want to know what those girls were saying.

So let me know what you want me to do with that tape and all and GET WELL SOON.

See you at the PGA, right?

Golfingly yours,
Norm Henley

I remembered what Cari Coleman, the cocktail waitress at Gents, had told me—that Tree would sometimes come in with two nerdy Asian guys wearing glasses. I looked at Tree. I'd never seen him more morose, like he knew his little bender was over.

With perfect gallows humor, Mr. Tremont said, "I believe we've entered the bad-to-worse phase."

20

"Norm, what's up? It's me," Tree said.

We had Tree call Norm on a speakerphone. Herb and Finkelman and I were all in the room, recording it.

"Pardsy!" Norm said. "You just made me two hundred bucks. Hank Haney gave me two to one, said you'd never call." He sounded like they'd been talking every day.

"Oh, I'm Pardsy again?" Tree said. "After that shit you wrote me?" His anger was surging through.

"You know I didn't write that," Norm said. "They made me write it."

"Bullshit. It's your handwriting and your signature."

We had told Tree that he had to tell Henley he was being taped, and Tree said, "Please note you are on a recorded line to ensure customer satisfaction."

"What?" Norm said. He was understandably confused.

"You told Hank Haney, Norm? Beautiful. Haney tells Charles Barkley. Barkley tells *everybody*."

"I don't think Hank would do that," Norm said.

"That letter, Norm. What the fuck?"

"I kinda knew the one girl from Gents," Norm said.

"The blonde."

"The blonde. And after you disappeared, she calls me and says a lawyer friend of hers is putting together like a book about your off-course life. That's how they put it."

"Why didn't you tell them to fuck off?" It took the prospect of being outed as someone interested in gay male sex to get Tree to finally take his predicament seriously.

"C'mon, Tree, don't make this harder for I than it already is."

"Harder for me," Tree said.

"Harder for you?" Norm said.

"Not harder for I. Harder for me."

"I must have bad reception here," Norm said. "I got no idea what you're talking about. If you have dick problems, that's none of my business. Like I tell people, you were always good on the range. But the lady lawyer asks me a question, I got to tell her the truth, right? So that's all this is."

"Norm, I swear to Christ, you are either a genius or stupider than my fucking sand wedge. You got two drunk girls talking on a tape about me supposedly saying I want to get boned by some Asian dude, which is the craziest shit I ever heard. You're telling a lawyer about it and now Hank Haney. You're slandering me and blackmailing me. You're hurting my rep and trying to get in my wallet. And you know what? That shit's illegal."

It was a pleasure to hear Tree fighting back.

"Whoa, right there," Norm said. "Illegal? That's rich. Last time I saw you, you were coming out of the St. Pete jail. I never got my British Open bonus. Finky said he'd get me a marketing guy for the Power of Oneness band. Never happened. You haven't told me crap about when you're gonna play again. What am I supposed to do? I got bills, like everybody else. I just want to get paid."

"Get in line, asshole."

"I'm the asshole?" Norm said. "You stiff me, but I'm the asshole?"

"You didn't even come to my mother's funeral."

"You know what? The lady lawyer told me I should just give you her number, so that's what I'm gonna do."

" 'Cause you always do what the lady lawyer tells you to do."

"Hey, she's the law expert. You got a pencil? She's out of L.A. Norma Blackwell."

When Finkelman heard the name, he took the little pink throw pillow that was wedged between his shaking knees and threw it like a Frisbee across the room. It struck a desk lamp that crashed on its side. Papers fluttered to the ground.

"Norma Blackwell is a one-man wrecking crew," Finkelman said as soon as Tree hung up the phone. I knew the name. Anybody with basic cable did. As a lawyer, she did it all, took on any client, as long as there was the promise of a huge payout and TV time. "She's me with a cunt times a hundred," Finkelman said.

In addition to being very crappy news, it was the most modest thing I had ever heard Andrew Finkelman say.

Finkelman thought we should have a face-to-face meeting with Miss Norma, as he called her. "I want to turn her around," he said. She was eager to do it.

He wanted her to come to the facility, since she knew where it was, and to have Tree leave the Jenkins estate presented security risks. It had been almost two weeks since Tree had arrived with his gashed face. It still looked mushy and inflated, but he was not the multicolored freak show he had been. I felt that if Norma Blackwell saw Tree in hiding, it would only embolden her, and she was already holding three aces (A&E, Shark Lady, and Norm). We took it to the Tremonts. Father and son both voted in favor of going off-campus. I got us ready for our road trip.

I rented an old tan Buick from Jenkins's head pool man. It would not draw attention even with its maroon-tinted windows. Tree wanted to drive, but we needed him in the backseat, where other drivers on the Long Island Expressway would not be able to see him.

I chose a thoroughly nondescript hotel, the Marriott in Islandia, right off the LIE service road, about forty miles from the facility. I had stayed in the hotel several times, for U.S. Opens at Shinnecock Hills and Bethpage, and I knew it would suit our needs. It featured a staff who knew how to mind their own business and then some. Tree wore a beard I had ordered from a costume shop, an oversize New York Mets cap, and large dark sunglasses. He made it from the Buick to the hotel elevator without incident, although a kid in a Yankees hat saw him and said with unusual bile, "Mets *suck*."

The great Norma Blackwell, born to an aristocratic Hungarian family, arrived in our suite at one P.M., two hours after us and right on time. (We spent the time eating and rehearsing.) She was in her mid-sixties, wearing war paint makeup and a hideous lavender suit jacket with shoulder pads so puffy she looked like a high school linebacker.

Finkelman, the lawyer in our group, jumped right in. "We have no recording devices," he said. "Would you like to frisk us?"

"No, I'll trust you on that," she said in her accented English.

"Well, we'd like to frisk you, Norma," he said.

She removed a tiny microphone from the inside lapel of her suit jacket and placed it on a coffee table. "You're good, Mr. Finkelman."

"We'd still like to frisk you," he said.

She consented with a nod, and Finkelman did a pat-down more thorough than anything in the TSA handbook.

"Have you grown a beard, Mr. Tremont?" Norma said to Tree.

"Mr. Tremont is here to observe, not to speak, Norma," Finkelman said.

"Very well, then." She looked around the thoroughly charmless suite. "I *love* what they've done with the place," she said. I suppressed a laugh. "Should we order up some food, maybe some wine or beer? My treat."

"That won't be necessary, Norma," Finkelman said. "This won't take that long."

"Oh," Norma said, pretending to be offended. "Since you seem to know how this will play out, why don't you start, Mr. Finkelman."

"Thank you, Norma, I will."

He had told us in our dry run that he'd be using her first name at every opportunity, to establish authority. Now that he was doing it, he sounded utterly ridiculous.

"Norma, you're trying to extort my client. When you dropped those letters in a FedEx dropbox at Wilshire and Fairfax, in Los Angeles, 90048, and had them sent to Southampton, New York, 11968, you engaged in interstate commerce and ran afoul of federal interstate commerce law."

"I'm sorry, Mr. Finkelman, I'm confused."

"Really, Norma? The great Yale Law School grad is confused?"

Finkelman had gone to law school at Michigan State.

Norma nodded slowly and surely. "You said I was trying to extort your client," she said. "You're not suggesting that anything in those letters violates the 1946 Hobbs Act, are you? Because I think you'll find that my clients wrote letters to your client on subjects of mutual interest and that there are no terms of business in any of those letters."

Norma Blackwell was on a roll, and it was not pretty, not for us. "But since you've brought up the subject of business—*commerce,* to use your word—let me tell you what I believe to be true, and what *I* have come here to tell *you,* face-to-face," she said. "I believe that you could buy the memory card containing certain pictures for two million dollars, although that's a special price for this week only. I believe that you could buy the results to Mr. Tremont's blood work for one million, but again, that's a limited-time offer. As for Mr. Henley's recording, I believe he would settle for one million for it and the Casio device in which it sits, this week only."

Tree was running his hand through his fake beard. Herb was shaking his head. I was thinking that if the photos and the test results and the gay-pride tape could be disappeared for $4 million, it was a bargain. Because if those things went public, it would cost us more than ten times that in lost income.

Finkelman said, "Four million, Norma? Even for you, isn't that a little outrageous?"

"That's the price this week," Norma Blackwell said. "If payment is not made in full by high noon on Friday, the price will go up, and I fear that there may be a reprisal of the Ten Plagues. I suspect Mr. Finkelman is familiar with the Ten Plagues. Are you familiar with the Ten Plagues, Mr. Tremont?"

"He's here to observe, not to speak," Finkelman said.

His voice was terribly soft. He was done using her given name.

The ride back to the Jenkins facility was tense. We got caught in a horrible LIE traffic jam. The air-conditioning in the pool man's Buick broke. I had to engage the child lock so that Tree couldn't roll down his tinted window. We had nothing to drink. Everyone was cranky.

Finkelman was absentmindedly singing the Michigan State fight song. ("Spartan teams are bound to win. They're fighting with a vim!") Big Herb was silent and stewing, staring at the scrub oaks and scrub pines on the side of the road. Tree couldn't stop talking about the vile Norm Henley. He said, "I guess I'm not shocked that those bitches would turn on me, but Norm? Where's the loyalty? If it wasn't for me, he'd still be teaching Kermit fucking Zarley."

You have to give Tree credit. Kermit Zarley had won twice on Tour long before Tree was even born. Tree knew golf—he knew it deeply.

By the time we made it back to Southampton, Tree and Finkelman had convinced themselves that Blackwell was bluffing about the prices and the plagues. I wasn't so sure.

"For four million, we can make all of this go away," I said. I gave my take on the accounting: Pay something now or lose a lot more later. "It's actually a bargain. I think you should write the check. You can make that in a week in China when you're back in action." Chinese tournament directors would pay anything to get Tree in their events.

Herb was shaking his head east and west, and Tree said, "No way. They've taken away my kids. They're killing my rep. They're not gonna get my money, too. I earned that money. That's payback for ten thousand hours on that sod farm. All those leeches did was have sex in nice hotel rooms or sit on a tape recorder. They won't see a dollar from me."

The custodian's basement closet in Dr. Matteo's building would never be confused for a nice hotel room. Still, he'd made his point.

Mr. Tremont said, "Once the money siphon starts, Josh, how do you shut it off? They'll suck us dry."

Fame and adulation and respect were all intangible and immeasurable. Money, in the end, was how the Tremonts kept score.

On that Friday, at exactly noon, Norma Blackwell called Finkelman. He was ready for her.

"Tree Tremont will not be bullied or blackmailed," he said. "You can tell your clients it's time for them to make an honest living, like my client does."

He theatrically pressed the END button on his phone. Tree went to give him a high five. Finkelman whiffed it.

I worried that the jubilation was premature. I knew Norma Blackwell had gossip-buying toadies at every major "media outlet" in the country. I was sure she'd retaliate quickly. I trolled the Internet constantly through the afternoon, expecting the worst. Nothing. I checked one last time before going to bed. Nothing. I was starting to believe that maybe Norma Blackwell was bluffing.

Then came the next morning. I was awakened by an awful droning noise. I stumbled into the hallway. Big Herb was emerging from his room.

"What kind of lawn mower is *that*?" I asked.

Herb sniffed the air like Robert Duvall in *Apocalypse Now* and said, "That's no lawn mower, son. That's a Sikorsky 92 at fifteen hundred feet."

We went to the backyard. There was one helicopter flying lazy circles directly above us and another coming in. Finkelman burst onto the veranda, waving his BlackBerry.

"We're on the front page of the goddamn *Post*!" he yelled over the whirring.

When Tree appeared in the doorway, Finkelman pushed him back inside, shouting, "Get down, get down, get down." Big Herb and I hustled after them. I took Finkelman's phone and read the *Post* story.

FUGITIVE TREE
LIVING LARGE!

Disgraced bogeyman Tree Tremont has spent the last two weeks hiding out in Southampton at the luxury estate of Dr. Lee Roy Jenkins III, Page Six has learned exclusively. Tree has been a virtual prisoner on the $50 million property, missing a court date and leaving the grounds only once, for a meeting with Super Lawyer Norma Blackwell at the Islandia Marriott. Hotel employees confirm that a man matching Tremont's physical description was spotted in the lobby two days ago wearing a ridiculous fake beard and the hat of New York's financially plagued No. 2 baseball team.

Blackwell declined to reveal her interest in the case but said she is not working for the golfer.

Tree's stay with Dr. Jenkins—the plastic surgeon to the stars who got his start by removing one of Cher's ribs—will surely increase speculation about what happened on the night of July 24, when Tremont was supposed to be en route to a Florida hospital but never arrived. His subsequent disappearance, and corresponding legal and marital woes, has captivated the world.

According to a source, Tremont was recently visited at the Jenkins estate by two buxom babes who enjoyed an eventful afternoon with the straight-arrow golfer with the bad-boy secret life.

According to a source. What a joke. With Blackwell doing the feeding, these baby stories would grow into giants.

Miles, Jenkins's freckly resident, ran up to us and said, "You guys need to see this."

He led us into a small windowless room. A grid of nine TV monitors displayed security images from around the estate. One of the screens was fixed on the imposing wrought-iron gates at the front entrance. Miles zoomed in. It was a melee of TV camera crews, coiffed talent, harried reporters, and perspiring photographers all pushing and shoving for a chance to peer through the gates. The crowd had to be at least two dozen strong and growing. In the distance, I could see a cadre of TV trucks and Ford Taurus sedans arriving.

Tree said, "Holymarymotherofchrist."

I wondered how it worked in Norma Blackwell's mind. The *Post* story identifying Tree's hiding spot had to be her Plague No. 1. I wondered if she considered the air attack and the hordes at the Jenkins gate to be Plague No. 2. If so, I didn't want to see the next eight.

The incessant hum of the helicopters was in my head until late morning, when Suffolk County police, working with the FAA, moved them out. Dr. Jenkins got in my face and said, "You told me this would never happen. Your words. Never happen."

There was no point in reminding him that it was Finkelman who had said that. He never distinguished between the two of us.

The fact was, Jenkins had extended a major courtesy to us—surely for his own selfish reasons, but still—and his reward was an assault on his property and privacy. The tabloid press, cable and radio, Internet and newspaper, opened the doors for the so-called mainstream media. It was easy to see where it was going. Before long, *The New York Times* would be running man-in-the-news sidebars on secondary characters like Dr. Lee Roy Jenkins III. Serious readers of the paper of record would be lapping it up. Dr. Jenkins's frenemies would be e-mailing the story to one another, showering him with support on the phone, mocking him behind his back.

In the early afternoon, Herb, Finkelman, Tree, and I met in the kitchen, where the windows could not be seen from any public street. Finkelman drew the shades to be safe. Herb announced that we'd be hitting the road again and that the leading contenders for our destination were Las Vegas, rural Louisiana in the vicinity of Fort Polk, the Italian countryside, and somewhere out to sea on *Off Course*.

"Andrew," Mr. Tremont said. "I'm sending you to L.A."

Finkelman looked like a confused dog.

Herb said, "Norma Blackwell's gonna be on TV, so we need you to be on TV. That means New York or L.A. Since she's in L.A., I need you in L.A., too."

I was stunned. I knew nothing about it. The idea of Finkelman on TV worried me.

"You don't need me in L.A.," Finkelman said. "What about Josh's guy?"

He meant Marlin Fitzwater, the Reagan and Bush I press secretary. I had talked to him. I'd thought that Fitzwater, with his conservative credentials, could make the case that I could not—that even a celebrity athlete straying from his wife was entitled to some measure of privacy. My efforts to turn reporters around on that question were going nowhere.

"No, Andrew, no Marlin Fitzwater," Mr. Tremont said. "I'm not firing you. I'm just telling you I want you in L.A."

Finkelman nodded gravely and said, "I'll catch the next flight out." He stood up. Tree gave him a halfhearted bro hug, and Finkelman left the kitchen without another word.

I couldn't imagine Herb firing him; for one thing, he knew too much. Still, as soon as Finkelman was out of earshot, Mr. Tremont said to me, "We need to tighten the circle."

I guess I should have been flattered. I was in and Finkelman was out. Instead of feeling elated, I felt emptiness. I went to the estate's library and called Lily.

"Are you okay?" she said. The kindness in her voice was a reprieve, like nothing I had heard in weeks. At the estate, every fourth word was *fuck*.

"I don't even know," I said. "This whole thing is so sordid, so sick, so unnecessary."

It felt good to say it.

"You should come home," she said.

I couldn't. I was in too deep.

A couple hours later, Tree and Big Herb and I climbed into a helicopter on the Jenkins lawn. Mr. Tremont was the pilot. *The Sapling*, the GV, was waiting for us at an airport across the Long Island

Sound in Connecticut. We boarded the plane and were greeted by one lone pilot. The circle really was tightening. We had settled on a deeply rural spread, a ranch and hunting property Herb knew near Fort Polk. Maybe father and son wanted to play soldier, I didn't know. In any event, it was the best chance to keep cameras out of Tree's face. We couldn't risk having him go ballistic in public again, not with the Fourth and Fourth incident hanging over our heads. The fewer people around, the better. Belinda and the twins had returned to Tree House, and they were under siege.

On the flight, Tree was silent. He wasn't drinking. Just the opposite—I had never seen him more sober. He had no Ziploc med bag, not that I saw. His world was getting smaller and tighter and more claustrophobic. They were coming after his family, his reputation—and his money. It was a trifecta of nightmares for him.

We were cruising at thirty thousand feet and it was long past midnight when Tree spoke for the first time in an hour or more.

"I want to see the twins," he said.

It occurred to me later that it was the first time I had ever heard Tree make an independent decision in the presence of his father.

And with the snap of a finger, we were flying home, into the cauldron.

21

Unfortunately, *The Sapling* was outfitted with Wi-Fi. I never got a break from my various screens. They taunted me even when I tried to sleep, blinking at me from the nearest night-stand. Pete had been working the story with Bob Woodward-like zeal for *The Rev-Am*, and his M.O. was to post tidbits as soon as he had them. In the middle of the night, while we were somewhere over South Georgia, he broke more news. On RevAm.com, Pete posted this gem: *Belinda DeCarlo Tremont is close to securing the services of Super Lawyer Norma Blackwell for her expected divorce from Tree Tremont. She will be seeking full custody of their two children, with legal authority to move with them to Italy. She will also seek half of Tree's earnings over the course of their marriage. That would place her pay demands at approximately $378 million.* It struck me as odd that Norma was representing Tree's girlfriends *and* his wife. But that was what she was doing, according to Pete, and Pete got stuff right.

I looked at Tree and Herb. They were asleep. I saw no point in waking them for this latest whack across the head.

We arrived at the St. Pete airport in the middle of the night. Tree couldn't walk through the front door of Tree House unannounced at three A.M., not after being away for two weeks, not given the way he'd left, and especially not with the news that I knew and he did not. "Why don't you just crash at my place?" I asked. He could get some sleep, and when he woke up, I'd tell him how Norma Blackwell was burrowing deeper into his deteriorating life. To my surprise, he said yes.

There were more surprises at my home. Josh Jr. was asleep in his bed (I'd thought he'd be at his mother's), and Lily was in mine (I'd thought she'd be at her apartment). I told Tree I'd move Josh to the living room sofa, change the sheets, and Tree could sleep in Josh's bed. But Tree welcomed opportunities to seem unspoiled. "No, you know me. I can sleep anywhere," he said. "Maybe I could use that?" He was pointing to a square macramé throw blanket on the back of the sofa. My mother had made it in the sixties. Tree put the blanket over his shoulders like a kid coming out of a pool and shoehorned his big self onto my little IKEA sofa. He looked like Bo, the kid I had met a long time ago.

I climbed into bed. Lily smelled like warm jasmine and her hair was splayed all over her pillow.

"Meg's mom is sick," she said, half asleep.

Meg must have asked Lily to stay with Josh. They had that kind of relationship. They were amazing women. I missed them both.

"Tree decided to come home," I said. "He's sleeping on the sofa."

"Not surprised," Lily said, and like that, she was asleep again. I used to be an all-world sleeper myself. Then I got my new job, and sleep became something I saw others do in magazine ads for Lunesta.

The macramé blanket, I noticed, had been returned neatly to the back of the sofa. From a small hallway that lead to the kitchen, I could see Tree and Josh sitting at our kitchen table, eating Cap'n Crunch and talking about the state pastime, Florida and Florida State football.

"FSU is gonna spread 'em out and light it up," Tree said. Not even four hours of sleep, and he was impressively alert. "You watch."

"Ten bucks says they won't win eight games this year," Josh said.

"You got ten bucks?" Tree asked him.

Josh nodded confidently.

"All right, Joshie," Tree said. "You're on, and you're going down."

Tree truly loved sports. He loved winning and hated losing. He loved action.

I entered, and Tree said, "Let's ask the sportswriter. What's the over/under on FSU winning eight games this year?"

"I'd take the under," I said.

I got a good look at Josh in the early-morning light. He was taller, blonder, and skinnier than when his school year had ended. Summer in Florida. I went to give him a hug and a kiss, but he sort of pulled away.

"When's swim practice?" I asked.

"Now," he said.

"I'll give you a ride."

"Why is Tree Tremont sleeping on our couch?" Josh asked.

"Home's not so good for him right now," I said.

We drove in silence for a while. The coarse Bermuda-grass lawns were dripping with dew. He found a station suitable to both of us, WMNF 88.5. They were playing Bonnie Raitt's cover of "Burning Down the House," the old Talking Heads hit. If your teenager likes the music you like, it's a wonderful thing.

"When's your next meet?" I asked.

"Tomorrow night," he said. "SPCC." St. Petersburg Country Club, his team's big rival.

"What do they have you doing?"

"A lot," Josh said. "Hundred free, hundred back, four by hundred IM free, maybe fifty fly."

"What, is he trying to wear you out? I'm gonna talk to your coach."

"Do *not* talk to Coach," Josh said.

It was a pleasure to be home and to remember again the high stakes of ordinary life.

We pulled into the parking lot. Two kids walked by and gave Josh the jock nod. He gave one back. I'd never seen him do that before.

"How long you home for?" Josh asked me.

Our windows were down. You could feel the morning heating up.

"I really don't know," I said.

Two old men in tennis whites started hitting balls on a nearby court.

"What does your mom think of this whole Tree Tremont mess?" I asked Josh. I probably shouldn't have asked, but I was eager to know.

"She never even mentions it," Josh said. I shouldn't have been surprised.

"How's she doing?" I asked.

"She doesn't think Grandma should ever drive again," Josh said. Meg's mother had suffered a minor stroke and was in the hospital. "She wants her to move in with us."

Josh grabbed his backpack and was out the door.

When I got home, Tree and Lily were sitting on the little cement patio on vinyl lattice chairs, the blue strips faded almost to white. My boss and my girlfriend, as different as two people could be, were drinking orange juice out of old jelly jars with the scrubbed faces of Fred Flintstone and Barney Rubble on the side. Lily was still in her pajamas, patterned with pineapples.

"You got a good one here, Joshie," Tree said. "What can she possibly see in you?"

He was totally at ease. Maybe the Dutra home was a better fit for him than Tree House. Why is it when people start making money, they always start leading such isolated lives? Bruce Springsteen wrote his best music when he lived on a crowded street in Asbury Park. He got rich and famous and moved to a farm.

The news about Norma Blackwell's newest client would break in to this idyll soon enough. Tree needed to hear it from me.

"I'll give you a ride home," I said to Tree. "Let me help Lily make the bed. I'll be out in five minutes."

"Take your time," Tree said. "I'll do some stretching."

He wasn't going to do any stretching. He hadn't done any stretching since he warmed up for the last round of the British Open.

Lily and I collected the juice glasses and deposited them in the kitchen sink. I followed her to the bedroom, where we sat on an old wooden chest.

"Let me remind you of something you once told me," Lily said. " 'Denzel Washington has nothing on this guy—he's the best actor I've ever seen.' "

I nodded, remembering.

"I get it, how he seduced all those women," Lily said. "There's something about him. It's hard to describe. I'm sitting there, sipping my O.J., and even I'm thinking, I'd go to bed with him."

She flipped her hair back like Rita Hayworth in *Gilda*. What a move.

"Are we all right?" I asked.

"We're all right," Lily said. "He thinks you can somehow make things right with Belinda. Go do your Gandhi thing and come home."

On the drive to Tree House, I told Tree the news: that Belinda was talking about divorce, that she had hired Norma Blackwell to represent her, and that they already had a settlement number in mind. He did not seize on the prospect of divorce, nor on Norma's conflict-ridden client list. He went right to the proposed payout number.

"Three-seventy-eight, double it, that's seven-fifty-six," he said. "Belinda must be showing her my returns. That's the number to the mil."

He had me call ahead to tell Belinda that he was coming home, that he wanted to see his children, and that he wanted to see them in his house. Belinda said, "That is his right. He is their father. This is his house."

There were maybe thirty reporters at the gatehouse to the development. We passed by undetected in my old beater, with Tree in the back on the Camry's thin floor in the fetal position, a beach blanket covering him. The last time he was at Tree House, he had left a bloody mess. This was a less than triumphant return. Tree went in the front door and, five minutes later, out the back, hand in hand with the twins. He was going to say hi to them, then come in for a sort of group counseling session with Belinda and me. She and I sat in the living room. She poured coffee.

"I shouldn't have done that," she said. She was talking about what Finkelman was calling the Birthday Attack.

"You were provoked," I said.

"I certainly was," she said. "How can you work for him, Josh? He makes you cover his lies."

I had never thought about it so starkly. "I don't know," I said.

Belinda looked tired. She looked at her watch. Tree would be coming in soon. "You know, I love your Lily," she said. "I talk to her more than my own mother." We sat in silence for a moment.

I asked, "Do you think this group session thing makes any sense?" If Belinda was already committed to Norma Blackwell and already heading down the divorce road, it seemed ridiculous. Plus, what qualifications did I possibly have to conduct such a session?

"I must keep myself open," Belinda said. "If I close up, it is not good for me. It is not good for the children."

Tree came in. The twins stayed outside with the nanny. He sat on the edge of an enormous stuffed chair. Belinda sat on a sofa, her feet underneath her thighs. I sat on a glass coffee table in between them.

"Belinda," I finally said, "do you want to stay married to Tree?"

"I don't know, Josh," she said. "We would have to start all over again. Like a new couple. I would have to have answers. Does he have an STD? Does he have herpes or syphilis or AIDS? Is he willing to have me as his only partner? Will I ever want to make love to him again? Can he be the man of the house again, as my father was, as his father was? Is he someone I can grow old with? Will the twins respect him? Will I ever be able to trust him? Can he control himself?"

Her questions came out in one burst, like she had been saving up. With every one, Tree seemed to sink deeper and deeper into his chair. His arms were crossed over his chest.

"What about you, Tree?" I asked. "Do you want to stay married to Belinda?"

"I do," he said.

"Why?" Belinda asked.

"Because divorce means failure, and I don't fail at things," he said. "Because kids from divorced parents are always shuttling back and forth, back and forth, and it's a waste of time. Because Mom and Dad had their share of problems, but they never took the easy way out and just split up." They had separated some years after Tree turned pro, but they'd never divorced.

"Maybe they should have," Belinda said.

"Maybe they should have?" Tree repeated. "Raising me was the thing that kept them together! Everything you have here, the pool the kids are in, the lifeguard watching them, the nanny with the fluffy towels, that hundred-thousand-dollar couch you're sitting on, none of it exists if they don't stay together. Do you not see that? Don't you get it? Marriage is— You know what marriage is to me? Marriage is sacred to me."

"You certainly proved that," Belinda said.

"I'm telling you, marriage is sacred to me. Being the father of our twins? There's nothing more important to me in the world. I'd take every one of my trophies and throw 'em in the fucking trash if that's what I needed to do to make this family whole again. Everything that got us—got me—in such trouble? It's just sex, that's all it is. It's just— How did you put it, Josh?"

I thought: *Please, please, PLEASE don't involve me any more than I already am*. I said, "I don't know."

"Yes, you do. You said it at Pebble."

"A hobby," I said quietly.

"A hobby!" Tree said. "A goddamn fucking hobby, is all it is. You're getting all worked up about a hobby!"

Belinda left the room. My stint as Gandhi was over.

• • •

The most wanted man in America, at least by the press, was sleeping on my sofa, and nobody knew it. Josh didn't tell a soul. Lily and Meg didn't breathe a word. Big Herb, of course, was a vault. Our neighbors never saw Tree. The circle was tight. I didn't even tell Finkelman.

One night Norma Blackwell went on *Entertainment Tonight* and said, "Belinda DeCarlo Tremont wants what every married woman wants: a faithful, dependable, loyal husband. She's committed to mediation and counseling to see if they can make things work. There's no evidence that Mr. Tremont is doing the same. This is not about the money. This was never about the money. This is about commitment."

Later that night, Blackwell met with Finkelman at the Griddle Cafe in West Hollywood, where she gave him the new price list: the A&E photos from the facility, $3 million; Shark Lady's blood tests and Norm's tape, $1.5 million each. The total tab for blessed silence had gone from $4 million to $6 million. Tree wasn't budging.

The next morning, this headline was posted on the plaything.com website:

**TREE'S PORN STAR GIRLFRIEND:
GOLFER IS "BEST SEXTER EVER"**

The porn star went by Creamy Butter, née Carolann Bartram of Racine, Wisconsin. I had never heard of her. She was the star of something called the HARDcore Series, which included *Long HARD Journey into Night* and *Bang the Drum HARD*. I had never heard of those titles, I'm proud to say. Evidently, Creamy Butter saved every text message Tree had ever sent her over the course of their "recently concluded 28-month affair, thousands of them." I was about to call bullshit on the whole thing, but then I got to this part: *Creamy's relationship with Tree ended in a fight in a rented castle in Pebble Beach in June over, of all things, Altoids.*

Some of Tree's texting highlights to Miss Butter:

I'm playing in Japan next week. Wanna cum? Hear it tastes great w/ sushi!
Tman out

Cum as a double entendre. Really, embarrassingly unoriginal. I knew that trip to Japan for the Casio World Open. He won.

Paired with Will Martinsen Thursday, Friday this week at Phoenix event. Need extra tension relief. HELP! Tman out

What was with *Tman out*? The sign-off was as awful as the messages.

Glad you like them! I've always been partial to the left. When I was a little kid, once heard Mom call them my "dangling participles." Tman out

Couldn't Tman have had the decency to keep his mother out of his sexting?

You rocked last night. What's your hourly rate—for teaching Belinda?!?! Tman out

That one was going to cost a lot.

The useful kicker to the plaything.com story: *Creamy says there are way more where those came from, and that they are much, much worse! More sexting, and their XXX-rated Skype sessions, too. Creamy says, 'Come see me on my brand-new website, TreeOnMe.com.'* "

I could see Norma Blackwell's fingerprints all over the story. Evidently, she had yet another new client. No doubt some of Tree's other lady friends would come out of the woodwork and find their way to the Super Lawyer. She was cornering the market. By my count, the release of Tree's sexts to Creamy Butter was Plague No. 3.

Things got even stranger, which I didn't think was possible. Belinda was on the phone with Lily, railing about her husband's affair with an obscure porn star and the complete idiocy of his texts to her. At the same time, Tree was on my sofa, humiliated to his core by being outed as the most uncouth sexter in America. Every comedian in the country was working up Tree Tremont texting bits. Conan O'Brien had a whole routine about a new sushi accompaniment called Tree Sauce. Howard Stern was so impressed by Tree's sexting and by his twenty-eight-month affair with a porn star that he started a "Tremont for President" campaign. Jay Leno took the other view. "You know how Tree Tremont always used to say, 'I let my golf clubs do the talking for me'? Kinda boring, right? But I gotta tell you, between his golf clubs doing the talking and his texting fingers? I'll take the clubs."

Meanwhile, Rush Limbaugh went on for an hour about the dangers of glorifying athletes "like this Tree Tremont." *The Wall Street Journal* ran a damning editorial under the headline TREE, WE HARDLY KNEW YE. At a White House press conference, Don Van Natta, Jr., of *The New York Times* asked the president, "Are you disappointed in your old golf partner?" The president said, "You know, as a golfer, I like Tree Tremont quite a lot. As a texter, not so much." The press corps laughed. In a twenty-five-minute session with reporters that touched on alternative energy and gun control and North Korea's nuclear capabilities, the president's comment about Tree was the only thing to make the nightly national news broadcasts. Tree Tremont was doing something almost historic. He had turned from athletic icon to national joke overnight.

Trying to engage Tree in any real conversation was impossible. You could stand there all day and not make it happen. At midnight on the night the Creamy Butter story broke, he was sitting in front of the TV, eating Fruit Loops with a plastic spoon, watching Golf Channel. They were reporting the texting news.

"Creamy Butter," I said. "Quite a name."

"She's a bitch," Tree said.

"Are there *lots* of others?"

"There are others," he said.

An instruction show came on. The host and a well-known Tour swing coach were dismissing the merits of a swing method called Stack and Tilt. Tree turned up the volume.

"After they sold everybody on Stack and Tilt, now they want to crap all over it. You know, build it up and tear it down," Tree said. He did not note the irony. "But I'll tell you what: Palmer stacked. He didn't call it that, but he did. I mean, he took divots with his driver. Top of his backswing, some of those swings, he's got all his weight on his left big toe. And you know what? For about five years there in the late fifties, early sixties? He probably drove the golf ball as well as anybody, ever, and I'm talking Hogan, Nicklaus, Curtis Strange, who drove it great. Hale Irwin. Shark. Me. Fred Funk and Jeff Maggert, I'm not counting them because they didn't win majors. I don't care what the stats say. Palmer drove it long, and he drove it in play. And he stacked. This guy doesn't know shit."

He drank the remaining pinkish milk right out of his cereal bowl. Then he muted the TV, rubbed his eyes, stood up, and, without warning, raised his right foot like he was going to smash the screen. He stopped himself. Somehow, he must have remembered that the TV was not his.

Belinda's humiliation was an open wound, one she wanted no one to see. She needed to escape. She asked Norma Blackwell if she could take the twins to her parents' villa in Italy for the month of August. Blackwell encouraged Belinda to do just that (Plague No. 4) but advised her to ask Tree for written permission first. So Belinda sent him a text, and he texted back, "Yes, you may take the kids to Italy. I'll miss them. I understand."

He read the text to me before sending it. It made me wish he had checked more of his texts with me before hitting the send button.

I found myself thinking that again the next day, when Creamy Butter posted a single choice sext from Tree on her website: *Playing Jack's tournament in the rain. Every time Mac puts the flagstick back in the hole, water spurts all over the place. Like the visual? Your flagstick, Tman out.*

Belinda, lucky girl, was already on her way to Tuscany by the time Rush and Howard and the rest of the gang weighed in on that one.

• • •

The Tremonts refused to cough up the $6 million to Blackwell. "It can't get any worse," Tree said, but that was quickly disproved. A day after the deadline came and went, *The View* devoted an entire episode to Tree. I watched it in horror at my house. Barbara Walters opened the spectacle, staring into the camera with jarring seriousness. "Today we have a very special show that will touch on all the big themes of the human condition: love, sex, and betrayal. Speaking out for the very first time are a trio of Tree Tremont's mistresses. And they have quite a story to tell." One by one, she introduced them: Laura Myers, whom I recognized as a waitress at the Great American Diner; Jenny Jamison, a stripper at the Mons Venus in Tampa; and Jessica Griffin, a onetime reality-show contestant turned Las Vegas nightclub hostess.

"I understand that the three of you are being represented by feminist attorney Norma Blackwell," said one of the hosts, Elisabeth Hasselbeck. Here it was: Plague No. 5. "Do you all want the same thing from Tree Tremont, and does that include money?"

"No, no, no," Jenny said. "All I want is for Tree Tremont to look me in the eye and say he's sorry he hurt me."

"But what did you expect?" Hasselbeck asked. "You knew he was married. Don't you think you should be the one apologizing—to Tree's wife?"

There was a smattering of applause from the studio audience.

"He told me they were separated and about to divorce," Jenny said.

"His story to me was that it was an arranged marriage for marketing purposes and they lived in different houses," Laura said.

"He told me his wife had terminal cancer," Jessica said. "I was just trying to comfort him."

A collective gasp could be heard from the audience.

Another host, Joy Behar, piped up. "Based on everything we've all read and now heard, I'm guessing these relationships featured a lot of sex. A lot of raunchy, down-and-dirty sex. Was there anything more to it than that?"

"There was," Laura said. "We spent a lot of time talking. Tree needed to talk."

"If you're asking about quote material things, Joy, there was none of that, not for me," Jessica said.

"Not for me, either," Jenny said. "When we ordered room service, I wasn't even allowed to get a side dish. And I had to drink water. Tap, not bottled."

The audience howled.

"Same," Jessica said. "Tree would *never* spend money on me. He said he didn't want me to feel like a streetwalker. His thing was that if he started buying me stuff, I'd only love him for his money, not the real him."

"Did you all love him?" Joy asked.

Laura and Jenny said no, but Jessica started sobbing and nodding. The audience, feeling her heartbreak, sighed a group "*Awwwwwwww.*"

Whoopi Goldberg jumped in, looking to change the mood. "Time out, time out," she said. "You girls are all very pretty and very, very white. Just like the other Tree girls, 'cept maybe that Creamy Butter, who's got a kinda trampy look. But what I want to know is, where are the sistahs? I mean, c'mon, Tree. Be true to your roots!"

"That's funny," Laura said. "I once asked him about that. Tree said that his second year on Tour, he was undressing an African-American woman, and as he ran his hands on her, all he could think about was Vijay Singh. After that, he could never get it up around any girl with dark skin." The audience booed and hissed.

Near the end, Barbara Walters asked, "What more can we expect to hear from you three gals?"

The girls looked at one another, and Jessica spoke for the group. "We're collaborating on a book about Tree," she said. "It's going to be an oral history. But with some anal, too."

The live audience was grossed out. No matter. Within an hour, Jessica was an Internet star, and pictures of her sunbathing topless on the hood of a Jaguar became an Internet sensation.

• • •

Finkelman and Norma Blackwell met at an In-N-Out Burger in Los Angeles, the one off the 101 near Universal Studios. The two lawyers were starting to like each other. Finkelman picked up their $12.67 tab. But the price for one seedy tape, a couple dozen raunchy pictures, and a blood test that would make Barry Bonds blush was up to $8 million. "I'll take it to my people," Finkelman told her. His people—the Tremonts, father and son—said no.

Then came Plague No. 6. It struck at the heart of darkness for all male professional athletes: the vague possibility that there could be homosexuals among them. Congress could have openly gay members. The army could have openly gay soldiers. TV sitcoms could have openly gay characters. Even a professional athlete could have an openly gay cousin, as long as he didn't come to the locker room. But there was no place for gay athletes or even gay daydreaming in professional men's sports. Not in the NBA, not in the NFL, not in the NHL, not in MLB, not in NASCAR, and not in the most conservative league of them all, the PGA Tour.

Enter Lu and Lau, two nerdy Asian guys in glasses. Dr. Lu was the exceedingly slender chief radiologist at Treasure Island Imaging in St. Petersburg. Mr. Lau was the owner of the five Shiny Happy People dry-cleaner locations in St. Petersburg. Their English was halting, the doctor's especially. That didn't stop Ellen DeGeneres from getting into the nitty-gritty of their lives on her syndicated chat show.

"Dr. Lu, Mr. Lau, I'm glad you're here today," Ellen said.

They gave her formal nods.

"Mr. Lau, let's start with you. How did you meet Tree Tremont?"

"Dr. Lu and I are partners."

"Oh," Ellen said playfully. "Just like Portia and me?"

"Ping-Pong partners," Mr. Lau said.

"I see," Ellen said.

"Tree comes to my dry cleaner, Shiny Happy People," Mr. Lau said. "Very serious about his clothes."

"And how about you, Dr. Lu?" Ellen asked.

"Tree patient," the doctor said. "We invite Tree to Ping-Pong. He invite us to Gents."

"And Gents is?" Ellen asked.

"Upscale dancing nightclub," Dr. Lu said.

"And what happens there?"

Dr. Lu and Mr. Lau looked at each other.

"Nothing," Dr. Lu said.

"Nothing?" Ellen asked.

"Tree gets drunk," Mr. Lau said.

The audience howled.

"*Oookayyy*," Ellen said. "What happens *after* Gents?"

"Tree says, 'Have you guys ever been with a guy?' " said the owner of Shiny Happy People.

There was a collective *oooohhhhh* from the audience.

"And I say no. But Dr. Lu says—"

"Can we hear from Dr. Lu about what Dr. Lu says?" Ellen asked.

"I tell Tree I like him," the radiologist said.

There was a collective *eewwwwww* from the audience.

"And *then* what happened?"

"Tree and I meet at Don Cesar hotel in St. Petersburg," Dr. Lu said. "Twice. Once the week before he play the Masters. Second the week after he play the Masters. He was very nice, very sensitive."

The audience went berserk.

"Well, well," Ellen said. "Lot of issues here. Are you a married man, Dr. Lu? No? But Tree Tremont is. The kids like to say it's all good. But this one? I don't know—it's a doozy. Before we go to a commercial break, I have to ask you, Dr. Lu, why are you going public with this very private, very personal information?"

"Tree tells his golfing teacher he was never private with a man. His golfing teacher tells Miss Blackwell. Miss Blackwell tells me. I was hurt. I don't like liars. He was trying to disappear me, like I never happen."

22

Within forty-five minutes of the airing of Ellen's show, Tree posted a personal letter on his website, which he dictated to me in a whisper:

> I have felt it's futile to rebut every outrageous lie and rumor that has been visited upon me. But I cannot let this latest one go unchallenged.
>
> I have met Dr. Lu socially a couple of times. We have no carnal knowledge of one another. I respect my many gay fans but I myself am strictly heterosexual.

He wanted to sign it "Tree Tremont, PGA of America's Man of the Year." I argued against it.

Tree and I sat in my small kitchen, monitoring the replies on Twitter. Hundreds were pouring in every minute. I read aloud a representative sample:

thanks for setting the record straight, T! Your real fans still love you. Don't let the haters bring you down . . . stay strong!

AT LEAST YOUR FINALLY LEAVING THE WHITE GIRLS ALONE YOU MORAN

Why so defensive, Tman? You sound like Magic Johnson talking to Arsenio Hall. Not cool, bro.

"Here's Corey Pavin, checking in," I said.

Tree groaned. He found the former Ryder Cup captain annoying.

Tree, we will all pray for you at Tour Bible Study. For guidance, read Corinthians 6:9–10. Peace and Love, Corey Pavin

Mr. Tremont arrived at my back door. I had never been so relieved to see him. He and Tree shared a long embrace. Herb began speaking in the nostalgic tone he reserved for his war stories.

"When we were in the jungle, men got lonely," Herb said. "It's one thing not to have sex for months at a time. It's another to never even lay eyes on a woman. A piece of you dies inside. Some of the soldiers went to each other for relief and comfort. I never judged them."

"I hear what you're saying, Pops, but I'm not gay, okay?" Tree said. "This Dr. Lu guy hung around Gents. He was always paying for the bottles, so I let him hang at my table a few times. One night he says to me, 'Tree, you ever consider doing it with a man? A man like me?' I said hell no. He's got something in his head that isn't true."

I didn't know what to believe. I don't think Big Herb did, either.

My phone rang. It was Belinda, calling from Tuscany.

"Do you think it is true?" she asked.

I slipped into my bedroom and closed the door. Tree and Herb probably thought it was Lily.

"He says it's not," I said. "I believe him."

"He is a skillful liar," Belinda said.

In the background, Belinda's mother said something to her in Italian about eating lunch. Belinda responded to her.

"How are you holding up?" I asked.

"The first girl, that Emerson, that was a shock. That my interior designer was with my husband, that hurt. Then the porn star, his texts to her, that was degrading to *me*. The three girls on the Barbara Walters American TV show, you start to think maybe Tree is sick, you know? But this Chinese doctor makes me wonder if I ever even knew who I was married to."

"Belinda, you don't know that the doctor is telling the truth."

She ignored that and said, "If Tree is a gay, he should be proud and gay. I think Rocco may be a gay."

The kid was not yet six. "You think Rocco might be gay?" To me, Rocco was a kid who liked to shoot Nerf arrows, eat chocolate-chip pancakes, and run around collecting high fives from strangers after his father won golf tournaments. I didn't imagine him having a sexual orientation, not at age five.

"Oh, Josh, don't you see? It does not matter. Maybe Rocco is a gay, maybe not. Maybe Tree is a gay, maybe not. I just want him to be honest about who he is."

Belinda had unearthed the root of the problem. Tree Tremont wanted to lead the life a lot of men want to lead—to have sex with whomever they want, whenever they want. A rich, famous professional athlete can actually do that. Every year, when the Yankees were in Tampa for spring training, I'd see Derek Jeter. He was the king of serial dating, but he never left a wake. He was never in the paper for doing the wrong thing. I was impressed. All the writers were. But Tree wanted *everything*. He wanted the hot nightlife *and* the kiddie-soccer home life *and* the glamorous wife *and* the get-rich-now corporate life that was the foundation of the PGA Tour. To keep it all going, he had to wallpaper his life with lies.

Finkelman called from Los Angeles. "Do you have him on suicide watch?"

"No, Andrew, he's not suicidal."

"He should be. I wonder what Miss Norma's price is gonna be now."

"It doesn't matter anymore, does it? We're done with the plagues."

"Really?" Finkelman said. "That blood work comes out, and there's an asterisk on everything he's ever achieved in the game."

I noticed Finkelman wasn't using *listen* with me anymore.

"Andrew, maybe he was on juice the whole time, I don't know. He still had to make the shots, hole the putts. He's not an Olympic weight lifter."

"That's not how people are gonna read it. They're gonna says he's a druggie and a cheater." When Finkelman reduced it to that, I knew he was correct. "Does he understand that he's gonna get killed in the divorce? His wife forgives him for his affairs in front of witnesses, and he *still* keeps fucking around? When this is all over, he could lose the jet."

How would he survive without a private jet? The day Tree was sweating twenty thousand dollars in credit-card debt, as I had been six months earlier, was the day I'd start worrying about his finances.

"Believe me," Finkelman said, "he *should* be suicidal. If it were me, I'd be dead by now."

There were three or four county sheriffs guarding the entrance to Tree's development. The space above Tree House had been declared a no-fly zone. Tree Tremont and his affairs with a growing list of women and one man was the biggest story not just in the United States but across the world. Tree returned to Tree House and was a prisoner there. Where could he go?

One day he had to leave. Fred Willoughby, the prosecutor in the Fourth and Fourth incident, had a plea deal in mind and wanted to see Tree in his office.

Tree had raised Willoughby's ire by missing his arraignment *and* a pre-trial conference during the holiday on the Jenkins estate. *The Review-American* was harassing the state attorney's office for failing to declare a trial date. The truth is, the state wasn't eager for a trial. Tree would spend millions on expert testimony to gain an acquittal, and the prosecutors didn't want to get in a high-profile pissing match they might well lose. They had to show that the rich and the powerful were not above the law, but putting Tree Tremont—a multiracial philanthropist and athletic icon, even with a sullied name—behind bars came with significant political costs. There was no obvious win-win.

Tree, Tulip Watkins, and I drove to Fred Willoughby's office in downtown St. Petersburg, in the impressively square 501 Building. There were at least two hundred photographers and reporters waiting at the front entrance. Sheriffs cleared a path, and Tree walked right through a split sea of recording devices, never looking left or right, almost like he was walking down the lined fairway on the last hole of a golf tournament. Scores of people were calling out his name, some were even calling out mine. I found it impossible not to look. I don't know how celebrities hear people scream their name and walk on by as if they're retrieving the morning paper from the driveway.

I hadn't realized that Fred Willoughby was black, which meant that in his office, I saw something I had never seen in person: Tree Tremont with two other black people. Tree almost never talked about his life as an African-American, despite his father's persistent efforts. He was never taunted or celebrated in school for his multiracial skin, because he was never *in* school. When he was with Michael Jordan or Magic Johnson at an awards show, the link was athletic celebrity and nothing else.

But this was different. I felt like Tree's blackness was on glorious display. Even though the two lawyers were combatants, they bonded in ways that took me by surprise. The topic could not have been more urgent: a criminal matter, a possible prison term. The setting was formal. Everyone was using honorifics. ("May I get you some water, Mr. Tremont?" "No, thank you, Mr. Willoughby.") I felt that Fred Willoughby didn't want to be just another person tearing down Tree Tremont. He might have been distressed by the idiotic behavior that had led Tree to his District 6 office, and dismayed by the reckless behavior that had put Tree on the front page of the *New York*

Post day after day, but something about Fred Willoughby made me think he had loftier goals.

"Mr. Tremont, if you were convicted by a jury on even half the charges facing you, any reasonable judge would send you to prison for at least a month and maybe twelve," Willoughby said.

His mustache covered his upper lip, and his suit was so worn that it sat on his shoulders like a loose T-shirt. Tree made more money in four hours than this man made in a year, but Mr. Willoughby had all the cards.

"Would a prison sentence deter others from committing the same crimes? I think it would," the prosecutor said. "Would it deter you from committing the same crimes again? I have my doubts. We all know about the personal travails in your life. These are not legal issues, but I have no doubt they have everything to do with why you are here today. Your celebrity may feel like a curse to you, but in fact it will be your salvation. What I am going to propose is that you plead guilty to some of the counts and plead no contest to others. I'll go over all that with Ms. Watkins. But as part of your plea agreement, I am going to ask you to agree to perform five hundred hours of community service. And when I say five hundred hours, I mean ten hours a week for fifty weeks, to be completed over the course of a year. And when I say community service, I mean something that will truly help the community. You can give golf lessons to senior citizens. You can ref in the summer basketball leagues. You can paint houses in the Kenwood section. The details will be worked out, but I assure you that if you take this plea agreement, you will do real work. If you go off and play a golf tournament for a week, that's fine, but then you're doing twenty hours the next week. All that is Part Two."

Tree nodded rhythmically while Willoughby spoke. When we first sat down Willoughby told us about his preacher father and his own weekend gig preaching at a small Pentecostal church in crowded, forgotten black St. Pete, far from his son's tennis tournaments.

"Part One comes first," Willoughby said. "Part One of the plea agreement would require you to spend a minimum of a month at an in-patient treatment center to deal with what we might broadly call your personal issues. Anger management? Impulse control? Maybe there are addiction issues. I can't pretend to know. We have a list of programs for you to choose from. There are excellent programs here in Florida and all through the South. There are two good programs in Mississippi—Pine Grove is one; the other's called WPWC. Two places that have a lot of experience with celebrities are Betty Ford and Hazelden. I went to a tiny place in southern Indiana. Didn't see another black person for six weeks. Left there and never touched a line of cocaine again and never wanted to."

One March during spring training, I was writing up Darryl Strawberry, who had been in and out of various prisons, hospitals, and treatment centers for years. Somehow he always looked great. I asked him how he pulled it off. He said, "It's the fitness center at Betty Ford. It's fabulous."

Willoughby said, "So we're asking a lot here, Mr. Tremont. We're asking you to do something very public, to make St. Petersburg a better place and to show that no individual, no matter how wealthy and successful, is above the law. And we're asking you to do something private that will, we hope, improve you as a person and make certain we never have this kind of incident again. But it'll keep you out of prison."

At the word *prison*, Tree closed his eyes.

"There's a conference room across the hall. You are welcome to use it, discuss it with your people, and let me know if you accept the state's offer or if you want to go to trial. I only ask that you give me your answer by noon today. This has gone on far too long already."

Tulip Watkins leaned toward Tree to speak to him privately, but he gently raised a hand in her direction and stood. "Mr. Willoughby, I don't need to go into a conference room. The community service you're talking about? I'd love to do that. Honest. I've never held a paintbrush in my life. It's about time. The treatment center, you know, that's going to be weird for me, but I'd rather do that than go to prison. My parents didn't raise a child who would wind up in prison. Not for a month. Not for a day. I'm ready to move on. Tell me where to sign."

Later that day, I wrote, and Tree approved, this letter for TreeTremont.com:

AN OPEN LETTER TO MY FANS

While I believe my minor traffic accident was blown out of proportion by the media, I have accepted the penalties imposed by the state. I will be undergoing in-patient therapy. I welcome this opportunity to learn more about myself. For the time being, I am taking a hiatus from golf. But make no mistake, I intend to compete again, and when I return to public life, it will be as a better player and a better person.

I ask that everybody, fans and media alike, grant my family and me privacy as we begin the process of healing.

I hope you can find room in your heart to one day believe in me again.

23

Tree settled on one of the Mississippi rehab places. Not Pine Grove, the other one, WPWC: Walden's Pond Wellness Center. No relation to Thoreau's off-the-grid spot in what is now suburban Boston, except that both were deep in the woods and tranquil. Tree didn't pick it for those reasons. He picked it because it required its "Residential Residents" to come with a "Supporting Residential Sponsor." (The names sounded like Finkelman inventions.) Tree chose it because he didn't want to march off to rehab alone. He asked me to be his sponsor. This was how he put it: "How much would I have to pay you to go with me to that fucking place?" For starters, WPWC didn't allow Supporting Residential Sponsors to be employees of the Residential Residents. I had to agree to a one-month leave from Tree Corp just to be approved.

I went pretty skeptically. It's kind of hard to take seriously a drug-free "wellness center" where an obviously stoned midafternoon male operator says, "Tranquil morning to you from Walden's Pond, and how can I direct your call?"

At Tree's request, I drove us there in my old Camry. Tree wanted a break from *Flying Tree*'s leather seats, thin-lipped water glasses, arctic air-conditioning, and cheerleader flight attendants. He got it. We took an old blue highway, U.S. 19, for the long first leg to Tallahassee, driving with the rear windows half down and the warm summer air rattling my dog-eared *Rand McNally Road Atlas* on the backseat. Tree seemed at home, like Herb at the diner. He talked.

"That goddamn *Eye*," he said maybe an hour outside of St. Pete. "That's where this thing starts, you know. Used to be the athletes got a pass. Something changed."

Herb had figured that out months earlier, but Tree was realizing it only now. It was true. As long as I had been looking at the *Eye* and various other scandal sheets, the bedroom lives of most stars were open game, whether you got famous from movies or music or politics or TV or business or even the pulpits of the megachurches. But one group of celebrities had been given a wide berth: megastar athletes.

I said, "It's like they changed the rules and didn't even have the decency to tell you."

"Exactly!" he said, oblivious to my sarcasm.

We stopped for gas and Orange Crushes at the Chevron in Salem, a speck of a town on the highway. Tree didn't venture far from the car. The world was searching for him but in the wrong place. Florida is a vast state in a vast country.

We got back on the road and Tree said, "I'm sure everybody's looking at Belinda and saying, 'She's so hot, how does the dude cheat on *her*?' " He chewed on his straw. The germophobe wouldn't drink straight from the bottle. "But you know what? Let's be real. It gets old. You know that. It gets routine. Right?"

He sipped his soda. I thought of Pete's comment: *Dudes want a piece of strange.*

"All these girls coming out of the woodwork," Tree said. "What a bunch of horse shit that is."

Our cell phones were off, and the car radio was, too. I wondered about the current number. By the last public counting, twenty-three different girls had given up voice mails or texts or photographs, outing Tree as a serial philanderer with something resembling proof. There was a Vegas betting line on what the number would be by Labor Day. The under/over was an even hundred. My guess was you could make easy money taking the over.

I asked, "Do you recognize them?"

"Most of 'em," he said absently. "In my mind, every last one of them violated a contract. I could actually sue them."

He wanted to *sue* them? Whatever kind of counseling was coming up at Walden's Pond, the therapist was going to need his A-game.

We arrived at dusk. The place was impossible to find, with an eight-foot-high fence surrounding its three-hundred-acre property. The check-in area smelled like lavender air spray. The woman at the reception desk, who had no idea who Tree was, said, "Tranquil good evening to you, and welcome to Walden's Pond. At WPWC, when we ask you how you are, we really mean it. So let me welcome you by asking, how *are* you?"

In Tree's case, his truthful answer would have been *Pretty fucking annoyed*. But he did what most people do, golf pros especially. He said, "Perfect. Great trip up, glad to be here."

A man drove us to our room in a golf cart. He was a black man, maybe seventy, his back stooped with age. He never acknowledged us once on the drive over. But when we reached our two-story building, he held Tree's backpack against Tree's chest and said, "I got this one grandson, eight or nine now, T'shawn. He worshipped you, man. Worshipped the ground you walked on. And right now, as I stand here today, that boy is broken."

We carried our bags silently into our room. It looked like a dorm at a rural state college. WPWC rules—and there were lots of them—allowed one suitcase and one backpack per resident. You had to use their sheets (polyester), pillows (foam), and soap (Ivory). We'd been in the room for maybe two minutes when the first words were spoken, and they were Tree's.

"Just thirty more nights in this dump, and we're outta here."

• • •

Wouldn't you know it? He got a female counselor.

On our first morning, after a seven A.M. breakfast and a tour of the place—there was no pond at Walden's Pond—Tree and I met with the counselor assigned to him, Delores Macatee, a chubby woman in her mid-thirties with a long, wavy ponytail, stonewashed jeans, and a playful manner. She introduced herself by saying, "I know I'm not beautiful. I compensate for it by feigning super-genuine interest in people." Tree smiled. "Now, if I may, Mr. Tree Tremont, world-famous golfer with one really lousy day on the road, why are you here?"

We were sitting on little wooden chairs in a hot, muggy room. The only artworks on the walls were thick rugs with blocky geometric patterns. I'd seen similar ones at Wal-Mart.

"It was part of my plea," Tree said. "Package deal."

Delores let her hair out of its ponytail and massaged her scalp with her fingertips. "Sorry," she said. "Okay, that's better. Sometimes my head just gets so *itchy*. Now, Mr. Dutra, why don't you tell me why you think your friend is here?"

I told her she was welcome to use my first name, and Tree invited her to do the same with him. I started to answer her question. Three words into my answer, she stopped me: "Sorry again! I missed a step here. Don't worry, I have actually done this before. Gotta establish the ground rules. Tree *is* your friend, isn't he?"

I said he was.

"Tree, do you consider Josh to be your friend?"

He said I was.

Delores pretended to be relieved. "Sometimes things blow up before we get even *there*," she said. "So, Tree, what does it mean to be a friend?"

Tree considered the question for several seconds and said, "A friend is someone you like to hang out with, someone you can talk to, like that."

"But what does it mean to *be* a friend?" she asked.

"I'm sorry—I didn't hear the question right. Correctly."

"You don't have to apologize to me."

"Well, I messed up your question there."

"And I'm guessing you're somebody who doesn't like to mess up."

"You musta watched the last round of the Masters this year."

"Actually, I didn't."

"I'm just busting on you," Tree said. "I made a big mess out of that round."

He hadn't. But he saw it differently.

"I think the answer is right there in your question," Tree said. "To be a friend, you're there for the other person. If you say you're going to be someplace, you're there. That's what it means to me to be a friend."

Tree wasn't fighting it, the whole how-did-it-make-you-feel thing. That had everything to do with Delores's manner. I noticed he had not used a single profane word with her.

"Interesting," Delores said. She started humming a few bars of Carole King's "You've Got a Friend." She was odd and direct. I liked her. She asked Tree, "Are you there for Josh, there for him as his friend?"

Tree looked at me. This was not the sort of thing we ever talked about. I couldn't imagine how he would respond.

"Tough one," he said. "I would be if the guy ever needed anything. He never seems to, though."

It was an insightful answer. The things I needed, I got from Lily, from Josh, from my parents, from myself. I prided myself in not needing much.

"How about you, Josh? How do you feel about Tree's definition of a friend?"

"I think it's good."

"Would you say you're there for Tree?"

"I would."

"Would you say that even if you didn't work for him?"

"I think so, yes. Hard to say, because if I didn't work for him, I wouldn't be in his life. But to answer your question, yes."

"So you're friends," Delores said. "It's good to be king. It's better to have friends."

From a file folder, she retrieved a piece of paper with a handwritten paragraph on it. She handed it to Tree. "Would you read this out loud?"

Tree read: " 'Friends are a man's priceless treasures, and a life rich in friendship is full indeed. When I say, with due regard for the meaning of the word, that I am your friend, I have pledged to you the ultimate loyalty and devotion. In some respects friendship may even transcend love, for in true friendship there is no place for jealousy. When I call you a friend, I am at once affirming my high regard and affection for you and declaring my complete faith in you.' "

He looked at Delores. His mouth curled in a wry smile. "Bobby Jones," Tree said. "To the people of St. Andrews when he got the key to the city, 1958. Barbara Nicklaus gave me a copy of that speech after I won there—what, three weeks ago. Man, does that seem like a long time ago. Very impressive, Delores. You got some major golf heads in your house?"

"I've got Google," she said. "You know why we require our patients to come to Walden's Pond with a friend? Because *something's* wrong if you're here. We can get the ball rolling, maybe. Hold your hand while you take baby steps toward healing. But you're going to need a friend to keep it going. Marriage comes and goes in our culture. It just does. Friendships are more likely to last. Friendship, like Jones says here, can transcend love."

Baby steps. Tree always talked about taking baby steps when he was learning a new shot or working on a swing change. I knew he'd pick up on that.

"Let's go back to where we started, but let's do it differently this time," Delores said. "I asked Tree why he was here. He said it was a condition of his plea bargain. Sounds like the truth but not the whole truth. So let me try the same question on you, Josh: Why is Tree here?"

She was basically asking me to call bullshit on Tree, but she did it in a way that was not threatening. She was loaded with game.

"Tree's right," I said. "The plea deal is what got him here. But the thing is, we drew a prosecutor with a big heart. This prosecutor has had problems of his own. He was a coke addict. He'd been reading about Tree in the paper like everybody else. And my guess is he saw Tree's behavior, saw that it was maybe narcissistic or compulsive, and felt that Tree needed a better understanding of himself."

I wasn't unloading on Tree; I was responding to Delores. We were in a room where the needling language of professional sports meant nothing and another language was able to rise in its place.

"Tree, what do you think of what Josh just said?"

Narcissism, compulsivity. Tree was smart. He'd know exactly what those words meant and how they applied to him. The stakes were quickly getting higher. He looked like he was enjoying the challenge.

"You know how on TV, a guy wins the MVP in the World Series and they put a mike under his chin and go, 'What are you feeling right now?' " Tree said. "And the guy says, 'It's still sinking in.' I feel like that. I can tell you one thing: I've never heard Josh talk like that before. Maybe he's been saving up, I don't know. I'm not sure what to think except that there's a lot in it."

The days were long and often boring. There was light in the sky until past nine. We shot baskets and pool and played cards. There was no TV at Walden's Pond. There was no Internet, no cell phones, no movies, nothing with a screen. Books were allowed. Newspapers and magazines were not. The food was bland but plentiful. We ate at cafeteria tables with other Residential Residents and their Supporting Residential Sponsors. They all knew who Tree was. Some were nervous or awed in his presence, but many were not. They had their own problems to deal with.

Everybody I met was trying to recover from some sort of addiction: heroin, cocaine, steroids, alcohol, cigarettes, eating, dieting, gambling, texting, bodybuilding, exercising, tanning salons, lying, sex. Sexual addiction was big at Walden's Pond, and everybody, both RRs and SRSs, had to take a no-sex oath for the duration of the stay. I heard about people addicted to phone sex, hooker sex, coworker sex, solo sex, Internet sex, bestial sex. Lying and sex and drinking were the big three at Walden's Pond. LSD, the counselors called them.

Multiple addictions were commonplace. I spoke to several people who were there for compulsive lying *and* drinking *and* fornicating. Many of the addictions were weirdly specific. One woman had to have sex in a turnpike dog-walking area every morning. Didn't matter with whom. She couldn't go to work without it. Once she got it, she was good for the day. One man was there for compulsive golf playing, of all things. He was retired. He was financially set. But he had to play every day. Even in lightning storms. Even when he was having a heart attack. Even when his wife was having her gallbladder removed. She was his Supporting Residential Sponsor. The couple asked Tree if he understood the man's compulsion. "I don't know about that," Tree said. "But I can tell you from the time I was three until the time I played in my first U.S. Open, I played or hit balls every single day. And I had the time of my life."

Walden's Pond was different from rehab places I had read about or seen in movies. There wasn't much group therapy, where people sat in a circle and said things like "My name is Tree, and I'm a sex addict," followed by a group sigh, "Hello, Tree." For the most part, we did our work as a threesome: Tree, Delores, and me. She had us in two-a-days, like a football coach in the late-summer heat, and our first dozen or so sessions were devoted to the question of why Tree was in therapy in the first place and who he hoped to be. Day after day, Delores went deeper and deeper and deeper. She was relentless, in an amusing and pleasant sort of way.

When it came to admitting to his golfing deficiencies, Tree was ruthless. One of his adages was "If you're not getting better, you're getting worse." He got better by really believing that and doing something about it. He never told other players or writers what he was working on. There are guys on Tour who have true friends and can talk about the problems with their swings and the problems in their heads. That was foreign to Tree. He admitted his golfing insecurities only to Herb and his real-world insecurities to nobody.

I saw that at his first Masters. He won despite some awful fairway bunker play. In the Thursday round he needed two shots to get out of one fairway trap, and then it happened again on Friday. It was not a shot he ever practiced at the Brooksville sod farm. In a crowded press conference after the second round, I asked Tree what he would do to improve his long shots from fairway traps. He said, "My fairway bunker play is excellent, Josh." But the next time father and son went to the sod farm, they brought two shovels and forty big bags of Home Depot sand and built a fairway bunker. Herb was the one who told me about it, of course.

For every three questions Delores asked Tree, I got two. Many of them were about Tree, but some were about me—or questions about Tree that got me thinking about myself. I thought often of Josh and Lily and Meg and our baby girl, lost seventy-two hours into her painful life. I thought about my father, who started me in golf and in newspapers (he read two a day himself). I thought about my mother, who bought me a newspaperman's hat for my eighth birthday, a boxy Royal manual typewriter for my ninth, and Strunk and White for my tenth. When I made my first newspaper, *The Elderberry Place News*, she went to the library, mimeographed thirty or forty copies, and together we distributed them up and down our broad, tidy suburban street. As Delores asked Tree questions about his mother and his wife, I started to realize that I took the women in my life for granted, my mother and Meg and Lily most significantly, but also others, like an old copy editor at *The Review-American*, Toni Smythe, who taught me that the flower worn in the wedding announcements I was writing was spelled *baby's breath*—lower case, singular, possessive, never hyphenated—and to spell it any other way was to risk losing savvy readers who knew better. She paid me one compliment in twenty-four years. " 'The children's shrieks were muffled by the crashing surf.' Good." In my own way, I was a self-absorbed, middle-aged child. Maybe not on Tree's epic scale. Still.

Delores was filled with surprises. In one session about a week into our stay, she handed Tree another piece of paper for him to read. It was the pre-surgery blood work done by Daisy Slauter in Dr. Matteo's office. Delores asked Tree to read it aloud, and he did. Faced with many polysyllabic pharmacological names, Tree was surprisingly fluent.

"How'd you get this report?" Tree asked when he was finished.

"The PGA Tour sent it to us. The investigators in the Matteo case sent it to them."

"That can't be legal," Tree said.

"I think the Tour is sending a message here, Tree," I said. I wasn't surprised. I had figured the Tour would try to get Tree's blood sample from the St. Pete police. "When you get back on Tour, they want you clean."

"Do you think the public should have this information?" Delores asked.

"Of course not," Tree said.

"Why not?"

Tree gave her a look, like *You know why.* He said, "Because it's embarrassing, and I've been embarrassed enough."

"Well, let me ask you this, Tree: Do you think you're a drug addict?"

"No."

"Do you know any drug addicts?"

I thought Tree would say he didn't. He had led such a sheltered life. But he said, "That guy across the hall from me with the braided ponytail and the missing teeth and the green skin? That guy's a drug addict."

"That guy," Delores said, "was once a concert violinist. I would call him a recovering drug addict."

Tree looked shaken. There was no way he could ever imagine such a descent happening to him.

"How would you define *drug addict*?" Delores asked.

"Dependency on drugs, legal or otherwise, to get through the day, having a desperate craving for drugs," Tree said.

"How'd you get so smart?"

He smirked. "Smart parents."

"Josh, you've been around Tree a lot this year, more than any other person. Based on Tree's definition, would you call him a drug addict?"

I said that I would.

"Why?"

"Look at that report he just read. Look at all those drugs in his system. Something to wake up, something to go to sleep, something to get hard, something to get big, something to grow hair."

"What do you think, Tree?"

"I don't think you'd ever confuse me with your classic drug addict."

"Like what?"

"That violinist. Or some guy on a curb with a rubber hose around his arm and a needle in his vein."

"You watch too many movies, Tree," Delores said.

"Joshie's way worse," he said.

She retrieved a tiny mirror from her pocketbook and handed it to Tree. He looked at it and caught a glimpse of himself. "Lemme guess," he said. "I'm looking at a drug addict."

"Are you?"

He handed the mirror back to her and said, "This is childish." Then he calmly walked out of the room, as if there were someplace to go.

Delores looked at me and said, "Think we should save the alcohol talk for next time?"

In actual fact, at our next session, and the fifteen or so after, the subject was drugs. Then came Alcohol Week, although we kept up our drug talk all the while. In time, the girlfriend parade was introduced, featuring the Pack of Lies Marching Band. Oh, we were having a good time.

Every day, twice a day, the intensity level increased. Maybe I'm flattering myself, but I think Tree saw that I was treating it seriously, so he did, too. Delores was excellent. We both felt that. Tree never had to admit to being a sex addict, a drug addict, an alcoholic, a compulsive liar. All he had to do was answer questions, the more thoughtfully the better, and think about why he did the things he did.

"Tell me a story about an addict," Delores said. "Not a drug addict or an alcoholic. Some other kind of addict."

In regular life, no one ever asks questions like that.

"My father had this army buddy," Tree said. "Once a day he'd go to Krispy Kreme and get this chocolate donut that was like a thousand calories. He wouldn't tell anybody about it. He was logging all this time on the StairMaster, but he wasn't losing any weight. Finally, he tells my dad about the donuts. Dad says, 'Raymond, from now on I'm your DA sponsor. Donuts Anonymous. The front wheel of your car even hits the Krispy Kreme parking lot, you call me.' Now the guy can run a sub-twenty 5K."

"Do you think he enjoyed those donuts?" Delores asked.

"I'm sure he did," Tree said. He had no impulse for gluttony himself. "But not the consequences."

"Did you enjoy all that sex you were getting?"

"Most of it, yeah."

"And how about the consequences?"

"There were no consequences until I got caught." His desire for sex overwhelmed his fear of germs.

"When you did get caught, why were there consequences?"

"Because what I was doing was outside the norm."

"So how are you different from the donut guy?"

"My dad's army buddy was only hurting himself. I was hurting my family."

Delores handed Tree a yellow legal pad and a pen and said, "I have an assignment for you. Write a true story from your childhood, come back, and read it to me."

"How many pages does it have to be?" Tree asked.

"Don't worry about that. I can get you more paper if you need it." She could handle this guy.

"Can I get help from OBK?" O. B. Keeler. Another one of his nicknames for me.

"Sure," she said, turning toward me. "Isn't that why he's here?"

• • •

When I asked Tree what he was planning to write about, he said, "I don't know, but the first thing that comes to mind is something with Mom."

We were in our dorm room, each sitting on our own bed, our backs against the same cinder-block wall. It was strange, to have a roommate for the first time since college. I enjoyed it.

Tree said, "When I was about fourteen, for my homeschooling English class with Mom, she made me read *Our Town*. I was struggling with it, so we read it together. And you know there's that scene at the end, where the girl is dead but she comes back for her birthday?"

I had read the play as a sophomore at my large public high school. I kind of remembered it. I said, "Is it Eleanor? She comes back for her sixteenth birthday?"

"Emily. It's her tenth."

"Maybe you're right," I said.

"I am right. So Mom and I read the scene, playing all the different parts, but it really isn't doing anything for me. You know, first she's dead in the graveyard, and then she goes to the kitchen and she's dead, but the parents are alive. I just found it unrealistic. I wasn't into it. But we get to the end, and Mom's eyes are all red around the rims. And I feel bad, like it meant so much to her and nothing to me. And she goes, 'There's a time for everything.' And then she starts talking about—I'll never forget this—she starts talking about the 1960 U.S. Open, when Palmer won at Cherry Hills. And she gives me that famous quote from Hogan, 'I played with a kid today who shoulda won by ten shots if I'd been thinking for him.' The kid, of course, is Nicklaus. Big Jack was twenty. Mom says, 'Jack wasn't ready to win the U.S. Open then. But two years later he was.' And then she says, 'To everything there is a season.' You know, the biblical verse. She says, 'Right now you're not ready for *Our Town*. Someday you may be.'

"So like a year later, there's this production of *Our Town* at her church. And I almost never go to her church. Or plays. I mean, I never go to plays. But you know, Mom wants to go, so we go. The church has got that stale churchy smell, and she knows everybody there. She's making me say hello to everybody. I am not into this whole thing.

"And it's very weird, the way they do the play. The first part they do in the social hall. Then the wedding scene they do in the actual church. Then they do the cemetery scene in the cemetery next to the church—they bring us all out there. And then we go to the church kitchen for that scene at the end in the kitchen, when the girl goes back home for her tenth birthday. Mom's church has this huge old-timey kitchen with this big black stove and warped floor. And it's really warm in there. It's winter. The windows are all steamed over. And Emily's calling out to her parents. They can't hear her, but she can see them, and I'll tell you what, JD, this time I'm crying my eyes out. I mean, I'm bawling. And my mother goes in her pocketbook and gives me a tissue. Nobody sees her do it. I can still smell her perfume on that tissue."

I was bowled over by the precision of his memory, by his devotion to his mother, by his honesty. It made me think of my own mother. I owed my newspaper career to her. It made me miss the paper. It made me miss the promise Tree represented on the day I met him, way back when.

Tree wrote up his *Our Town* story and asked me to read it to Delores. I think he wanted to hear it—and watch Delores. When I was done, I saw him looking at Delores closely, and he could see what I saw, that now it was her eyes that were red around the rims. Tree handed her a box of tissues.

Mr. Tremont arrived early in the morning of Day 22. He was welcomed to Walden's Pond in all its tranquility. "How *are* you?" somebody asked him, and he answered in a clipped way: "Fine." In their lives, Herb and Tree had never spent three weeks apart, and I was sure he resented the place that had kept them separated.

"Pops, this is Delores Macatee," Tree said. "And I got to warn you about her: She will get under your skin, in bad ways and good. She's one of a kind."

He said it as if Delores were his new best friend. I didn't feel at all threatened. I doubt Herb felt the same.

At the Great American Diner, on any driving range anywhere, in the Champions Room at Augusta, Mr. Tremont always seemed comfortable. But he wasn't comfortable at Walden's Pond. His public role, as the father of the great Tree Tremont, didn't mean anything there. He viewed Delores, understandably, as a Johnny-come-lately who hadn't earned her place in the Tremont Family Circle of Trust. When it was just the two of us in the Welcome Center, Herb said to me, "Do they have him on anything?" I think he meant some sort of downer or tranquilizer, maybe truth serum.

Before long, we were in our customary meeting room in our regular hard chairs with the familiar odd rugs on the wall, this time as a foursome. It was all routine to me and to Tree, but it had to be strange for Herb. As a foursome, the atmosphere was different.

"Mr. Tremont, your son's a remarkable person, and not just because of his golf," Delores said. Herb held a tiny Styrofoam cup of coffee in his immense hands and looked at her. "I'm sure I'm not telling you anything you don't already know."

She knew she had about two minutes to have any chance at all of winning this tough old man over, and she was going to make every word count.

"One of the themes that comes up with Tree is that there's a time for everything," Delores said. "He's struggled with that in his life, even though he knows there's a time to hit it in the middle of the green and a time to—what's that phrase, Tree?"

"Take dead aim."

"Take dead aim," Delores said.

"I find that interesting," Herb said. " 'To everything there is a season.' Tree's mother loved that verse. Ecclesiastes. 'To everything there is a season, and a time to every purpose under heaven.' But sometimes events get imposed on you. Have you played hide-and-seek, Miss Macatee? At some point, somebody yells, 'Ready or not, here I come.' And all hell breaks loose, right?" Mr. Tremont made an exploding motion with his fingers and hands. "In Vietnam, I had a boy in my unit who was like a kid brother to me. He was eighteen and got sent home to the South Bronx in a bag. Sniper got him. Was it his time to die, Miss Macatee?"

The question might have been rhetorical, but Delores didn't treat it that way. She said, "No, it's like you say—events got imposed on him, tragically. Like you say, ready or not. We used to see a lot of Vietnam vets here. Now we see young men who have been through Iraq and Afghanistan. They come here after three, four, five years in the military, and they're still kids. How old were you, Mr. Tremont, when you went to Vietnam?"

"I was twenty-seven, turning twenty-eight. I had my BS in engineering. I had been working. I was ready."

"How old were you when you got married?"

"Twenty-seven."

"Twenty-seven," Delores said. She turned to Tree. "How old were you, Tree, when you got married?"

"Twenty-one," he said.

"Twenty-one," she repeated.

Twenty-one without a day in college, without ever really being away from Herb and Helene, I thought.

Herb said, "You see, Miss Macatee, the golfers tend to marry young. Palmer was twenty-four when he got married. Nicklaus was twenty. Hogan was twenty-two. Tom Watson was—how old was Watson, Bo?"

"Twenty-two."

"Twenty-two. Tom Watson was twenty-two. See, there are lots of distractions on Tour. Guys tend to marry young because it keeps them focused, gets them to the range, gets them to the practice green, gets them to bed early. You don't want to chase tail all night long, then have to be on the first tee at Doral for a seven A.M. tee time."

Tree was just listening. Not nodding, just looking at his father and listening.

Delores said, "Is that right, Tree?"

Tree bobbed his head first to one side and then to the other. "Right then or right now?" he asked. "I remember thinking all that when I got engaged. You know, focus has never been an issue for me. Sleep, either. There's some weird thing about my body. It functions well on almost no sleep."

Delores let those words sit in the air and did just what I'd do in interviews. She waited for someone to fill in the silence.

"I'm not sure what you're getting at here, Miss Macatee," Herb finally said. "Not sure at all. Are you implying I pushed Tree into marriage when he was too young for it, for the sake of his golf game? Golf was *in* him, Miss Macatee. It was in him from the day he was born. He was always going to be a champion. I knew that when he was two. He was going to be the best the world had ever seen, and he was going to do the things you needed to do to make it happen. Yes, he made sacrifices. Of course he made sacrifices. So he missed Little League and senior prom and sleeping till noon in some college dorm that smelled like old socks. He spent that time playing golf against men, Miss Macatee, playing grown men for millions of dollars. He's won tournaments at country clubs where I never could have walked through the front door when I was Tree's age. He's played golf with the president, Miss Macatee. He's had tea with Nelson Mandela. He's rung the bell at the New York Stock Exchange. He talks to Bill Gates about his foundation once a month. He's done more at thirty than anybody in the history of the world, including Jesus Christ. And the world cannot stand that much success, Miss Macatee. Not from Tree Tremont. Not when his father looks like me. And they have tried to bring him down. For what? For the things men have been doing for a million years. But they will not bring him down. He will get stronger and stronger and stronger. That's what he will do."

I looked at Tree. He was sitting in his hard wooden chair, staring at the toes of his Arrow running shoes, absentmindedly running his thumb along a tiny roll of stomach fat, the way a toddler seeks comfort from the corner of a familiar pillow.

Mr. Tremont stood up and walked to the door. He reached for the knob, turned around, and said, "As for pussy, it remains undefeated."

• • •

Day 28 of a patient's stint at Walden's Pond was called Disclosure Day, the day the Residential Resident lays it all out to the person he has most aggrieved. Belinda was coming for D-Day, and Tree was a wreck. Patients who had relapsed and returned to Walden's Pond warned us that the day could leave you feeling skinned and filleted. I had never seen Tree so on edge, not even on Sunday mornings at majors.

An unmarked black WPWC van arrived from its airport run, and Belinda stepped out. She looked different, as if she had been robbed. She was wearing jeans, a gray sweatshirt, no makeup. Somehow she looked shorter, and it wasn't just the tennis shoes. Tree went to hug her but got nothing back. After that, I didn't know how to greet her. Did she view me as an extension of Tree's debauchery or as an independent friend, brought closer to her by her growing friendship with Lily? I was worried I might get one of her smother hugs, when her perfect breasts come up against you so tight you couldn't *not* feel self-conscious, even if you were wearing a windbreaker or a golf sweater or a parka at the British Open. She gave me the full treatment. I stuck my bottom out and tried to diminish the impact.

Delores led the three of us to the usual room, assigned us seats, and asked Belinda, "Would you be up for playing a version of Twenty Questions?"

Belinda forced a smile. "I can try," she said.

"That's the spirit," Delores said. "It's something we do here on Disclosure Day. Belinda, you'll ask Tree any question you like. He may answer at length, or just say yes or no, but he's required to tell you the truth. Then Tree goes. You alternate questions. It's usually enlightening. Tree, let's start with you."

He exhaled audibly, like he did when lining up a do-or-die eight-footer, and asked, "How are the kids?"

"They love Italy," Belinda said. "Your daughter has a gift for language. Your son has a gift for boccie. They've heard nothing about your affairs, but they will in time. They wonder how you are. They miss you."

When Delores was sure Belinda had completed her answer, she

asked her to pose a question to Tree. Belinda didn't hesitate. She asked her husband, "Do you have any STDs?"

"No," Tree said. "I got lucky."

It sounded bad the second it came out of his mouth, and Belinda pounced on it. "*You* got lucky?" she said. "You could have infected *me*. You put my life in danger with all your fucking around."

"Belinda, I understand your anger," Delores said. "But it's Tree's turn. Save all that for your questions, if you like. Tree, your question."

He asked, "Are you okay?"

"No, I'm not okay," Belinda said. She folded her arms over her chest.

"Anything you want to add to that?" Delores asked.

Belinda shook her head. She tugged on her baggy gray sweatshirt like she was trying to get air in it. Delores asked if she was ready to ask Tree a question. She was: "How many were there?"

"Let me jump in here for one quick sec," Delores said. "We did anticipate this question. It always gets asked. Tree prepared for it. Belinda, are you one hundred percent sure you want to hear his answer?"

Belinda, now sitting with her fingers under her slender thighs, said yes. Tree retrieved a folded paper from an envelope in his back pocket. It was actually three pieces of yellow legal-pad paper stapled together, crowded with his handwriting.

He said, "It started six years ago, when we were pregnant. When you were pregnant. The first one was a massage therapist. I was playing at La Costa. I don't know her name. It began as a legitimate massage. The second one was a cocktail waitress in Hawaii. Don't know her name, either. That was at the Kahala, the old Hilton hotel. She knocked on my door when she got off her shift. The third one was her friend, later that night . . .

"Number 87 was Emerson Wright, who I met at Gents. *Whom* I met at Gents. Number 88 was Laura Myers, a waitress at the Great American Diner. Number 89 was Creamy Butter. I met her on the set of a movie she was shooting. Norm Henley took me there . . .

"Number 173 was Natalie Gonzalez Jennings, I think. Some of

this ordering is not exactly scientific. She was celebrating her election to the board of the Tour Wives Association at Le Méridian in New Orleans. Number 174 was Eva Fenimore, the commissioner's ex-wife. The day before she got re-married. Numbers 175, 176, and 177 were all Dallas Cowboy cheerleaders, during the Colonial . . ."

I was numb. Some of the girls I knew about. Numbers 248, 249, and 250 were all notched on our trip to Arrow Golf, when the Tree Trunk clothing line was announced. But many were new to me.

I couldn't fathom how he was able to keep this immense number of affairs quiet for as long as he did. Part of it, I'm sure, was what Herb had told me early on, that the girls kept quiet because they were hoping for more. The TV, newspaper, and website tabloids—the few that might have known anything—were somehow bought off, either with actual cash or with the vague promise that Tree would do something for them. Still, how could every busboy, valet, chambermaid, girlfriend, cocktail waitress, and suspecting Tour caddie, hundreds and hundreds of people over the course of six years, *all* keep their thoughts off the Internet? With a million cell-phone cameras on the loose and tweeters and bloggers, anonymous and otherwise, on every street corner? All those valet guys who must have seen *something* but never said *anything*? Somehow Tree kept them quiet, just as for years he stopped his opponents from making putts they had every right to make.

Tree helped his cause by being such a skillful liar, constantly able to cover his tracks until he no longer could. But the bigger thing he had going for him was nobody wanted to be first, at least not within the friendly confines of the golf world. Nobody wanted to be the person to land a big right hook to the face of a once-in-a-lifetime athlete who was doing so much good. Nobody wanted to be the person who took the cover off a great national myth. I remember the kid down the block who first denied the existence of Santa Claus to Josh. I could have clocked him. Whistle-blowers are never popular, marital whistle-blowers least of all. Even as the foibles of real life are further degraded by reality TV, *mind your own business* is still the rule of law in the everyday world.

Tree continued to read from his list, and I felt like I needed a shower. I could see that I was sucked into the orbit of a star, just like all the girls in bed with him. Like a lot of reporters who grew up on broadsheets when they were fifteen inches wide, I'm naturally inclined to reserve judgment. In Tree's case, I was in no position to wag a finger, not with an affair in my own closet, the marriage I had breached, the pain I had wrought.

So the easiest thing was to tell myself that what Tree did in various beds with various women had nothing to do with my relationship with him. The problem was that I had continued to say that long after it stopped being true. Belinda had become someone I cared about. I owed her something. In my silence, I was perpetuating Tree's fraudulence but making him happy and keeping my job. The fact is, I was damned either way. There's mind your own business, but that's not the end of the line. My parents used to say, "You're responsible for what you know." I used that same phrase with Josh when a friend of his stole a pair of Nikes from the Foot Locker in the Tyrone Square Mall. Josh told me, and I told the kid's parents. It was awkward and uncomfortable but had to be done. Yet when I found it convenient and exciting and remunerative to turn a blind eye to Tree's nightlife, I forgot all about the old Dutra family dictum.

Tree droned on. His memory for his sex partners was like his memory for golf holes he had played. As he continued, Belinda seemed to get smaller and smaller. I put my arm on her shoulder, but it was frozen stiff. I slinked my hand back to my lap. The salesgirl from Saks, the waitress from the Loews on South Beach, the nanny who worked next door to Tree House on the occasion of her twenty-first birthday. It was a repulsive confessional.

"This is the last one," Tree said finally, close to an hour after he had started. I realized that he must have believed in what he was doing. He must have been clinging to the hope that the truth, as Emerson Wright had supposedly told the *Eye*, would set him free, that Belinda would consider taking him back if he came clean. He wanted the marriage to work. He didn't want to fail. He didn't want to be an absent father. He didn't want to write a settlement check for north of $100 million. For a man who kept score in a ledger book, that idea pained him to his core. But happily ever after? I couldn't see it. Even if Belinda took him back, what were the chances of those two ever enjoying an unencumbered sex life—or any sex life—again? Not much. So what was he going to do for the next half century? Lead the life of a monk? There was no way.

"Number three-forty-two," Tree said. "Stephanie Stayman, legal assistant to Tulip Watkins."

He lowered his head. He had been living with so many lies for so long, he seemed almost relieved.

"That's it?" Belinda asked.

"Yes," Tree said.

"What about the Chinese radiologist?" she asked.

"I met Dr. Lu for drinks twice at the Don Cesar. I was curious to learn more about his life as a bisexual. I'd never known a gay man. Nothing ever happened. I think things just got lost in translation."

The room was still. The color had drained from Belinda's skin. Delores offered everybody Munchkins from a big Dunkin' Donuts bag. There were no takers.

There was nothing for me to say. I hadn't talked the whole session. Twenty Questions was over. Delores looked at Tree and at Belinda, taking the temperature from afar. Belinda exhaled audibly and asked quietly, "Why?" The room belonged to her now.

"I was bored, and the girls were available," Tree said. "It came to me. When I got away with it once, I wanted it again. It made me feel like I was in the heat of competition. It was like a drug. It made me feel alive. I'm trying to answer you truthfully."

Belinda, I could tell, was beyond hurt. She was just looking for information that she could process later. "That quote in the *Eye*," she said, "when you called me an ice queen. Do you really think that?"

Disclosure Day was being pushed to its sensible limits. Tree looked down and then right at Belinda. "At times, yes," he said. "I know how much this must hurt."

Suddenly, there were tears streaming down her face, but her voice was not halting at all. Belinda looked at Tree and said, "You couldn't. You couldn't possibly know my hurt. My hurt, my sorrow, my anger is more than you are capable of knowing. But I am not broken. I would like to move with the children to Italy, but maybe that is running away from the inevitable. I must think about that. I wish you well, Tree. I know you will be the best father you can be. I hope you have learned something here. Our marriage is over."

And so ended a fairy tale, with Belinda and Tree sitting on small, hard chairs in a hot, stuffy room somewhere in rural Mississippi where they had never been before. Tree looked flattened. But Belinda did not.

"I see you have learned something here," Belinda said. "You are lucky to have met Delores. And to have Josh in your life. For your sake, and for the sake of our children, I hope you can find your way back."

24

After listing all the actors in the movie of his secret life, all 342 of them, it was inevitable that Tree was going to get killed on the divorce settlement. He knew it. His great strength as a golfer, his realism, served him well in the dissolution of his marriage, too. His goals were to prevent the divorce from dragging on and to keep the twins in the United States. Given his attachment to money, the division of assets was going to be painful whether the final payout was $100 million or $500 million. As it turned out, Belinda settled for $300 million and Tree House.

She kept the house name but changed her own. As a single woman, she was Belinda DeCarlo again. With her independence and her wealth, she was looking for something meaningful to do, and she found it. She bought, for the fire-sale price of $8 million, *The St. Petersburg Review-American* from Charles B. "Salty" Morton IV. The Morton family of St. Petersburg had owned the paper for exactly ninety-nine years, and now they were out.

"If you could have any job at any newspaper, what would it be?" Belinda asked me.

"Sports editor, *Review-American*," I said.

The job was open. Pete had left the paper to become the first credentialed White House correspondent for the *Eye of the World*. I was trying to figure out what to do. After we left Walden's Pond, I never resumed my job as director of communications at Tree Corp. I wanted to be Tree's friend, not his employee. He gave me three parting gifts: a signed first-edition copy of *Golf Is My Game* by Bobby Jones; a personal check—*Herbert X. Tremont, Jr.*—for a hundred thousand dollars; and a handwritten thank-you letter. I tried to return the check, but he wouldn't take it. We compromised by putting it in a college fund for Josh.

"You've got the job if you want it," Belinda told me.

That was how I became sports editor for *The Rev-Am*. I made myself a columnist, in the old-time tradition of a paper's sports editor doing double duty as its voice-of-the-department column writer. I tried to shelve the old-timey pomposity. When Tree made his return to tournament golf at Augusta, nine months after the British Open, I was there with a badge that said WORKING PRESS. What a difference a year can make.

Tree's scheduled visit to the press building on the Monday of Masters week was the most widely anticipated press conference in sports history. Salty Morton, in his capacity as the new chairman of Augusta National, introduced Tree, in a manner of speaking.

"Ladies and gentlemen of the press corps, on behalf of the Augusta National Golf Club, welcome to the Masters tournament as we mark the return of a golfer whom some regard as one of the all-time greats."

This was a ridiculous piece of private-club understatement. In the week before the Masters, a Golf.com poll asked the top hundred golf historians to name the greatest golfer in the history of the game. How the editors found and ranked a hundred golf historians is beyond me, but evidently, they did. There were eighty-three votes for Tree, sixteen for Nicklaus, and one vote for Young Tom Morris, a nineteenth-century golfer from St. Andrews who played with a wide stance, an impressive mustache, and a ball made from the gum of a gutta-percha tree. I would have voted for Nicklaus, based on his longevity. He had four more majors than Tree, a career that time could not kill, and nineteen second-place finishes in majors. Tree had one, to Will Martinsen, at the Masters one year earlier. That was it. Tree dominated his competition far more than Nicklaus did his, although I think Nicklaus faced a group of tougher men. When it comes to greatness, there are other factors that tip the scales toward Nicklaus, including his grace in defeat, his relationship with fans and sponsors and the press, his exemplary public life, the eighteen majors, the nineteen major runner-ups—all of it. I knew at least one interested party who agreed with me: Tree Tremont.

As the new chairman spoke, Tree was nowhere in sight. He must have been nearby. The whole thing had the orchestrated feel of a made-for-TV cable show. *Keepin' It Real: Augusta Style!*

"We all know that Tree Tremont has the ability to do magical things with a golf ball," Morton said. "He has thrilled youngster and oldster alike in his illustrious career. But if he wants to be regarded as a truly great champion, he will have to make amends with all of us, most particularly his fans across this great country and even across this great world. Sadly, Mr. Tremont has stained the game. I'm not saying anything to you all that I haven't already said to Mr. Tremont in private. I hope and pray that today Mr. Tremont is ready to start that healing process. It's time for him to beg for forgiveness." He paused. "I say, it is *time* for him to beg for forgiveness."

And on the second cue, a side door opened and Tree appeared. He had not done a single interview since his British Open victory. The few published photographs had revealed little. One showed Tree officiating teenagers as they played night basketball in a St. Pete rec league. Another had Tree weeding a lawn in the early-morning glare at a shelter for battered women in St. Pete. Another captured Tree and his kids snorkeling in the Bahamas, off of *Off Course,* the shots taken from a helicopter. The most widely circulated picture was of Tree leaving a tiny restaurant in rural New Zealand with a beautiful red-haired older woman. That one ran in the *New York Post* with the headline WHO IS SCARF LADY?

I knew the answer, but I wasn't writing about it. The rest of the *Rev-Am* staff could do as they saw fit, but in my own column, I was treating Tree as the friend he was. In a piece explaining how I would handle this delicate situation, I told readers that I'd give insights when I could and write nothing when I couldn't. I wasn't pretending to be objective. People seemed to think that was reasonable.

After leaving Walden's Pond, I'd see Tree two or three times a week, often for meals at my house; a few times in the guesthouse at Tree House, where he was staying for the time being; sometimes at the sod farm in Brooksville. He was working on his game there in secrecy, occasionally with Herb standing beside him, more often going solo. We talked on the phone almost every day. When bloggers wrote that Tree would never play golf again, I wrote, *Not only do I think Tree will come back to golf, I think the game means more to him now than it ever has.* That's what I was hearing, and that's what I was seeing.

When Tree emerged from the side door of the press building and stepped up to the dais, reporters gasped. They were getting their first real look at his full-blown makeover.

He was wearing his hair in a shaggy Afro that rivaled that of Dr. J in his ABA days (it was either a wig or the Rogaine was working). But he was dressed like Jimmy Stewart out for a Sunday stroll, in a tan hard-collared Sea Island cotton golf shirt, a charcoal-gray cashmere V-neck sweater, and navy blue wool trousers. No logos, no hat. I couldn't remember the last time I saw a player come into a press conference without a hat. Except at Arnold's tournament, golfers usually seized any chance to sell some product on the brim of their lid. Tree had lost at least twenty-five pounds over the previous nine months. He looked fit and nervous and young. When he was in his late twenties, he looked like he was in his mid-thirties. Now he was thirty and looked it.

Tree went to shake Salty's hand. It was never consummated. While Tree was reaching toward the chairman, Morton was dipping into the right pocket of his club coat from which he retrieved reading glasses and a small pile of index cards.

As Morton spoke, he alternated between looking at his notes and the TV cameras. There were stands from the four networks plus Golf Channel and ESPN, all carrying it live. As the chairman spoke, it was as if Tree were not even there.

"You taught us the term *fisting,* when what we really want to see is your fist *pump,*" Morton said. He made a slow-moving, halfhearted fist pump himself. I thought he might fall over. "You taught us about *golden showers,* but what we really want is to see you play through *April* showers." He flittered his fingers vertically through the air to signify spring rain. "In text messages, you wrote of *wearing out* your lady friends, but how pleased we would all be to simply see you wear out your driver." He made an air-golf swing, like the one David Letterman sometimes made.

I knew from my years of working for the man that Salty Morton had a tin ear, but this diatribe was all-world in its awkwardness. Everyone in the room was visibly cringing, except Tree, whose expression never changed.

"This club has given you three club coats, just as it has given four to Arnold Palmer and six to Jack Nicklaus and two to Tom Watson and three to your contemporary Will Martinsen. Think about what those living legends have given back to us. And what, pray tell, have we received from you? Reason to improve the security of our wine cellar."

I started to wonder if the man was actually drunk. Others had to be thinking something similar. Peyton Williams Armstrong, the previous club chairman, an admired banker who had turned the Atlanta Marathon into a sparkly international event, approached the dais and spoke directly into Salty's ear. When the exchange was over, Morton returned to the microphone and said, "I believe I've made my point. I shall cede the floor to you, Mr. Tremont, with the hope, on behalf of all of golfdom, that your best days are ahead of you."

Morton made a move to exit through the same door where

Tree had just entered, but Tree had enough presence to stop him. "Mr. Chairman?"

Morton turned around. Tree looked Salty in the eye and said, "The things you just said, they were hard to hear. But I had it coming. I have the exact same hope: that my best days are ahead of me. And I'd like to give you my word on that, because this club has given so much to golf and so much to me. I know my word doesn't mean much right now, but I'm going to change that by my deeds."

And then, like a high school debater demonstrating his ownership of the room, Tree walked off the dais and toward Morton, who was frozen in shock. Tree put his left hand on Salty's shoulder and stuck out his right hand in such a way that Morton had no choice but to shake it. It was an amazing moment. After Morton's insane remarks, Tree could have tried to turn the Morton sideshow into the main event.

As they shook hands, dozens of cameras started clicking away all at once. You could actually hear 180 reporters (the room's legal capacity) furiously scribbling notes. The level of white noise was almost deafening. The handshake ended quickly, and Salty slipped out the door. Tree returned to the podium, looked at the room, and for a moment seemed completely petrified. Nobody had any idea what he would say, and I, for one, wondered if Tree had any idea what he would say.

"It's embarrassing, standing up here, knowing how much you guys know about my private life," Tree finally began. "It's also kind of strange, that because of my success in golf, my private life—my sex life, really—is public fodder. I don't want to make anyone uncomfortable, so I'm not going to ask for a show of hands from any reporter sitting here today, or any member of Augusta National, who has ever cheated on his or her spouse. I don't think that would be right."

Tree made eye contact with a certain celebrity reporter for one of the cable channels, a noted player who for months had been calling for Tree's castration. Many others had done the same. If looks could kill, this woman would have fallen dead right then and there.

"Of course, my level of infidelity was on an epic scale, and I am well known. So I get that people are interested and that the rules are different for me. And after my arrest, I opened the door for all manner of questions. When I didn't have anything to say publicly, people filled in the blanks on their own. I get all of that. It's human nature. I'm just saying I don't think it's right. My mother would often cite the verse 'Let he who is without sin cast the first stone.' I think there's a lot in that."

At the mention of his mother, Tree started to well up. He looked down at the podium for a long moment and composed himself.

"Last summer, after the British Open, my reckless life caught up with me. After my arrest, I went for therapy. It was part of my plea agreement. To be honest with you, I went into it cynically. Sometimes in life you surprise yourself. I learned an incredible amount about myself in therapy. But as my new friend Delores told me there, the month of therapy was just a little step in the right direction. A baby step, if you will. I can't undo the past. I have caused so much hurt with my selfish behavior, more than can be measured. I'm not going to talk much about that. I want to protect the privacy of people I love, Belinda and our children in particular."

I looked at my BlackBerry. Somebody had just tweeted, *Tree has new girlfriend. Delores. Terribly unsexy name.* It was from a veteran British scribe on an old broadsheet whom I used to take seriously.

"There are things about me that I'd rather you hear from me. I've disbanded Tree Corp. My only employee now is Mac McCausland, my faithful caddie, and sometimes I feel like I work for him. Plant a Tree is now part of the Bill & Melinda Gates Foundation. Some of the generous members of this club, including Mr. Gates himself and Mr. Armstrong here, helped me set that up. I've sold the planes. I'm selling the boat. Henceforth, I'll be changing planes in Atlanta and renting from Budget, just like you guys. I'm buying my own clubs and my own clothes, just like you guys. I don't want to appear in ads anymore. I don't want the public ownership of my life that comes with it. I'm still going to play Arrow clubs, but not because anybody is paying me to play them. They work for me. For somebody else,

I can't say. I am carrying a new putter this week. It's an exact replica of Calamity Jane II, for those of you who know her."

I knew her, and I'm sure all the top-hundred golf historians did, too. Calamity Jane II was Bobby Jones's favorite putter.

"Before I get to the really crazy part, I just want to say one thing about blame. I know some of you want to blame my behavior on golf or on how my parents raised me. One of you wrote something like, *What do you expect from an only child playing such a selfish game?* I'm telling you, the problem was me. I had so much discipline for golf that I had nothing left over for the rest of my life. As for my parents, let me just say that I only hope I can be the kind of parent to my kids that my parents were to me."

He nodded to Big Herb, who was holding up a back wall. They made eye contact for a second. Mr. Tremont made a measured nod back.

"Okay, the really crazy part. There's no easy way to do this, but I think it's important for you to hear it from the source. I had three hundred and forty-two different sex partners outside my marriage."

Every reporter looked up almost at once. All around me, I heard people ask each other some variant of "Did I hear that number right?"

Tree said, "When I was doing it, I was having a good time. I'm just being honest here. For some of you dieters, it might be like going to Krispy Kreme and getting a chocolate-glazed donut with the cream filling. You don't tell anybody about it. You can't help yourself. You just inhale the thing. If I hadn't gotten caught, I'd probably still be at it now. Really, I was an addict. I know a lot of people will think that's a joke. But I believe I was an addict. I lied all the time to cover myself, and addicts have to be good liars. My behavior was compulsive and narcissistic and self-destructive but had the benefit of giving me a momentary high. Any addict can relate to what I just said."

He stopped for several seconds to take an inventory of the room. His confessional was becoming intensely personal, and his nervousness was abating.

"I'm not doing any brave thing here. People in recovery often become pathological truth-tellers. I've been reading about 'rigorous honesty.' It was familiar to me because I practiced it on the golf course. Now I'm trying to do it off the course. Confession, that's part of the healing process, too. So I'm confessing to those I've hurt. The fact is, I don't know how many I've hurt. I've hurt total strangers. Chairman Morton made that point, and I know it's true. I've heard from people I've hurt, people I don't even know. A boy named T'shawn. He might be eight or nine. I've never met him, but I know I hurt him. And I want to win him back, if I can. Because, you know, I had a sports hero growing up, too. Big Jack. And Jack Nicklaus never let me down. He inspired me to become the golfer I became. And I owe it to the game to be that person to somebody else, if I can be."

He had no notes or papers with him. The words were coming easily not because he had practiced them but because he believed them.

"Anyway, the *Eye* has the number at 128 already, right?"

"*Eye*'s got it at 129," somebody said from the middle of the room.

"Good, thanks for that: 129. I didn't check their website today. Sooner or later, it'll get to 342. But I got to tell you something: I'm calling BS on anything over 342."

Tree sort of laughed, and all the reporters did with him. The mood was changing so quickly, I could barely keep up with it. It went from flat-out weird to tense to *Oprah*-like confessional to church-pew sober to humorous about as fast as you could tap your foot. But I felt Tree was winning over the room and the many people in it who had spent most of the last nine months bashing him for real crimes and imagined ones.

"There's something else I want you to know. For a thirty-month period, concluding at last year's U.S. Open, I used steroids and other performance-enhancing drugs."

It was another moment when people turned to each other and basically said, "Did I hear that right?" After the little laugh line—BS on anything over 342—people had reclined in their seats. With this news, they were perched forward again.

"My use began before the Tour had implemented a policy banning these drugs, but I know that doesn't matter. It was wrong, and I knew it. I got big over the course of my career by using every single product you can buy at GNC and working out early and often. But I got bigger over that thirty-month period with drugs. They hurt and helped my golf. I think I lost some touch. I know there were chips and putts I played too aggressively because the steroids had me so amped up. I know the drugs helped my clubhead speed, my play out of the rough, and my stamina. They allowed me to train harder and to spend more hours on the range.

"I consider myself a recovering drug addict. I'm playing naked now, as the ballplayers say. If the PGA Tour wants to suspend me for this admission, I understand. Maybe they'll want to withdraw my titles from that period, I don't know. I earned twenty-seven million in prize money during those thirty months. I have written a check to the PGA Tour for double that amount, fifty-four million, in my shallow effort to make things right. I understand that Commissioner Fenimore will have more on that later, but I know they are putting a lot of that money in the Tour's pension program and in a special fund for Neckbone Circuit golfers who never had the chance to play on Tour because of the Caucasian-only clause. Given what Lee Elder and Charlie Sifford and my father's uncles from Greensboro did for me and for golf, it's the very least I could do. That twenty-seven million was tainted anyhow. If fans want to put asterisks on my thirteen wins in that period, I understand. To the players who feel I cheated to beat them, I agree with you. As the chairman said, I *have* stained this great game, and I can only say that I will spend the rest of my career trying to undo the damage."

You could practically hear the reporters on deadline suffering from what's-my-lede overload: How in *hell* do I write this thing up?

"I know some will hear me talking here and think I've lost my mind. Or that I'm oversharing. Maybe I am. But if I'm going to be a public person, I might as well be an honest one. It's got to be easier than what I was doing before. Maybe the single greatest thing you learn from golf is to look at things realistically, and that's what

I'm trying to do. Since the British Open, at least four people have attempted to extort me. One with a lab report, two with compromising photographs of me, one by making vague claims that I'm gay. That lab report and those photographs will be available on my website. To get access to them, all you have to do is make a donation to Plant a Tree or the charity of your choice. As for the gay question, I addressed that before I went into rehab. But really, who cares? Does it matter whether an athlete is gay or straight or, for that matter, bicurious?

"I'm probably going on too long. I know a lot of you have questions, and I'll ask you to save them for any other time after this week. I wanted to get this out of the way early so that we can all concentrate on golf and on the Masters. This week is about golf, it's about spring, and it's about friendship. This *club* is about friendship. If you read Bobby Jones, the cofounder of this place and this tournament, that's the message you get. I treasure the friendships I have. I see my dad in the back there. I see Mr. Armstrong, who showed me all the ins and outs of this club after my first win. I'll always treasure that memory, Mr. Chairman. I see Josh Dutra here in the first row, scribbling away. He knows more about me than I know about myself. I hope I can start being as good a friend to him as he has been to me."

I felt my cheeks get hot. I also felt scores of eyeballs looking at the back of my head. I had always prized being an anonymous reporter. Those days were over, at least when I was covering golf.

"Most of you in here know I've always been a grinder. You'd see me on the range, or in a press tent, and you'd ask me, 'What are you working on?' Well, this is what I'm working on: trying to be as good to others as they've been to me."

I watched Tree from behind the ropes and spoke to him each night. During his Monday-morning practice round, before the press conference, he got polite clapping here and there. By Tuesday, after the session in the press building, he got hearty, sustained applause on every tee and green. A year earlier, the swinger didn't even bother to play in the Wednesday Par-3 Tournament. This time he was happy to play in the event, held on the cozy course hard by two ponds, one of them named for Eisenhower, who fished it. During the contest, the fans were right on top of the golfers. There were no nasty comments directed toward Tree. Just the opposite. People welcomed him back. It helped that he was playing with Arnold and Jack, that the magnolias were in bloom, that the sun was so strong you could practically see the grass growing. It was as if a new lease on life had been granted to the entire world, or at least to our little green corner of it.

After Tree stiffed yet another wedge off the seventh tee, Jack put his left arm around him while Arnold gave him one of those neck twists with his meaty and tanned right hand. Arnold said to them, "They tell me I used to play shots like that back in the seventies, but I really don't remember." The threesome, in perfect unison, threw back their chins in laughter. That moment was all over TV, and it was an important step for Tree in his return to public life.

No player has ever won the Par-3 Tournament and then the Masters in the same week. As Tree stood on the ninth tee, he was six under par and in position to win the ultimate booby prize. The first time Tree went into his backswing, Nicklaus and Palmer threw clubs at his ball. Tree laughed and teed up his ball again. As he did, Nicklaus and Palmer began leading the gallery in a group singing of "Row, Row, Row Your Boat." Tree couldn't stop giggling. He called off his own second backswing.

"Arnold, Jack, I gotta ask you guys something," Tree said, loud enough that the crowd could hear him. "What do you think I would have to pay some kind soul from the gallery here to take me out of my misery and play this shot for me?"

"Now, that would be a wise way to spend your money," Jack said.

"You could probably get somebody to do it for ten bucks," Arnold said. "But I'd make it a hundred to be on the safe side."

Tree went fishing in his golf bag for his wallet. People were loving the whole routine.

"Okay, I got a hundred-dollar bill right here," Tree said. He held it up. "Legal tender. Show of hands. Who's willing to play this shot for me?"

Scores of hands went up. Tree pointed to a man about his own age but quite overweight, wearing golf shoes, long shorts, and a Masters visor. His red arms were streaked with white sunblock.

"Sir, what can you shoot?" Tree asked him.

"Depends," the man said. "On a good day?"

"Yeah, on a good day."

"Ninety-seven, ninety-eight."

"Perfect," Tree said. "Would you play this shot for me for a hundred dollars?"

"I'd pay *you*, Mr. Tremont."

All through the crowd, you heard people say about the same thing. The man did a limbo dance with the gallery rope and came on the tee. Tree gave him an 8-iron, plenty of club for the 130-yard shot. The designated golfer was a natural ham, and he made practice swings that brought to mind Jackie Gleason's goofy move. After about a minute, Palmer said good-naturedly, "Any time you're ready, fella."

"Please, Arnold," Tree said. "Don't rush my man here."

The man teed the ball about two inches off the turf and never touched a blade of grass. He hit a short, high pop-up to first that had splash written on it from the get-go. When the ball disappeared, the gallery let out a collective moan of disappointment, but Tree seized the moment and said, "Sir, that was perfect." He slipped the hundred in the man's pants pocket. "I could not improve on that."

Luke Donald won the Par-3 event, and Tree said to me, "One less guy to worry about."

I was back in my old seat in the press building again, sitting next to a legend, the golf writer from the Jacksonville paper. He was the only person to ask me questions about Tree during his self-imposed exile. Maybe the others were embarrassed for me for having been around so much unseemly activity. More likely, they thought that talking about the scandal was ancient history. "I told my sports editor to let the entertainment reporters take care of it," one fellow sportswriter said as we ate at lunch. The reporters at Augusta wanted to report on Tree Tremont the athlete. Everywhere I went, with Tree and without him, I found that people liked the new Tree, open and imperfect and unique. It seemed like his regrets and pain were their own.

Tree seemed to care what fans, players, reporters, and the Augusta National members thought of him. His approach to the week was like nothing I had seen from him before. He buried the thousand-yard stare and replaced it with casual nods. The new Tree often walked near the ropes, responding to high-five requests from the ten-and-under crowd. Arnold Palmer had the uncanny ability to look into a crowd and make every last person feel connected to him. Tree was showing he had that trait, too.

On the driving range and practice green, he was a different man. Tree was hanging out, inviting conversation. I can't say it was natural chitchat. How could it be, after his long absence from the game and all the sordid revelations? But I didn't think Tree was using his superior acting skills, either. He was trying.

"Nice run your Bulldogs had," Tree said one day to Zach Johnson on the putting green. Johnson looked at him quizzically. He was an Iowa boy and one of the most religious men on Tour. When he won the Masters, he said, "This being Easter, I cannot help but believe my Lord and Savior, Jesus Christ, was walking with me." He had nothing but respect for Tree's golf game and was, I'm sure, genuinely dismayed to learn how Tree had led his private life. But like nearly every Tour player, he said nothing negative in public about Tree while the scandal was erupting. It would have been bad form, and one thing Johnson and his brethren understood was that the great Tremont had brought billions into the game, particularly by quintupling the value of the Tour's TV contracts over the course of his career. A lot of that new money had found its way to the players and had bought them Hummers and hunting lodges and ski trips to Aspen.

"Tree Tremont, *starting* a conversation with *me*?" Zach said to me later. "He's talking about the Bulldogs in the NCAAs, and I'm figuring he's talking about Georgia, because I didn't even know he knew I *went* to Drake. And when he leaves the putting green, he says, 'Tell Kim hey for me.' That blew me away. Don't put that in the paper, but you know?"

I knew, and Tree did, too. Tree had always known. He studied the annual PGA Tour media guide like a med student studies *Gray's Anatomy*. He had always wanted to know the facts about his opponents, their Sunday scoring averages, their histories in majors, their putting stats, their sand-save percentages. Along the way, he had picked up on the names of their wives and where they went to college and what they considered their official hobbies (hunting and fishing, typically). Until then Tree had seldom seen a reason to use what he knew in the interest of friendly conversation. The whole notion of friendly conversation was foreign to him. He was there to beat you.

One afternoon I was walking through the player parking lot with a faintly famous player who said to me, "You know, it's not like Tree is the only guy out here trying to live like Vinny in *Entourage*. The difference is that your boy is the only guy out here so big, he *had* to get caught." The player opened the trunk of his Mercedes tournament courtesy car. There were a dozen putters in there, and he tossed in another two. "You know what? He'll probably win even more now. 'Cause every other guy out here is now even *more* scared of getting Tree big. They don't want the attention."

A veteran caddie, a noted conspiracy theorist who knew more about the Tour than most, told me, "If the Tour asterisks his wins, they might as well tear up the whole record book, 'cause Tree can't be the only one doing something. I mean, c'mon. Weed, Valium, beta-blockers, booze, steroids, HGH—they're everywhere, so why wouldn't they be on Tour? Thing is, the Tour drug testing's not designed to catch guys. It's designed to make fans think the sport's clean. And it probably is pretty clean. But it ain't squeaky clean."

In the first two rounds, when Tree played with Hyung Young, the former Asian Amateur champion, and the veteran Stephon James from Jamaica, I saw him do something I'd never seen him do. It had always been his habit to look away when his playing partners made their swings. "I don't want *their* swings in *my* subconscious," he had told me long before we ever heard of Walden's Pond. But it was bad golf manners. For one thing, it's harder to help a playing partner find an errant shot if you haven't seen the ball leave his clubface. In that first round in his return to golf, Tree was really watching. That could not have been easy for him, particularly with Hyung, now a twenty-one-year-old professional whose swing was wildly unconventional. After the first round, Hyung and Tree spent a half hour on the range talking about swing mechanics. When I asked Tree what he had told Young, Tree said, "The real question, Joshie, is what did Master Young tell me. He thinks my left arm is way too stiff at the top of the backswing. He likes Bubba Watson and John Daly. Kid doesn't know it, but he's talking about Jack in the sixties. The kid likes that feeling of a little bit of flex and softness. He thinks it prevents injury and frees you up. He gave me a lot to think about."

Even more amazing was to see Tree so engaged with Stephon James, one of the few players on Tour with skin darker than Tree's. When Tree first got on Tour, some people tried to push the two together, but there was never any rapport. If anything, the blood between them was bad, stemming from a comment Stephon once made about Tree's wild driving: "If Hogan saw the places where Tremont wins from, he'd be embarrassed for the guy." I loved Stephon James. All the deadline writers did. He was a quote machine. Tree had no use for him.

But there he was, making small talk with James and watching his gorgeous swing. In the second round, with James's ball in the air on the par-3 twelfth, a boom mike picked up Tree saying to Mac, "How pure is that?" The ball finished six feet below the hole.

Tree's Augusta nights had a whole new pattern, too. Instead of hiding out in his development fortress, he was staying in a hotel and going out to eat. On Friday night he and I went to the Downhill Grill, a greasy spoon favored by Augusta National's older and retired club caddies, black men in their seventies and eighties with fishhook scars who knew wild, secret things about the club. The restaurant had a wall-size mural depicting various legendary Augusta loopers, including Tommy "Burnt Biscuits" Bennett and Nathaniel "Iron Man" Avery and Willie "Cemetery" Perteet, Ike's regular man.

I sometimes wondered if Tree and his black ancestry would ever reconcile. I had my doubts. Until we got to Walden's Pond, I hadn't even known about Big Herb's stepbrothers and uncles who had grown up caddying and working at Greensboro golf courses with the golfing Thorpe brothers. Herb had pushed Black History Month too much on Tree, and Tree had rebelled. He had grown up on Michael Jordan. Not Muhammad Ali. Not Bill Russell. Not Althea Gibson. Not Jesse Owens. Not Josh Gibson, the Babe Ruth of Negro League baseball, beloved by Mr. Tremont. That night at the Downhill Grill, it wasn't like Tree was suddenly home. It was more like he was making an effort.

One of the old Augusta caddies, a man called Sandman, said to Tree, "You a student of the game, Mr. Tree, I know that, but do you know what I'm talking about when I say to you Eugene Saraceni?"

"You mean *Eugenio* Saraceni?" Tree said.

They were referring to Gene Sarazen, winner of the second Masters, in 1935.

"Oh, the Sandman forgets—you an expert on all that Italian shit, ain't ya now?" The old caddie, remembering Belinda's accent, was riding Tree. "But do you know this?" The caddie cupped his hands and said something into Tree's ear.

Driving back to the hotel—we were both staying at the Partridge Inn, old-fashioned and near the course—Tree said, "Let's make a stop at the club."

We talked our way past the security guards and, under the moonlight, walked down slippery hills covered with dew. After a few minutes, we arrived at Sarazen Bridge, which leads the golfers from the fifteenth fairway to its green. We read the plaque honoring the double eagle Sarazen made there in 1935. Tree would never get a similar plaque for his two on thirteen from the previous year. For one thing, Sarazen went on to win, and Tree did not. For another thing, Sarazen had never appeared on the front page of the *New York Post* in his Masters jacket under the headline GREEN, GREEN SEX MACHINE!

"You know what that old caddie said?" Tree said in the cool dark.

"You talking about Sandman?"

"I'm talking about Sandman. He said Sarazen's remains were scattered right here."

I thought of Tree at the Old Course, standing over the Road Hole Bunker with his mother's ashes.

"I hate to do it," I said, "but I gotta call bullshit here. I covered Gene Sarazen's funeral. The man is buried on Marco Island."

"Yeah?" Tree said. "Did you look inside the casket before they lowered it?"

I acknowledged that I had not.

"Okay, then," Tree said. "You should know this, Josh: You can't believe everything you read."

We were silent for a while. Tree lowered his chin and seemed to say a little prayer. Within seconds, he was gasping for air, overwhelmed with sadness for all that he had lost.

He was back at fifteen late the next day, in his Saturday round. He was paired with Will Martinsen, and they were tied for the lead. It was delicious. Both went for the green in two. Will hit a soaring, drawing shot, a thing of beauty that finished fifteen feet beyond the hole. Tree's second shot finished over the green. He needed to run his third shot up one hill and down another. He'd be playing it on the ground and was worried that the coin Will had used to mark his ball might be on Tree's line.

"Will, can you move your mark two to the right?" Tree asked.

Will, maybe a little chagrined that it hadn't occurred to him to offer to move the coin first, promptly moved his ball marker two putter heads to the right. Tree stood over his ball, 8-iron in hand. He put it back in his stance so he'd catch it on the downswing. He wanted to play a low, spinning shot that Nicklaus had taught him.

And then, for the first time all week, Tree's nerves betrayed him. Afraid that he might hit the ground before he hit the ball, he hit the ball thin, catching the top half of it with the leading edge of his 8-iron. The ball went scurrying across the green and into the pond protecting the green. After taking a penalty drop, he chipped the next one—using an 8-iron again—within inches and tapped in his bogey putt. It was devastating. Sarazen had once told Tree, "Never make a six or worse, and you'll be fine." Tree had made a six, and he wasn't fine. He was steaming, just like he would have been in the old days. There was murmuring among the spectators, more than usual. A large cloud suddenly blocked the sun.

Will put down his ball, picked up his coin, and settled over his putt, ready to attempt his fifteen-foot eagle putt. He was hunched over his ball when Tree, calmly but quickly, walked over to him and said, "Will, wait."

Martinsen backed away. Tree got right next to him and said something that nobody else could hear. Will put down his coin again, picked up his ball, and moved the marker by two putterheads, so that it was back in its original spot. He went through his whole routine once more and calmly stroked in his putt for three.

Had Will putted from the wrong spot and realized it before he left the scorer's hut beyond the eighteenth green, he would have been required to add two shots to his score on the par-5 for playing from the wrong place. Had he left the scorer's hut after signing an incorrect scorecard, he would have been disqualified from the tournament. Such is the ruthlessness of the rules of golf.

As they walked to the sixteenth tee, Will said to Tree, "You did me a solid there." He marked his card with a 3. His lead was three shots.

"You would have done the same for me," Tree said, marking his own card with a 6. He always marked his card immediately after making a bogey, as a sort of punishment.

"I'll tell you what," Will said. "Not every player trying to win the Masters would do that."

Tree said, "Guy compliments Bobby Jones for playing by the rules. Jones says, 'You might as well praise a man for not robbing a bank.' "

"Pretty fucking good," Will said.

The spectators on the sixteenth tee gave the two players a

standing ovation for the quality of their golf and their sportsmanship. It was so loud, you couldn't hear yourself think.

I wondered how that whole thing might have played out, pre-scandal. If Tree had seen the mistake with the ball marker, I'm sure he would have told Will to move it back to its original position. But I doubt he would have seen it. He would have been too absorbed in his own little world.

In his time away from golf, nothing had changed in Tree's game. It may have improved. One morning at Walden's Pond, Tree told me about a dream in which he made a smoother transition from backswing to downswing. At Augusta, his dream was coming true. In the fourth round, Tree and Will were paired again. Will had played the final three holes on Saturday in par, par, bogey, and Tree played them in birdie, par, par, meaning that Will began Sunday with a one-shot lead. The afternoon was cool and blustery, and distances were hard to judge. Putts wobbled like an overserved groomsman.

Tree went out in 35 and Will in 36 in Sunday's final round, but it wasn't really that close. Tree hit every fairway and green but couldn't get a putt to fall. Will's ball-striking was erratic, but his short game was allowing him to hang around. On the eleventh hole, Martinsen stirred the ghosts of Larry Mize with a hundred-foot chip-in for birdie from off the right side of the green. The crowd roared. After Tree made par, Martinsen had a one-shot lead again.

I couldn't detect a rooting interest among the fans. At times I thought there were more people pulling for Martinsen, but then Tree would get some serious applause. When they arrived on the twelfth tee, everybody was standing for them. Will did his old bashful, dimpled nodding thing. Tree saw a small group of men and women in military fatigues from nearby Fort Gordon and gave them a brief salute.

Will, with his birdie on eleven, had to play first on twelve. It's not a hole where you necessarily want the honor. The par-3 is set in an amphitheater of pines, creating swirling, baffling winds. The green is about the size of a tongue and slopes madly. It requires only a short-iron, but Jack Nicklaus once told Tree there was no shot in golf that scared him more.

Will hit a towering 9-iron that was swatted down by the wind. The ball landed on the front left of the green, spun backward, and trickled down the shaved bank and into Rae's Creek.

Rehab had changed Tree in many ways, but his cutthroat competitive instincts remained intact. He stepped up and hit his purest shot of the day, a sawed-off punch 7-iron that whistled through the breeze and settled three feet right of the flag. The shot was greeted with a throaty roar.

Martinsen walked slowly to the drop area. He knew Tree would be making a two. He was desperate to salvage bogey and maybe even make a three. The safe play for him would be to pitch long and left of the flag, but that would leave a twenty-footer for bogey to stay within one of the lead. Will Martinsen hit lob shots as well as anybody in the game and decided to play the hero shot. He laid open his lob wedge so that it was almost flat on the ground and hit a soft, high cut that looked like it might go in the hole for a three on the fly. It glanced the flagstick on its way down and finished four feet above the hole. Tree stood on the side of the green and applauded with his hands over his head. This was golfing masterpiece theater.

Four feet for bogey on Augusta National's billiard-table greens is pure hell, especially when you're putting downhill and downwind. It's as if the greens have a built-in device to read your level of putting insecurity, and if they register any queasiness at all, they make you suffer. Will hit his putt hard enough to keep the ball on its line. But it caught an old ball mark that made his ball veer to the right, where it caught the edge of the hole, spun out hard, and started a slow, agonizing downhill, downwind trickle toward its grave. Will watched his ball slip off the green, down a bank, and into the creek.

The 9-iron tee shot that finished in the creek (one). The penalty shot (two). The lob that hit the flagstick (three). The downhill four-footer that finished in the creek (four). The second penalty shot (five). A second lob shot, this one to ten feet (six). Two putts (seven, eight). By the time Will had finished, he had made a snowman, as we in the duffing game call scores of eight.

Tree tiptoed through Will's funeral proceedings and calmly made his three-footer for birdie. He had trailed by one. Now he led by five. All he had to do to win was play smart golf. Tree's stock-in-trade was smart golf. It was over.

Tree told me later what happened next. He and Will walked wordlessly to the thirteenth tee. It's the most secluded spot at Augusta. The nearest fans are a couple hundreds yards away. Tree stopped at what used to be the back edge of the old teeing ground, a spot hidden from the gallery and invisible to the TV cameras. The group in front of them was held up by a rules question, and Will and Tree sat on a bench. Tree ate almonds from a plastic bag and offered some to Will, who took several.

"Just think if you could build the perfect golfer from everybody who has ever sat here," Tree said. "Hogan's one-iron, Norman's driver, Crenshaw's putter, Seve's heart, Nicklaus's brain, your lob wedge—"

"—and your steel balls," Will said.

"That nine-iron you just hit?" Tree said. "It was perfect until that gust came up and knocked it down. Your lob wedge was perfect, but the flagstick decided to play goalie. You hit the right putt, but the ball mark got you."

"Is your point that I got hosed?" Will said.

"You got hosed!"

They laughed, and Tree gave him a fist bump.

Given the conditions and the state of his private life, Tree's 66 had to be one of the best rounds of golf ever played. He won by four but lost a thousand dollars to Will on the last, after a one-hole side wager they made on the eighteenth tee. Will ran in a long birdie there, to Tree's par. When Will's ball disappeared, he winked at Tree. It was the ultimate inside joke understood by only those two, a light moment at odds with the powerful emotion of the afternoon.

When Tree made his par putt from five feet on the last, his

cheeks, stiffened by the cold wind, immediately became streaked with tear tracks. There were spectators crying with him, maybe out of happiness, maybe because they were looking at Delores's mirror and seeing themselves. In victory, Tree went to the edges of the eighteenth green, where the spectators stood ten deep, and made his way around the entire horseshoe. It wasn't a racer's victory lap. It was more like a leisurely stroll. He applauded the fans as they applauded him. Will Martinsen stood on the back of the green with his wife and five kids and clapped slowly and rhythmically. I heard later that in the clubhouse and locker room, dozens of players and attendants and Augusta National members stood in front of TVs and clapped nonstop for several minutes. In a Butler Cabin interview with Jim Nantz on CBS, Nicklaus said, "Look, in my day, I'm sure there were guys who weren't angels, but they didn't have the kind of scrutiny that these guys have today. Tree Tremont is a staggering golf talent, the best the game has ever seen, and he wants to make things right. And people can see that."

At the awards ceremony, Tree dedicated the win "to my kids, for their love, and to their mother, for her grace." Will, as the defending champion, slipped the winner's green coat on him, and Tree gave him a long hug. It was the start of a beautiful friendship.

Lily and I were married two months later, on the Saturday after the U.S. Open. I had originally suggested U.S. Open Saturday as a wedding date, but Lily thought that was a showboat move on my part to prove to her and everybody else that the wedding meant more to me than covering another golf tournament. It occurred to me that if I could somehow hang around her for another forty years, I might get halfway to smart.

As we made an invitation list for the wedding, we were able to figure out the important people in our lives. I surprised myself by finding that I wanted to invite Finkelman and his wife. We invited Delores from Walden's Pond. We invited Mac McCausland. We invited every last faculty member at Lily's school because she didn't want to leave anybody out, even the teacher who always brought malodorous egg-salad sandwiches into the teachers' lounge. We invited Fred Willoughby, the prosecutor and weekend preacher, and asked him to officiate. We invited Tree and Big Herb. We invited Belinda and the kids. Belinda said to Lily, "I want to see you in a wedding dress, even if it means I have to see Tree." We invited the "Chief Matchmaking Officer" of whatdoyouhavetolose.com, Mrs. Edgar Buxbaum of Kew Gardens, Queens. We sent her one of Lily's handwritten invitations along with a picture of us taken just after I popped the question, which I did while we were floating downstream in tire tubes on the Mississippi.

"You're not the first of my couples to invite me to their wedding," Mrs. Buxbaum wrote us in an e-mail, "but you're the cutest!"

As Lily and I had almost nothing in common on paper, we asked Mrs. Buxbaum how she thought to put us together. She wrote back, "You know the expression 'opposites attract'? It wasn't that." She would have killed on Johnny Carson. "But you both listed reading as a hobby, so I figured you were both curious, and curious people at the very least usually get along."

Mrs. Buxbaum didn't have anything to do with getting Tree together with Meg, who was also on our invitation list. Lily was the one who saw the potential there. If your new wife and your ex-wife are close friends, and mine were, you're beyond lucky. By the time of our wedding, Tree and Meg had been dating for close to five months. The beautiful, mysterious redheaded older woman wearing the scarf in the picture near the tiny restaurant in rural New Zealand? That was Meg.

Tree was open to the idea from the start. He knew from Josh and Lily and me that Meg was funny, beautiful, smart, caring, and independent. At first I was pretty weirded out by the idea of Tree dating Meg. But since Lily had initiated the idea, it made me think that she saw Tree maybe not as a reconstituted person, but at least getting there. The notion came up for the first time at my house one night when Meg was dropping off Josh and I was manning the grill. Lily was pouring homemade Arnold Palmers and didn't realize that I could hear her.

"Why would I possibly want to go on a date with Tree Tremont?" Meg asked. "I really have no interest in being number three-forty-three."

"Consider the positives," Lily said. "You have to think he got it all out of his system. He's interesting. He's smart. You know he's going to try. And he's hot!"

I was shocked, Lily, using the word *hot* that way. It was so girlish and sexy. I flipped the hamburgers with a he-man metal spatula and gingerly turned Lily's veggie burger with a fork. They're prone to crumbling, those things.

Meg and Tree went to see a Coen brothers movie on their first date (Tree's arty, trying-too-hard choice). They went bowling on their second (pure Meg). Tree didn't even know how to bowl. Meg had a 150 average.

"Is this whole thing okay for you?" Tree asked me.

"Let me tell you the part I wouldn't be able to handle," I said. "If Josh ever starts calling you Pops."

Tree offered to rent *Off Course* from its new owner for the wedding, but Lily and I wanted something simple. We were married on a beautiful beach in St. Petersburg, at Fort De Soto Park, on a still and humid June night when the air smelled like clam broth and the sand was firm and cool. Nobody wore shoes. Fred Willoughby presided magnificently and nondenominationally. You can't keep a good preacher down, and we wouldn't have wanted it any other way. This was his kicker, if I may use that newspapering term to describe the end of a nuptial blessing: "And so, by the power vested in *us*, vested in us by this great sea beyond these breakers, and by the ancient rocks tumbling on its sandy floor—"

"Amen, brother!"

Without looking, I could identify the shouter: Delores, our resident Holy Roller.

"And by the power vested in *us* by the collected love of the good folks gathered here on this ancient beach and in the powerful name of love and hope—"

"Love and hope!" shouted Delores.

"And by the power vested in me by the great state of Florida and with the good tidings and blessings from the hands of God, whomever, however, wherever, *whatever* you may conceive that spirit to be—"

"Spirit in the night!" shouted Delores.

I felt a Springsteen song coming on.

"With all these powers trembling through me, I do hearby pronounce you, Mr. Josh and Miss Lily, I do hearby pronounce you man and woman, partner and partner, friend and friend. I do hearby pronounce you husband and wife!"

"*Hallelujah!*" said Delores.

"You may kiss the bride," Reverend Willoughby said.

We kissed until Finkelman yelled, "Get a room!"

At one point near the end of the wedding, Belinda and Rocco and Isabella, Finkelman, Big Herb, Tree, Meg, Josh, Lily, and I found ourselves standing around a smoldering beach fire, making s'mores and poking at the red-coal embers with long sticks that Herb had whittled for us as a wedding gift. Josh was doing that thing where you carefully rotate the stick as if the marshmallow is a rotisserie chicken, to assure even browning. Tree was following suit.

"I probably shouldn't admit this," Tree said.

"But you are the pathological truth-teller," Meg said, almost singing. She had just the right sense of humor for him.

He nodded in agreement and said, "This is the first time in my life I've cooked marshmallows."

"You poor underprivileged child," Big Herb said.

"Oh, you've got the child part right," Belinda said.

Isabella giggled.

"You don't cook 'em, Mr. Tremont," Josh said to Tree. "You *roast* them."

I was glad to hear him use the honorific. Josh had given up lacrosse and was playing a lot of golf. He was spending some of his weekends at the Brooksville sod farm, working on his swing with Big Herb, a fine teacher and a fine man.

I said, "Joshie, you remember Flanders in *The Simpsons Movie*? He takes a blowtorch to his marshmallow. I wouldn't call that roasting."

"This court will not consider cartoon examples in the roasting-versus-cooking marshmallow debate and sides with the junior Mr. Dutra," Finkelman said. "For the rest of this wedding, marshmallows prepared under open fire shall be deemed to be roasted and not cooked."

All these months later, I could smile at Finkelman. He had left Tree Corp and been hired immediately by, of all people, Norma Blackwell.

Big Herb said, "When I was in the army—"

"Here we go again," Tree said.

"I'm sorry. Maybe some of you don't know: I had three tours of duty in Vietnam. And in the second tour, I had a little guy in my platoon from some itty-bitty place in Kansas. Every time he'd see a fire, and that was often, he'd go, 'I wish I was home, toastin' a marshmallow.' *Toasting*. That was his word."

Rocco loaded up two marshmallows on a single stick, and Belinda asked Isabella, "Marsh-a-mellows, what do we call these? Is it the *caramella*?"

What an accent. She was turning into a superb newspaper publisher, too. Everything they do right on the Italian papers, Belinda was doing with *The Review-American*. She had one rule: Make the stories interesting.

Meg burned the outer shell of the marshmallow intentionally and lifted it off, using her fingers as pincers. She then carefully roasted the molten remains. "We used to call this the twice-baked marshmallow," she said.

Its namesake, the twice-baked potato, was the special-occasion starch of my simple boyhood (one house, two parents, one school system, K–12). I used to do the same thing with my boyhood marshmallows. It was funny. In all our years together, marshmallow-roasting methods had never come up.

Meg ate her innards while they were warm and gooey, right off the stick, like a kid. I thought of the child we had lost. You couldn't compare the circumstances, but Meg and Tree both knew something about the frailty of life and relationships. Lily knelt low and blew hard on the embers and breathed new life in them. She stood up, and I put my arm around her, feeling wistful and happy in the warmth of the fire.

I've been writing this at my desk at the paper. I've been paging through old notebooks, looking for quotes and phone numbers, sometimes closing my eyes while trying to re-create scenes that played once and will never play again. The drive to the *Review-American* building from our house, the house I share with Lily, takes you on some of the same downtown roads Tree tore down on the day of his Fourth and Fourth fiasco. Every day I drive by the St. Pete airport and the Great American Diner and the domed stadium where Herb will never root for the home team. In a crowded desk drawer, I have a letter from Tree, written by hand on Tree House stationery. It's the letter he gave me when I left Tree Corp. In it, he writes about his golf and his kids and his parents, but at the end it changes tone:

> *I hope someday you'll still want to help me with my book. But before that, if you want to write your own, you should. Write it as you see it. Tell it all. And whatever happens in the future, Josh, I want to thank you. I couldn't have come this far without you.*
>
> *Your friend,*
> *Tree*

As for what the *X* stands for, I'm keeping that to myself.